The Bones Of Odin

(Matt Drake #1)

By

David Leadbeater

Thriller, Action, Adventure, Bestseller, Odin, Thor,
Mystery, Fantasy,

Other Books by David Leadbeater:

The Matt Drake Series
A constantly evolving, action-packed romp based in the escapist
action-adventure genre:

The Bones of Odin (Matt Drake #1)
The Blood King Conspiracy (Matt Drake #2)
The Gates of Hell (Matt Drake 3)
The Tomb of the Gods (Matt Drake #4)
Brothers in Arms (Matt Drake #5)
The Swords of Babylon (Matt Drake #6)
Blood Vengeance (Matt Drake #7)
Last Man Standing (Matt Drake #8)
The Plagues of Pandora (Matt Drake #9)
The Lost Kingdom (Matt Drake #10)
The Ghost Ships of Arizona (Matt Drake #11)
The Last Bazaar (Matt Drake #12)
The Edge of Armageddon (Matt Drake #13)
The Treasures of Saint Germain (Matt Drake #14)
Inca Kings (Matt Drake #15)
The Four Corners of the Earth (Matt Drake #16)
The Seven Seals of Egypt (Matt Drake #17)
Weapons of the Gods (Matt Drake #18)

The Alicia Myles Series
Aztec Gold (Alicia Myles #1)
Crusader's Gold (Alicia Myles #2)
Caribbean Gold (Alicia Myles #3)
Chasing Gold (Alicia Myles #4)

The Torsten Dahl Thriller Series
Stand Your Ground (Dahl Thriller #1)

The Relic Hunters Series
The Relic Hunters (Relic Hunters #1)
The Atlantis Cipher (Relic Hunters #2)

The Disavowed Series:
The Razor's Edge (Disavowed #1)
In Harm's Way (Disavowed #2)
Threat Level: Red (Disavowed #3)

The Chosen Few Series
Chosen (The Chosen Trilogy #1)
Guardians (The Chosen Tribology #2)

Short Stories
Walking with Ghosts (A short story)
A Whispering of Ghosts (A short story)

All genuine comments are very welcome at:

davidleadbeater2011@hotmail.co.uk

Twitter: @dleadbeater2011

Visit David's website for the latest news and information:
davidleadbeater.com

DEDICATION

I would like to dedicate this book to my daughter,
Keira,
promises to keep,
and miles to go . . .

And to everyone who has ever supported me in my writing.

PROLOGUE

Some of the greatest treasures from history are not on display in a museum. They are not presented grandly on a silken cushion for the admiring eyes of the multitudes. Instead, they are ignored, allowed to gather dust and rot. They are disregarded and refuted, largely because they are too advanced to be explained within the accepted framework of historical narrative.

It was depressingly gray outside. Professor Roland Parnevik sighed and walked to the window, studying the middle distance. The moment it had come to his attention he'd known that this mission, this quest, would consume him. It wasn't every day that questions raised by a life's work offered up a potential answer.

Outside, the streets were empty—the hour relatively late—as a brisk wind scoured the open roads before whipping up and rustling through the rows of trees, gusting against the unassuming car showroom opposite, before blasting over the rooftops and away.

Parnevik shivered despite the warmth of the room. The facades of the street were gray, burnt orange and dirty white, lackluster at best, offering the aging professor not an ounce of inspiration.

Still, his heart beat wildly.

The older professors of archaeology behind him were all talking at once. "It's the bell and the hammer all over again," one of them said in Swedish. "It's the eight-carat gold chain ambiguity, and we'll never be allowed to continue to research it."

Someone else spoke up. "Not this time; surely not. With a find of this magnitude, of this *importance*. They cannot ignore it."

"Pfft," still another voice added, one Parnevik easily recognized, as he did each and every one. They had, after all, been working together for countless years. "The conformists will seek to debunk the find. They'll scientifically refute its age; discredit the source. And then they'll banish our artefact, our findings...and us."

Parnevik turned. His mind flitted through countless old discussions with these men, sorting through their relevance. The artefacts his colleagues referred to were now legends of archaeology, some even thought of as *urban* legends. And that, of course, was what the conformist scientific community wanted the vast majority to believe. The real truth was so hot to touch, it would be like trying to pick up lava.

First: the hammer. In June 1936, a couple of walkers noticed a small rock from which jutted a lump of wood . They decided to take the peculiarity home and what they found shocked the scientific world to its foundations.

Fixed in the rock was an ancient, man-made hammer.

Later, dated and analyzed, the rock was found to be four hundred million years old. The hammer itself was over five hundred million. A part of the handle had already begun the metamorphosis into coal. The head was so pure it was unlikely that such a thing could have been made without assistance from modern smelting methods.

Just the one, Parnevik thought. Of course, if the hammer had been the only artefact ever found, then a hoax or misreported-story theory might have been plausible. But there were literally thousands of these artefacts collecting dust in dozens of museums around the world, hidden from public view, explosive secrets buried beneath layers of dust that were surely profound in more ways than one.

And then there was the bell. In 1944, a boy dropped a large lump of coal in his basement. The coal had split open to reveal a secret that defied current scientific belief: a handcrafted brass alloy bell with an iron clapper and sculptured handle.

The seam from which this coal had been mined was three hundred million years old.

Scientists and geologists accepted that coal was a by-product of decaying vegetation, which, in time, was covered by sediment. This sediment then fossilized and became rock. Evolutionists believed that the natural process of coal formation took between thousands and four hundred million years. Creationists and evolutionists had battled over this question for many years.

Finally, and to him most importantly, Parnevik mulled over the as-yet unanswered question of the ancient footprints.

In 1968, a paleontologist excavated a track of fossilized dinosaur footprints found near a town in Texas. The findings, again, were dumbfounding. Running parallel to the dinosaur tracks, in exactly the same hundred-million-year-old Cretaceous period's fossilized strata, were human footprints.

The naysayers had piped up—yelling hoax at the top of their expert lungs. The TV stations loved these experts, calling on them whenever a new crisis popped up, allaying the public's fears.

Or did they? Parnevik himself remembered suspicion and even a little fanciful thought at the news, and he'd been just a young boy at the time. Experts said the human tracks were actually those of dinosaurs, eroded to appear human, but had never explained why the three-toed dinosaur's own had not similarly been eroded.

The human tracks were later found to continue under bedrock that was later removed from the riverbed. And there were other footprints, later found all over the world.

Parnevik looked away from the window, and back into the room. The group of older men sat on sofas, with cups of coffee and bottles of water to hand, the blinking computer screens, the wide table full of dusty books and scrolls.

All eyes had turned to him.

He didn't say anything however. He took his time, considering the currently accepted beliefs about the ancient world alongside the facts that had now presented themselves. There was one more, of course—the best one yet...

"Roland?" A voice interrupted his train of thought. "Well, what are your thoughts, man? Does this upheaval of scientific beliefs not interest you?"

"On the contrary," Parnevik said, "but I think we have to choose our words and our methods very carefully. You know our own world will seek to discredit us. Our peers will shun us. This new find, well, it challenges more than just scientific belief; *it points the way to the existence of beings even we dismiss as mere myth."*

"An interesting day," another guffawed, and was joined by an aging chorus of laughter from the other men, that quickly degenerated into much throat-clearing and wracking coughs.

Most importantly, Parnevik thought, *one of the leading organizations on the planet has already acknowledged the problem.*

In 1987, and again in 1992, the Smithsonian published an article relating to the "Petrified Footprints", acknowledging the mystery and labelling them what established scientists liked to call "problematic". It described large "mammal" and bird tracks that had "evolved long after the Permian period, but these tracks were clearly Permian".

Clearly Permian, Parnevik thought. *A huge statement for the Smithsonian to make.*

But while it was commendable that the Smithsonian had acknowledged the mammal and bird tracks found, it did not make reference to the human footprints found with them.

"I am thinking of the spheres of South Africa," he said aloud. "The so-called Klerksdorp spheres." Found over decades by miners, the spheres measured 25-100 mm in diameter and were etched with three parallel grooves around their circumference. The spheres had been reported to be so carefully balanced that it would take a zero-gravity environment to achieve such a feat.

Because it was refuted so ardently by the scientific community, it was therefore not surprising to find that the spheres had been found in rock dated back to the Precambrian era—2.8 billion years old.

"How many people even know about the Klerksdorp spheres?" Parnevik said to prove his point. "How many mainstream documentaries have they been featured on? And who even remembers the poor archaeologists who attempted to reveal to the public the true age of these anomalies? Not even I, since the men's careers were ended when I was just a boy. The public," he sighed, "is already indoctrinated. This," he pointed a finger to the new object at the rear of the room, "is revolutionist's gold."

Many of them smiled.

"If we weren't all so old," and Parnevik himself smiled, "we might not feel so radical."

"All these hidden discoveries need to be re-examined," a close friend of his said. "If just a single one of them is verified by the scientific establishment, it would force a reappraisal of either the process of geology or the theory of human development."

A silence fell, weighty and insightful, thick with nervous tension and suppressed excitement.

Parnevik again indicated the newly found object. "Its age has been doubly confirmed?"

"Yes" many of them said at once. "More than that," a lone voice added.

"And it is—" but he dared not put the words into the mouths of his colleagues.

"It is the shield," came an answer. "Odin's Shield."

He smiled. Feeling happy. Excited, even. Not realizing that his idle scientific curiosity would soon place the entire planet in danger.

ONE

YORK, ENGLAND

The darkness exploded.

"This is it." Matt Drake fixed his eye over the viewfinder, and tried to ignore the surrounding spectacle, focusing on the outlandishly clad model prowling down the catwalk.

Not an easy task. But he was a professional, or at least trying to be. No one ever said the transition from SAS soldier to civilian would be easy. But he'd struggled more than most over the last seven years. He'd jumped from vocation to vocation—each one a leap of folly—but now he'd finally discovered his calling: photography.

Especially tonight. The first model gave a wave and an experienced, haughty little smile before sashaying away amidst a rising din of music and cheering. Drake kept the camera clicking as Ben, his twenty-year-old, long-haired lodger, leaned in to shout in his ear.

"Program says that was Milla Jovovich. I quote: 'A movie star and also a chic Frey designer model'. Wow, is that one Bridget Hall? Hard to say, under all that Viking gear."

Drake ignored his commentary and stayed on his game, partly because he wasn't sure if his young friend was being serious. He tried to capture the vivacious catwalk images along with the disparate play of light across the crowd. The models were decked out in Viking ensemble, carrying swords and shields, helmets and horns—retro costumes conceived by the internationally renowned designer Abel Frey, who had weaved new season vogue with ancient Nordic battledress to commemorate the evening.

Drake now switched his attention to the head of the catwalk and the object of tonight's celebrations— a shield. A recently discovered relic ambitiously named "Odin's Shield". Ambitious because, to Drake's mind, Odin was a god and well. . .mythical. Found recently in Iceland and now on a worldwide tour, the shield had been hailed as the greatest find in Norse mythology and had been dated to *before* Viking history began. Way before. "Just an anomaly," the experts had said, adding that they needed more time to study the shield.

The ensuing mystery was immense and intriguing and had captured the attention of the world. The shield's value and renown had only increased when scientists joined the publicity circus after some other unclassified element was discovered within its makeup.

Ben tugged at Drake's arm, meaning he missed the model and came up with a snap of the moon instead.

"Whoops!" Ben laughed. "Sorry, Matt. This event is pretty good. Apart from the music; that's crap. They could have hired my band, The Wall of Sleep, for a few hundred quid. Can you believe that *York* has landed something as awesome as this?"

Drake waved his camera in the air. "Truthfully? No." Having lived here a while, he knew all about the city council and their odd visions. The future is in the past, or so they kept saying. "But listen, *York's* paying your landlord a fair few quid to take pictures of models and shields, not *The Sky At Night*. And *your* band's crap. So, chill, will you?"

Ben rolled his eyes. "Crap? The Wall Of Sleep are even now considering, umm...multiple offers, mate."

"Just trying to focus on the nice models." Drake was actually focused on the shield itself as it glimmered under the catwalk lights. A stunning object to be sure, it was made up of two circles, the inner overlaid with what looked like ancient depictions of animals and an upside-down triangle, the outer a mishmash of animal characters and symbols.

Great for the conspiracy fruit and nuts, he thought.

"Hold there," he whispered to himself as a model went over to pose with the shield and he recorded the digital contrast of youth with age.

The catwalk had been erected outside York's renowned Yorvik Center—a museum of Viking history—after Sweden's Museum of National Antiquities had granted them a brief loan during early September. The importance of the event had increased exponentially when reclusive superstar designer Abel Frey had offered to fund a catwalk event to kick off the exhibition.

Another model stalked the makeshift tiles, her face holding the expression of a cat seeking its nightly bowl of cream. Spotlights rolled and raked the dark sky behind her. Bright light bounced from shop window to shop window, often ruining what little artistic aura Drake was managing to muster. The distracting dance music of Cascada battered his ears. *Bloody hell*, he thought. *Missions in* Bosnia *were easier on the senses than this.*

The crowd swelled. He took a moment to scan the faces around him, all hoping for a glimpse of Abel Frey, their idol, who was nowhere to be seen. People in fancy dress added a carnival atmosphere. He smiled. The watchful urge was admittedly duller after seven years out—the army alertness wearing off—but if he let them, the old instincts rose like the new dawn, fresh, unsullied and ready to take charge. In a perverse sense they'd gained strength since Alyson, his wife, had died in a car accident two years earlier. One of the last things she'd said to him was that he might have quit the Army but the Army would never quit him. At the time his self-confidence had pushed the comment away. What the hell did she even mean?

Now...

Something remembered from the old days snapped Drake back to the present, a distant *thunk, thunk,* long forgotten...just a memory now...*thunk*...

Drake shook away the fog and focused again on the catwalk show. Two models were staging a mock battle beneath Odin's Shield, nothing spectacular, just publicity fodder, but the crowd cheered, the TV cameras whirred, and Drake clicked like a dervish. In the heart of the crowd, he felt its beat like a happy cadence.

And then he frowned. He lowered the camera. His soldier's mind, may have become lethargic but it was by no means decayed. The *thunk, thunk* was instantly recognizable. Why the hell were two army Apache attack choppers approaching the event?

"Ben," he said, carefully, asking the only question he could think of. "If you're the geek I think you are you will have researched this evening's program extensively. Did you hear about any surprise guests tonight?"

"Well, it was tweeted that Kate Moss might show up."

"Kate Moss?" Drake doubted she'd make her appearance rappelling from a military helicopter.

The helicopters blasted overhead, circled around then hovered in sync. They made a spectacular sight, the moon glistening behind them. The crowd cheered ecstatically, expecting something special. All eyes and cameras turned to the night sky.

Ben cried, "Bloody hell..." as his cellphone chirped. His family kept in constant touch and, as a well-raised boy with a heart of gold, he always answered.

Drake ignored Ben, and scrutinized the helicopters' positions, the fully loaded rocket pods, the 30 millimeter chain guns visibly housed under the aircrafts' forward fuselages, and quickly assessed the situation.

The crowd was crammed into a small square bordered by shops, with only three exits. Ben and he only had one choice if ...*when* ...the crush came:

Head straight for the catwalk.

And then all hell broke loose.

Without warning, dozens of ropes slithered down from the second chopper, which Drake now realized must have been an Apache hybrid: a machine modified to house multiple crew members.

Masked men descended the lines, disappearing behind the catwalk. Drake noticed guns strapped across their chests as a wary hush began to spread through the crowd. The last voices were those of children asking why, but soon even they went quiet.

Local security rushed toward the back of the stage, speaking rapidly into handsets.

Then, with a hiss like a million gallons of steam escaping, the lead Apache unleashed a Hellfire missile into one of the empty shops. There was a roar like the collision of two locomotives. Fire, glass and fragmented brick exploded high across the square.

Ben dropped his cellphone in shock and scrambled to retrieve it. Drake heard the screaming rise like a tidal wave, and sensed the mob instinct now gripping the crowd. Without a moment's thought, he grabbed Ben and manhandled him over the railing before vaulting over it himself. They landed heavily next to the catwalk.

The Apache's chain gun rang out, deep and deadly. The sound was deafening. Drake instinctively threw his body across Ben's, but the rounds had been fired above the crowd, invoking pure panic, their screams only adding to the noise level.

Drake signaled that Ben should follow and raced around the foot of the catwalk. A few of the models reached down to help. Drake gained his feet and looked over the surging wave of people now streaming toward the exits. Dozens were clambering onto the catwalk, helped by models and staff. Terrified screams laced the air, causing the panic to spread. Fire lit the dark, and the heavy *thunk* of helicopter rotors drowned out most of the tumult.

The chain gun rang out again, sending heavy lead into the buildings above the crowd. It was the kind of nightmare sound no civilian should have to endure.

Drake turned. Models cowered behind him. Odin's Shield was in front of him. Drake turned to help some of the models climb to safety. Quickly, he waved them to cover just as soldiers in bulletproof jackets appeared from backstage. Drake's first concern was to position his body between Ben, the escaping models and the soldiers, but he risked a few snaps of the shield for himself, which made him the centre of attention. Better the soldiers were focussed on him than some innocent who didn't know what they were doing.

With his other hand, he pushed his young lodger further away, in the direction the models had just ran.

"Hey!" a soldier cried out, eyeballing Drake, and swinging his machine gun around. This kind of thing didn't happen in York, not in *this* world. York was tourists, ice-cream and American day trippers. It was safe, it was prudent, and it was the place Drake had chosen to start a quiet new life.

The soldier was suddenly in his face. "*Give me that!*" he screamed, speaking English, but with a thick German accent. "*Give it to me!*"

The soldier lunged for the camera. Drake chopped at his forearm and twisted his machine gun out of his grasp. Surprise lit the soldier's face. Drake palmed the camera off to Ben behind his back and heard him move away.

Drake was careful to point the machine gun at the floor as three more soldiers started toward him.

"*You!*" One of the soldiers raised his weapon.

Drake half closed his eyes, but then heard a raucous shout; "Give him the camera *idiot*. I don't want to shoot someone in cold blood on national television."

The new soldier nodded at Drake. "Give me the gun first, and then the camera." His German pronunciation carried a lazy twang.

Drake let the gun clatter to the floor. "Don't have it."

The commander nodded to his subordinates. "Check him."

"There was someone else..." The first soldier picked up his gun, looking embarrassed. "He...he's gone."

The commander stepped right up into Drake's face. "Fool. We want those pictures. One way—" his mouth turned up behind his mask. "Or the other."

A muzzle pressed against Drake's forehead, his vision filled with angry German and flying spittle. "I said *check him!*"

As the soldiers frisked him, he imagined it appeared as though he'd been taking their pictures and, despite the face masks, had orders to risk nothing as regards their identities. He watched the orchestrated theft of Odin's Shield under the direction of a newly arrived masked individual wearing a white suit. The man waved his arms around as if directing people and scratched his head, but never spoke aloud. Once the shield was safely away, the man waved a walkie in Drake's general direction, seemingly trying to attract the commander's attention.

The masked man in charge sighed audibly and placed his own walkie to his ear, but Drake kept his eyes on the man in white.

"See you in Paris," the man's lips said into the mouthpiece.

The commander murmured, "At six tomorrow."

Special army training, Drake reflected, *still came in handy.* Lip reading was a special requirement.

The commander then said, "Dah," and was back in Drake's face, brandishing his credit cards and photographer's credentials. "Lucky snapper," he drawled lazily. "The boss says minimal casualties, so you live...for now. But," he waved Drake's wallet, "we have your address. And," he added with a cold smile, "trouble *will* find you."

TWO

YORK, ENGLAND

Much later, at home, after some interminable questioning by the local authorities, Drake handed Ben a filtered decaf and joined him to watch TV coverage of the night's events.

Odin's Shield had been stolen. The good news was that no one had died. The burning helicopters had been found miles away, abandoned where three motorways converged, their occupants long gone.

"Ruined Frey's show," Ben said, only partly serious. "The models are already packed up and gone."

"And I changed the bloody bed sheets," Drake said with a wry grin. "Well, I'm sure Frey and Prada and Gucci will survive."

"And they cut my dad off in mid-flow."

Drake shook his head. "Don't worry. He'll ring back in three minutes or so."

"Making fun, crusty?"

Drake laughed. "No. You're just too young to understand."

Ben had been rooming with Drake for about nine months now, during which time they had grown from strangers to good friends. They had met at night school, at an eight-week photography course Ben had been running, as part of his ongoing college degree. When Ben mentioned that he was broke and needed a place to stay, Drake subsidized Ben's rent in return for his photographic knowledge. Ben was the kind of guy who wore his feelings on his sleeve, a sign of innocence maybe, but admirable too. Drake found distraction in the boy's enthusiasm. It helped keep at bay memories of his own wretched past.

Drake himself was an easy-going, capable man with a soldier's sense of camaraderie and humor. Someone had once called him "James Bond in jeans". Though flattered, Drake wasn't exactly comfortable with the comparison. It did nothing to help him keep a low profile, or move on from the army days.

Ben put down his mug. "Night, mate. Guess I'll go ring Sis."

"Night."

The door closed, leaving Drake able to kick back and watch Sky News for a while. When a picture of Odin's Shield appeared, he sat up to take notice.

After watching a re-run of an earlier newscast, he picked up the camera that represented his livelihood and pocketed the memory card with a mind to view the pictures later. He was still intrigued by what the soldier had said to him, how they would "see him later". They had clearly wanted his pictures for themselves. But why? He headed to his PC, pausing on the way to double check the doors and windows. This house had been safe-proofed years ago when he was still in the Army. He liked to believe in the rudimentary goodness of every human being, but one thing war—and his old friend and girlfriend, Mai Kitano—had taught him was never to put his blind trust in anything. Always have a plan and a good backup—a plan B. Mai had taught him more about warfare than anyone else in his life, including the SAS, but time and hard life experience made them drift apart. Now, she was a world away.

He googled "Odin" and "Odin's Shield". The wind picked up outside the house, rushing around the eaves and wailing louder than an investment banker who had had his bonus capped at four mil. He soon realized the shield was big news. It had been a major archaeological find, the biggest ever in Iceland. Some Indiana Jones types had strayed off the beaten track to investigate an ancient ice flow. A few days later they'd unearthed the shield, but then one of Iceland's largest volcanoes had started rumbling and further exploration had had to be postponed.

The same volcano, Drake mused, *that had sent the ash cloud across Europe recently, disrupting air traffic and people's holidays.*

Drake sipped his coffee and listened to the wind howl. The

mantle clock chimed midnight. The information he had found with just a few Google searches was overwhelming. Maybe he was getting older, but he thought that Ben might make more sense of it than he could. The biggest news appeared to be that the shield had been dated beyond anything previously accepted, challenging all current beliefs.

He started to read a small essay on the formation of coal, felt his eyelids starting to droop, and quickly moved on. The next revelation was that some unknown material had also been discovered in the shield's makeup, an apparently manmade property that most historians would argue should not have existed so long ago.

The boffins had likened this new material to *Starlite*, a very real invention of the '70s and '80s. Prior to any expensive development, NASA and the Atomic Weapons Establishment had conducted live tests of the material, coating it with eggs. They had then applied a blowtorch to the eggs for five minutes before proving that despite this, they remained cold enough to be picked up by bare skin. The material could withstand temperatures of up to 10,000°C. NASA and many other cutting-edge companies showed interest but the material's composition was never revealed by its inventor, and never handed over for fear of reverse engineering. Whether the inventor feared new weapons development or some other misuse, the world never knew for he died in 2011 without disclosing the fabrication process, and to this day it had never been replicated.

Drake read that the shield was made up from at least some of the same claimed polymers and co-polymers and other barrier ingredients used in Starlite, but this only fuelled the fire of mystery that already surrounded the artefact. He read further articles, and learned that the surface of Odin's Shield sported many carvings, all of which were being studied by scientists, and that J.R.R. Tolkien had based his wandering wizard, Gandalf, on legends of Odin.

But most of this was simply random information, uncorroborated. Not a reason to commit a dangerous and very public crime. The symbols or hieroglyphs that ringed the outside of the shield had been translated and were believed to be an ancient form of Odin's curse:

Heaven and Hell are but a temporary ignorance,
It is the Immortal Soul that sways toward Right or Wrong.

No script existed to translate or otherwise explain the curse, but still everyone believed in its authenticity. At the very least, it was attributed to the Vikings, if not to Odin himself.

Drake sat back in his chair and ran through the events of the night.

One thing cried out to him. The guy in white had mouthed "*See you in Paris*", and the other had replied "*At six tomorrow*". Worry ate at Drake when he considered how dangerous the men were, and how directly they had warned him off.

Trouble *will* find you.

But if Drake followed the obvious path, he could be putting Ben's life, not to mention his own, in danger.

Maybe they'll let it go.

A civilian would drop it, but a soldier would reason that he didn't like being threatened, that their lives were already in danger, and that new information was always good information. The police had lost the thieves. They were in the wind, and they knew Drake's identity. The thought unsettled him. Whilst he knew, after tonight's restlessness, he would let this go, he was nevertheless intrigued by their audacious attack, theft and future plans.

He googled "*Odin + Paris*".

One entry leapt out at him.

Odin's Horse, Sleipnir, was on display at the Louvre.

Odin's *Horse?* Drake scratched his head. For a god, this guy was laying claim to some exceptionally material things. With a click, Drake brought up the Louvre's home page. It seemed the small sculpture of Odin's fabled horse had been discovered years ago in the mountains of Sweden. Drake read on, and soon became so wrapped up in the many tales of Odin that he almost forgot he was, in fact, a Viking god, simply a myth.

The Louvre? Drake chewed it over. *Maybe they'll let it go...* but the thought was more a world-weary hope than an actual belief.

He finished his coffee, suddenly feeling tired, and pushed away from the computer.

In another moment he was asleep.

*

He woke to the sound of the croaking frog: a motion-activated device and his little sentry. An enemy might expect an alarm or a dog, but would never suspect the little green ornament nestling beside the wheelie bin—and Drake had been trained to sleep light.

He'd fallen asleep at the computer desk with his head in his arms; now he came instantly awake and slipped into the darkened hallway. The back door rattled. Glass smashed. Only seconds had passed since the frog had croaked.

They were in.

Drake ducked below eye-level and saw two men enter, sub-machine guns held competently but a little shabbily. Their movement was clean, but not graceful.

No problem, he thought, *seven years ago maybe.*

But now? They were about to find out.

Drake waited in the shadows, hoping the old soldier in him wouldn't let him down.

Two came in. An advance team. Not a good sign because it showed that the intruders knew what they were doing. Drake's strategy for such a situation had been planned years ago when his particular regiment had come under direct threat from a group of extremists. In the years that followed he'd simply not bothered to change anything. The extremists had managed to come by personal information, but had been neutralized in Britain before they could act on it. Now, Drake's old plan refocused in his mind.

When the first soldier's muzzle poked out of the kitchen, Drake grabbed it, jerked it toward him, then twisted it back. At the same time he stepped toward his opponent and spun, effectively wrenching the gun away and finishing up behind the man.

The second soldier was momentarily taken aback. That was all it took. Drake shot him in the head. Then he spun, firing another round at the first soldier before the second had even crumpled to his knees.

Run! he thought. Speed was everything now.

He sprinted up the stairs, shouting Ben's name, and squeezed off a burst of automatic fire over his shoulder. He reached the landing, shouted again, then hit Ben's door at a dead run. It burst open. Ben stood in his jogging bottoms, cellphone in hand, sheer terror etched into his face.

"Don't worry," Drake said with more assurance than he felt. "Trust me. This is my *other* job."

To his credit, Ben didn't ask questions. Drake focused hard. He had disabled the house's original loft hatch, then installed a second in this room. After that, he'd reinforced the bedroom door. It wouldn't stop a determined intruder for very long but it would certainly slow them down.

All part of the plan.

He bolted the door, making sure the integral bars were fixed to the reinforced frame, then pulled down the loft ladder. Ben shot up first, Drake a second later. The loft space was large and carpeted. Ben just stood and gaped. The entire wall space to east and west was dominated by a large bespoke bookcase overflowing with vinyl records, by the 70s and 80s rock bands that he loved the most, CDs and old cassette cases.

"These all yours, Matt? I knew you were into old rock, but. . ."

Drake didn't answer. The real truth, that they were almost all that remained of the things Alyson and he used to collect and enjoy, was too complicated to confront right now. He crossed over to a pile of boxes that concealed a door tall enough to crawl through, a door that led to the roof.

Drake upended a box on the carpet. A fully packed rucksack fell out which he secured over his shoulders.

"Clothes?" Ben whispered.

He patted the rucksack. "Got 'em."

When Ben still looked blank, Drake understood just how scared he was. He realized he'd turned back into the army guy a little too easily. "Clothes, cells, money, passports, iPad, ID."

He didn't mention the gun, the bullets, the knife...

"Who's *doing* this, Matt?"

A boom came from below: their unknown enemy hitting Ben's bedroom door, perhaps now realizing they'd underestimated Drake.

"Time to go."

Ben turned without expression and crawled into the windswept night. Drake dived after him and, with a last glance at the walls full of CDs and cassette tapes, pulled the door shut behind him.

The wind tugged at them with eager fingers as they crossed the treacherous roof. Ben stepped carefully, bare feet slipping across the concrete tiles. Drake held his arm tightly, wishing they'd had time to find him some shoes.

A strong gust howled around the chimney breast, struck Ben full in the face and sent him stumbling toward the edge. Drake pulled him back hard, heard a shriek of pain, but maintained his grip. After a second he reined his friend in.

"Not far," he whispered. "Nearly there, mate."

Drake could see that Ben was terrified. The young man's eyes darted between the loft door and the edge of the roof, then to the garden and back again. Panic made a twisted mask of his features. His breathing was coming too fast; at this rate they'd never make it.

Drake stole a glance at the door, steeled himself, then turned his back to it. If anyone came through they would see him first. He took hold of Ben's shoulders and locked eyes.

"Ben, you have to trust me. *Trust* me. I promise I'll get you through this."

Ben's eyes refocused and finally he nodded, still terrified but putting his life in Drake's hands. He turned and stepped forward gingerly. Drake noticed blood seeping from his feet, draining into the gutter. The roof tiles were more than sharp enough to cut into flesh. They traversed the neighbor's roof, stepped down onto his conservatory and slithered to the ground. Ben slipped and fell halfway, but Drake had landed first and broke most of his fall.

Then they were on solid ground. Lights were on next door but no one was around. Hopefully they'd heard the automatic fire and the police were on their way.

Drake gripped Ben tightly around the shoulders and said, "Fantastic stuff. Keep it up and I'll buy you a new climbing frame. Now, let's go."

Ben sniffed. "Who the hell's up there?"

Drake was looking up at the loft and its secret door. The lead they had gained was quickly wasting away.

"Germans."

"*What?* Like World War Two *Bridge over the River Kwai* Germans?"

"I think those were Japanese. And no, I don't think these are anything like World War Two Germans."

They were already at the rear of the neighbor's garden, and now clambered over its sturdy wooden fence.

Straight out onto a busy street.

Two minutes away from a cab rank.

Drake walked toward the waiting cars with murder in his mind. His soldier's insight had resurfaced. Like Mickey Rourke, like Kylie, like Hawaii Five-O it had been lying dormant, waiting for the right time to make its glorious comeback.

Now he was sure the only way to protect the two of them was to get the bad guy first.

THREE

PARIS, FRANCE

The flight into Charles De Gaulle touched down at 09:00 that same morning. Drake and Ben landed with nothing but Drake's rucksack. New clothes were on their backs, new burner cellphones prepped. The iPad was charged. Most of their cash was gone—spent on transport. Drake's weapon had been ditched as soon as he decided their destination and before boarding the plane.

During the flight, Drake had brought Ben up to date with all things German and Viking, and had asked him to help with the research, whilst he focused on who might be targeting them. The more he understood about them, the quicker he would be able to deal with the threat. Ben's only comment was, "Maybe I could draft Karin in to help."

Drake talked him out of it. The last thing they wanted here was more of Ben's family involved, and his sister, though extremely computer literate, would only add danger and distraction to the situation.

They exited the airport into a cold Paris drizzle. Drake had half expected the bad guys to be waiting, but now assumed they didn't have the resources to react this quickly. Ben found a cab and waved at it with a guide book he'd bought. Once they were inside he said, "Umm...Rue..._Croix?_ Hotel opposite the Louvre?"

The cab shot off, driven by a man whose face betrayed that he himself was driven by nothing. The hotel, when it appeared forty minutes later, was refreshingly atypical for Paris. There was a large lobby, elevators that could accommodate more than one person, and several twisting corridors of rooms.

Before they booked in, Drake used the cash machine in the lobby to withdraw the rest of his money—about five hundred Euros. Ben frowned, but Drake tried to reassure him with a wink. He knew what his smart friend was thinking, even as Ben said it aloud: "You're flaunting electronic surveillance and creating a money trail."

"That's the idea, mate. Wait and see."

He paid for one room by credit card, making sure he could acquire the room opposite with cash. Once upstairs, they both entered the "cash" room and Drake set up surveillance.

"Our chance to kill a few birds with one stone," he said, watching Ben scout the room with a critical eye.

"What do you mean?"

"This is the way we see how good they are. If they come soon they're capable, and probably trouble. If they don't, well, it's important to know that too. And you get a chance to break out your new toy."

Ben switched on the iPad. "It's definitely happening today, at six?"

"It's an educated guess." Drake sighed. "My lip-reading's pretty rusty, but it was only a few words. And it fits the few facts we know about the Louvre and Sleipnir."

"Well, step aside, crusty..." and Ben made a show of cracking his fingers. His confidence shone now he was assisting rather than fleeing, but then he'd never been a man of action. To Drake's mind Ben was the kind of person identified by his *first* name, or by a nickname—mostly Blakey—never cool enough to earn a dynamic last name moniker.

As if to reinforce this, as Ben sat down, he turned his worried eyes on Drake.

"Why are they targeting us?"

Drake shrugged, reluctant to get to deep into this conversation for fear of freaking his friend out. "Bad luck," he said. "They didn't like me taking photos."

"But how did you know they would come after us?"

"I didn't." Drake frowned.

"But you researched everything last night as if. . .as if. . ." his already weak comment trailed off to nothing.

"I know bad men," Drake admitted. "And I know what they can do. And how they operate. One way to survive is to be prepared and stay ahead."

Drake fixed his eye to the peephole. "The longer they take," he murmured, "the better our chances."

It took longer than he'd expected. Ben was able to shrug off his fears, and was thoroughly engrossed in the iPad by the time Drake saw half a dozen big guys gather outside the door opposite. The lock was picked and the room invaded. Thirty seconds later the team reappeared, looked around angrily and dispersed.

Drake set his jaw.

Ben said. "This is really interesting, Matt. It's believed there are actually *nine pieces* of Odin scattered throughout the world. The shield is one, the horse another. I never knew that, but it's all here."

Drake barely heard him. He racked his brain. The bad guys might not be Special Forces, but he and Ben were still in big trouble if they truly wanted them dead. They could hide, or they could run, but neither option was part of Drake's makeup. He knew from experience that if a criminal organization really had its black heart set on finding someone, there wasn't a whole lot could stand in their way. Who were they? Just thieves intent on selling the shield? Or had Ben and he stumbled into something more? All he knew was they wanted him for something he'd either seen or snapped back on that catwalk and every instinct told him to stay ahead of them. To do that, he needed to learn who they were.

Without a word, he backed away from the door and tapped a number into his cell. Almost immediately the call was answered.

"Yes?"

"This is Drake."

"I'm shocked. Long time, pal."

"I know."

"Always knew you'd call again."

"Not what you think, Wells. I need something." He paused, waiting for the inevitable reply. Wells was his old SAS commander and a man he'd kept in touch with since leaving the regiment. He was one of the few people Drake knew that he could fully trust.

"Of course you do. So talk to me about Mai."

Wells was being cautious, testing him with a pre-agreed code to show Drake wasn't under duress. Problem was, Mai was an old flame from Chechnya, Tokyo and Thailand before Drake was married to Alyson—and even Ben shouldn't be party to those old, cherished secrets.

"Codename—Shiranu.   Location—Phuket.   Type—let's see...occasionally exotic...mostly lethal."

Ben's ears were twitching.

There was laughter in Wells' voice as he said, "Exotic? That the best you can do?"

"At the moment—yes."

"Someone there?"

"Very much."

"Gotcha. Okay pal, whatcha want?"

"I need the truth, Wells. I need the raw intel' that the news and the Internet aren't allowed to broadcast. The truth about Odin's Shield being stolen and the Germans that stole it. Especially the Germans. Real MI5 and SAS intel', not the public drip feed."

"You in trouble?"

"Immense." You don't lie to your commander, former or not.

"Need a hand? Sam, Jo and the boys would drop everything to help you. Off the books, of course."

"Not yet."

"You've earned a hand, Drake. Just say the word and they're yours. Any time."

"I will."

"Okay. And by the way—you still telling yourself you were plain old SAS?"

Drake hesitated. "It's an acceptable term of explanation, that's all."

Drake disconnected. Asking his former commander for help hadn't been easy, but Ben's safety overrode all sense of pride. He checked the peephole once more, got an eyeful of empty corridor, and then went to sit next to Ben.

"Nine pieces of Odin, you say? What on earth does that mean?"

Ben pointed at the screen. "Well...I'm following the trail of these nine pieces of Odin. Not that they're carefully hidden or anything. It seems that nine is a special number in Norse mythology. Odin was self-crucified on something called the World Tree for nine days and nine nights, fasting, with a spear in his side just like Jesus Christ, and many years *before* Jesus. This is *real* stuff, Matt, catalogued by real scholars. It might even be the story that inspired the tale of Jesus Christ. The spear is a third *piece,* and is linked to the World Tree, though I can't find any references as to its location. The *Tree's* legendary location is in Sweden. A place called Uppsala."

"Slow down, slow down. Does it say anything about Odin's shield or his horse?"

Ben shrugged. "Just that the shield was one of the greatest archaeological finds of all time, and that around its edge are the words: *Heaven and Hell are but a temporary ignorance. It is the Immortal Soul that sways toward Right or Wrong.* Apparently, it's Odin's curse, but no one has ever been able to figure out what it means."

"Maybe it's one of those curses where you just have to be there." Drake smiled.

Ben ignored him. "Says here that the horse is a sculpture. Another sculpture, 'Odin's Wolves', sits in the New York National History Museum."

"His wolves?" Drake's brain was starting to fry.

"He rode two wolves into battle. Apparently."

Drake frowned. "Are all the nine parts accounted for?"

Ben shook his head. "Several are missing, but..."

Drake paused. "But what?"

"Well, it sounds daft, but there are bits of a legend building up here. Something about uniting all of Odin's pieces and finding the tomb of the gods. Several scholars have made reference to it."

"Standard stuff," Drake said. "All these ancient gods have fables attached to them. What gets me is all these physical references to Odin when the guy's supposed to be a God."

Ben studied him. "Ever hear of Euhemerism?"

A grin cracked across Drake's face. "*Yoohoo*-what?"

"Euhemerism. It's a rationalizing way of interpreting mythological references and figures as a true reflection of actual historical events and people. The original stories were reshaped, exaggerated or altered as each tale got retold and retold again. Many people believe King Arthur was real, but he sure didn't possess a magical sword and live in a fairytale castle. The legend *becomes* legend through rich embellishment. Euhemerus said mythology was 'history in disguise'. It could explain the Odin references."

"But didn't Odin live long before humans were around? His shield dates back millions of years, so they say."

Ben shrugged. "Let's not forget the actual historical references to the fact that Zeus's tomb is in Crete, discovered by Pythagoras in the third century. Varro and others also claimed the tomb, but nobody agreed on a location."

Drake sighed. "A bloody shame, I should say."

Ben nodded and looked at his watch. "Look, us Internet wizards require sustenance." He thought for a second. "And I think I can feel some new band lyrics coming on. Croissants and Brie for brunch?"

"A bacon sarnie sounds better."

Drake cracked the door, checked around, then motioned Ben out. He saw the smile on his friend's face but also read the strain in his eyes. Ben was hiding it well, but was floundering badly.

Drake went back into the room and stowed all their belongings in the backpack. As he was securing the heavy strap, he heard Ben say a subdued "Hi", and felt a heart-stopping jolt of fear, for only the second time in his life.

Oh no.

The first was when Alyson had left him on that fateful night, citing that irreconcilable difference—*you're more soldier than a friggin' boot camp.* It was the last sentence she'd ever spoken to him before she died in the car accident.

He ran for the door, every muscle in his body coiled, then saw the old couple toiling their way along the corridor. *Thank you.* He took a deep breath, reprimanding himself.

But Ben noticed the stark terror that had filled his eyes a brief second before he'd managed to mask it. *Stupid mistake.*

"Don't worry," Ben said with a pale smile. "I'm okay."

Drake took a shuddering breath and led them down the staircase, constantly alert. He checked the lobby, saw no threat, and stepped out onto the street.

Where was the nearest back street eatery? He took a guess and headed away from the Louvre.

The fat man from Munich with the brain-surgeon's touch saw them straight away. He checked the photographic likeness, and recognized the well-built, capable Yorkshireman and his long-haired friend in two heartbeats, and fixed them in his crosshairs.

He shifted his position, not liking the high vantage point or the white chippings that were digging into his fleshy extremities.

Into a shoulder mic he whispered, "Got them on a hair trigger."

The answer was surprisingly immediate. "Kill them now."

FOUR

PARIS, FRANCE

Three bullets were fired in quick succession.

The first deflected off the metal doorframe beside Drake's head, then ricocheted down the street, striking an old woman in the arm. She twisted and fell, leaving a question-mark pattern of blood in her wake.

The second whipped past Ben's head.

The third hit the concrete where Ben had been standing, a nano-second after Drake tackled him roughly around the waist. The bullet glanced off the concrete and smashed through the hotel window behind them.

Drake rolled and crab-walked Ben behind a row of parked cars. "I've got you," he whispered fiercely. "Keep going."

Staying low, he risked a glance through a car window and saw movement on a rooftop, just as the window shattered.

"Shite shooting!" His Yorkshire accent thickened as the adrenalin pumped. He surveyed the area. Civilians were running, screaming, causing all sorts of distractions. But it didn't matter. The shooter knew exactly where they were. He was a professional.

And he wouldn't be alone.

Drake recognized three guys he'd seen earlier on lock-picking duty, as they stepped out of a big dark-colored Mondeo and strode purposefully toward him and Ben.

"Time to move."

Drake crab-walked them two cars down to where he'd already spied a young woman crying hysterically in her car. To her surprise, he cracked open her door and felt a quick rush of guilt at her terrified expression.

He kept a poker face. "Out."

Still no shots. The woman crawled out, fear icing her muscles to dead slabs. Ben slithered inside, keeping his body mass as low as possible. Drake followed him in a hurry and turned the key.

Taking a breath, he jammed the car into gear and shot slantwise out of the parking space. Rubber smoldered and smoked across the road, marking their trail.

Ben cried, "*Rue de Richelieu!*"

Drake swerved in anticipation of a bullet, heard the metallic twang as it bounced off the engine compartment, then sped forward. They left the surprised lock-pickers standing at the side of the road, saw them hurrying back to their car.

Drake flung the wheel into a right, then left, and left again.

"*Rue Saint-Honore,*" Ben shouted, craning his neck to see the road name.

They entered a flow of traffic. Drake made haste as best he could, zipping the car—which to his appreciation, being a petrolhead, was an old style Mini Cooper—in and out of the lanes, keeping a steady eye on the rearview.

The rooftop shooter was long gone, but the Mondeo was back there, keeping pace with them.

Drake turned right, then right again, and got lucky at the lights. The Louvre shot by on the left-hand side. This was no good: the roads were too crowded, the lights too frequent. They needed to get away from central Paris.

"Rue De Rivoli!"

Drake frowned hard at Ben. "Why the hell do you keep shouting out street names?"

Ben stared at him. "I don't know! Is it helping?"

"No!" Drake cried back above the roar of the engine as he zoomed down a slip road and away from the Rue De Rivoli.

A bullet ricocheted off the car's rear end. This was bad; this was serious stuff. These people were arrogant and powerful enough not to care who they hurt, and could live with the consequences.

Why were the Nine Pieces of Odin so important to them?

During the plane journey he'd again questioned himself about the importance of this trip, and why he should pursue it, but a second attempt on their lives in twenty four hours affirmed the danger tenfold. Both Ben and he were a number on some person's kill list, and they needed to find out why.

Drake firmly believed it to be the photos he had taken, capturing the figures of the men engaged in a daring robbery, recording the build and stature of the man in white. It had to be – there was no other explanation. The man in white and his mercenary friends didn't want to be recognized.

There would be no hiding and they would never stop seeking.

Bullets struck concrete and metal and zinged in errant patterns all around the speeding Mini.

At that moment, Ben's cell rang. He made a complicated shoulder-wrenching maneuver to twist it out of his pocket. "Mum?"

"*Bollocks.*" Drake cursed quietly. The lad could never ignore a call from his mum. She suffered from stress, and even one missed call would cause anguish.

"I'm fine, ta. You? How's Dad?" Ben's face was twisted in discomfort as he fought every nerve in his body to remain calm.

The Mondeo powered its way up to the Mini's back end. Glaring headlights filled the rearview, along with the faces of three jeering Germans. The bastards were loving this.

Ben was nodding. "And Sis?"

Drake watched as the Germans pounded the dash with their guns in a frenzy of excitement.

"Nah. Nothing much. Umm...what noise?" Ben paused. "Oh...Xbox."

Drake floored the pedal again. The engine responded quickly, the car an eager sprite. Tires squealed, even at sixty miles an hour.

The next bullet destroyed the back window. Ben scrambled down into the front crawlspace without being asked. Drake allowed a moment of assessment, then bounced the Mini up onto the empty walkway alongside a line of parked cars.

The Mondeo's occupants fired recklessly, bullets passing through the windows of parked cars to strike the bodywork of the

Mini. After a few seconds Drake bounced the car back out onto the road, tramped on the brakes and reversed with a screech. Without losing a beat, he threw the little car into a quick one-eighty, then raced off back the way they'd come.

It took the Mondeo precious seconds to realize what had happened. Their own one-eighty was sloppy and dangerous, and took out two parked cars with an awful crunch. Where were the bloody police?

No choice now. Drake threw the car around as many corners as he could. "Get ready, Ben. We're gonna run."

If Ben hadn't have been there, Drake wouldn't have avoided a confrontation, he'd have formulated a plan of attack; but the first priority was his friend's safety. And getting lost was the prudent move now.

"Okay, Mum, catch you later." Ben flipped the cell closed with a shrug. "Parents, eh?"

Drake rode the Mini up the curb again and braked hard halfway across a manicured lawn. Before the car stopped they flung open their doors and jumped out, heading for nearby streets. They mingled with a horde of tourists and Parisians before the Mondeo was anywhere in sight.

Ben managed a little croak and blinked at Drake. "Aren't you the action hero?"

They hid out for a while at a little Internet cafe near a place called Harry's New York Bar. To Drake this was the wisest move. Inconspicuous and cheap, it was somewhere they could continue their research and deliberate on the Louvre's imminent break in without too much concern or interruption.

Drake set up muffins and coffees whilst Ben quickly logged on. Drake then slid into the booth across from Ben and met his gaze.

"How you doing with all this crap?"

"I don't know," Ben said truthfully. "Haven't had time to take it in yet."

Drake nodded. "That's normal. Well, when you do..." he gestured at the PC. "Whatcha got?"

"I logged back onto the same website as before. Amazing archaeological find...nine pieces...yada, yada, yada...I was reading about Odin's spectacular conspiracy theory."

"And I was saying—"

"It was a load of bollocks; yeah, I know. But not necessarily, Matt. Listen to this. As I said, there *is* a legend, and, unusually, it's been translated into many languages over the years. Not just the Scandinavian ones. It seems pretty universal, which is unheard of according to the crusties that study this sort of thing. It says that if Odin's Nine Pieces are ever assembled at Ragnarok they will reveal the way to the Tomb of the Gods. And if the tomb is ever desecrated, or if the nine pieces are assembled inside...well, sulfur and brimstone is just the start of our problems. Notice I said *gods*?"

Drake frowned. "Nah. How can there be a *tomb* of the gods? They never *existed*. Ragnarok never existed. It was just the mythological Norse place for Armageddon."

"Exactly. So what if it did exist? Imagine the value of a find like that."

Drake whistled softly. "A tomb of the gods? It would be beyond everything. Atlantis. Camelot. Eden. They'd be nothing compared to that. So you're saying that Odin's Shield is just one piece of a larger puzzle?"

Ben bit off the top of his muffin. "I guess we'll see. There's no solid evidence yet, no reference to any hidden data that needs extracting. I guess that's just for the movies. But there are eight other pieces to go for, and if they start disappearing." He paused. "You know, Karin is the brains of the family, and Sis would love making sense of all this Internet crap. It's all just bits and pieces."

"Ben, I feel guilty enough involving you. And I promise nothing's gonna happen to you, but I can't involve anyone else in this." Drake frowned. "I wonder why the bloody Germans kicked this off now, though. Surely the other eight parts have been around a while."

"Less with the soccer descriptions. And they have. But if there's no hidden data, no secret conspiracy, then maybe the shield was special in some way? Something about finding it may have started a sequence of events."

Ben tapped the screen. "It says the sculpture of Odin's horse was found in a Viking longship, one of the oldest and most complete ever discovered, which is actually the Louvre's chief exhibit. The horse is inside the longship. Most people wouldn't even notice the horse sculpture itself whilst walking around the Louvre."

Ben read on. "And see here," he pointed at the screen, "this part focuses on the other pieces of Odin I mentioned earlier. The wolves in New York, and the best guess is that the spear is in Uppsala, Sweden, having fallen from Odin's body when he climbed down from the World Tree."

"So that's five." Drake settled back into the comfy seating and sipped his coffee. Around them the Internet cafe buzzed with restrained activity, and the smell of roasting coffee and specialty teas infused the air. The pavements outside, in contrast, were filled with busy people zigzagging their way through life.

Ben had been born with a steel-lined mouth, and downed half of his hot coffee in a single gulp. "There's something else here," he tapped away. "It looks complicated. A story about someone called a volva. Which means—seeress."

"Maybe they named the car after them."

"Funny. No, it seems Odin had a special volva. Wait—this could take a while."

Drake was so busy switching his attention between Ben, the PC, the stream of information, and the bustling street outside, that he didn't see a woman approach until she stood right next to their table. She was medium height and build, and wore a dark pant suit. Her hair was long and black and held back only because she quickly tucked it behind her ears.

Before Drake could move, she raised a hand. "Don't get up, boys," she drawled in an American accent. "We need to talk."

FIVE

PARIS, FRANCE

Detective Kennedy Moore had been evaluating the pair for a while.

At first she'd thought them harmless. But, after a while, analyzing the younger man's scared but determined body language and the older dude's vigilant demeanor, she'd come to the conclusion that these two weren't Parisians. And they were definitely in trouble.

She wasn't a cop here. But she was a cop in New York, and that island with its big concrete towers was a tough place in which to grow up. There, if someone's mindset was right, they developed cop's eyes before they even knew their destiny was to join the NYPD. Later, they honed and recalculated, but always had those eyes and that hard, calculating stare.

Even on vacation, she mused bitterly. *Even now....*

After an hour of sipping coffee and aimless surfing, she couldn't help herself. She might be on vacation—which sounded better than "forced leave" to her—but that didn't mean the cop in her just gave it up quicker than a guy surrendered his virtue on his first night in Vegas.

She sidled over to their table. *Forced leave,* she thought again. Two words that sure put her glittering NYPD career in perspective.

The older guy looked at her with distrust. Something in his expression put her on alert. Her instincts had been correct. Something was wrong here. "Don't get up, boys," she drawled disarmingly. "We need to talk."

34

"American?" the older guy said with a hint of surprise. "What do you want?"

She ignored him. "Are you okay, kid?" She flashed her shield. "I'm a cop. You be honest with me, now."

Older Guy clicked immediately and gave a grin of relief, which lightened her mood. His friend blinked in confusion.

"Sorry?"

The cop in Kennedy pressed the issue. "Are you here by choice?" It was all she could think of to get next to them.

The younger guy looked pained. "Well, the sightseeing's okay, but the rough sex ain't much fun."

Older Guy grinned "Trust me. There's no problem here. It's good to see the law-enforcement community doing their job even this far from home. I'm Drake, Matt Drake."

He held out a hand.

Kennedy ignored it, still not convinced. Her mind focused on that phrase "doing their job" and flicked back over the last month where it snagged on the same barbed obstruction it always snagged on. On Kaleb's unconditional release. Kaleb had been her biggest takedown, and now a fellow cop's greed had set the serial killer free to murder once more, bestowing upon Kennedy a world of guilt. *And forced leave*, she thought.

"Well...thanks, I guess." She raised a half smile.

"So, you're a cop from *New York?*" The younger man looked at his friend, and raised his eyebrows.

"Bloody subtle." Matt Drake laughed. He seemed confident in himself and, though he sat easily, Kennedy could tell he had the competence to react in a second if the situation turned. The way he constantly surveyed his surroundings made her think he could be a cop. Or maybe military.

She nodded, wondering if she should invite herself to sit down. It would be good to have someone to talk to. Keeping her own company was more akin to demonic possession these days.

Drake indicated the free space, at the same time leaving him a clear way out. "Polite, too. I heard New Yorkers were the most overconfident people in the world."

"*Matt!*" The kid frowned.

"If by overconfident you mean awesome at the same time as

being extremely modest, I heard that too." Kennedy slid into the booth, feeling like a bit of a dweeb.

"An American alone in Paris. I guess you're on holiday?"

"So I'm told."

The guy didn't push it, just held his hand out again. "I'm still Matt Drake. And this is my friend, Ben."

"Kennedy. I overheard what you were saying, the headlines anyway. That's what hit me up. And what's that about wolves in *New York?*" She raised her eyebrows in imitation of Ben.

"Odin." Drake was studying her closely, watching for a reaction. "Know anything about him?"

"He was Thor's dad wasn't he? You know, in the Marvel comic."

"He's all over the news." Ben nodded at the PC.

"I've been keeping well clear of headlines lately." Kennedy's words came fast, wrung out with hurt and frustration.

"You make it sound like you've created a few."

It was a moment before she could carry on. "More than is good for my career." She gazed out through the dingy cafe windows into the street.

Drake followed her gaze, wondering if he should push her, and then his eyes locked onto those of one of the German mercenaries from earlier, peering through the glass, his gaze quickly sweeping the café.

"These guys are more annoying than a call center."

The German's face lit up with shock and recognition when Drake moved. Again, they were in trouble, and Ben's life was in danger. Drake made a decision. The gloves were well and truly off now. He moved fast, picked up one of the armchairs, and flung it through the window with an almighty crash. The German flew backwards and collapsed to the ground.

Drake waved Ben to the side. "Come with us, or don't," he called to Kennedy as he ran. "But stay out of my way."

He moved quickly to the door, flung it open, and paused in case there was gunfire. Those who hadn't noticed were standing about whilst one foolish tourist snapped away at the action. Drake cast a probing gaze down the street, recognizing faces from earlier and counting five enemies approaching.

"Suicide." He ducked back in.

"Rear entrance." He dragged Ben toward the counter. Kennedy hadn't moved, she was thinking hard, but it didn't take a cop's analytical mind to see these people were decent and, being a bit of a troublemaker herself, she recognized a kindred spirit in Drake.

"I'll help cover you for now."

Drake strode past the frightened counterman into a dingy corridor lined with boxes of coffee, sugar and stir-sticks. At the end was a fire exit door. Drake hit the push-bar, then peered cautiously outside. The afternoon sun stung his eyes, but the coast was relatively clear—that meant there was only one unarmed enemy racing around the corner toward him.

Drake motioned the others to hang on, then strode purposefully toward the running German. He didn't avoid the man's punch, but took it hard in the solar plexus without flinching. The shock on his opponent's face gave him a momentary satisfaction.

"Wimps aim for the plexus," he whispered. Experience had shown him that a trained opponent would strike at one of the body's pressure points and pause for effect, so Drake compartmentalized the pain—as he'd been endlessly taught—and ploughed through it. He broke the guy's nose and shattered his jaw with two strikes, and then left him sprawled on the floor without breaking stride. He waved the others out.

They exited the cafe and looked around.

Kennedy said, "My hotel's three blocks over."

Drake nodded. "Bloody awesome. Let's go."

SIX

PARIS, FRANCE

A minute later, Ben said, "Wait."

"Don't say you need the toilet, mate, or we're gonna have to buy you some nappies."

Kennedy hid a grin as Ben flushed.

"Don't be a dick, old man, but it is nearly time to visit the Louvre. The guy in white said six pm, remember?"

Drake had lost track of time. "Bollocks."

"The Louvre?" Kennedy said, glancing at him.

"About turn." Drake waved at a passing cab. "Kennedy, I'll explain."

"You'd better. I've already been to the Louvre today."

"Not for this..." Ben murmured as they climbed into the cab. Drake said the magic word and the car sped off. The journey was undertaken in silence and lasted ten minutes through streets clogged with traffic. An ambulance and a police car blasted through the crush, sirens shrieking. When they finally reached the Louvre, the pavements were no less hectic. The three of them tried to hotfoot it toward the museum.

As they did so, Ben brought Kennedy up to speed. "Someone found Odin's Shield in Iceland, then someone stole it from an exhibition in York, completely *ruining* Frey's catwalk show."

"Frey?"

"The fashion designer. Aren't you from New York?"

Drake shook his head in resignation at Ben's naivety.

"I *am* from New York," Kennedy said. "But I've always been a *cop* before a woman. And I'm not liking being dragged into this conflict. I really don't need any more problems right now."

Drake almost said "There's the door", but stopped himself at the last second. A New York cop might prove useful tonight for many reasons. As they approached the glass pyramid that marked the entrance to the Louvre, he said, "Kennedy, these people have tried to kill us three times now. It's my responsibility to make sure it doesn't happen again. We can't run because they've already proved they can find us. My only solution is to gather more information about what's happening, or go hide in a rat hole somewhere, which isn't my style."

Kennedy rolled her eyes. "I noticed."

"For some reason these people are interested in something called the 'Nine Pieces of Odin', and it all began with the discovery of the first piece—the shield. We don't know why yet, but in here," he pointed past the glass pyramid, "is the second piece."

"They're gonna steal it, tonight," Ben said, then added, "Probably."

"And what's the New York angle?" Kennedy appeared to be hovering between retreat and intrigue. Perhaps that was exactly what she needed: something to take her mind away from the harsh glare of stark reality.

"New York could be next. Another of the Odin artefacts is on display at the Natural History Museum."

"But you're not sure?"

Drake was studying a map and ignored the question. "Seems the Louvre doesn't normally display Viking collections. This one's also on loan. Says here, the biggest Norse interest is the Viking longship, one of the finest ever discovered. It's displayed on the lower ground floor of the Denon Wing, near some Egyptian...*Coptic*...*Ptolemaic*...*bollocks*...*bollocks*... whatever. It's this way."

The wide, polished corridors gleamed as the trio merged with the throng. Locals and tourists of all ages filled the grand old space.

Ben said, "Oh crap, it's already six o'clock."

Seconds later there was a thunderous boom, like a concrete wall collapsing. They all paused. Drake turned to Ben.

"Give us half an hour. When they evacuate, just leave with the crowd. I'll call you."

He didn't wait for an answer. Ben was fully aware of the danger. Drake watched him shaking his cellphone free and hitting a speed dial number. That'd be Mum, Dad or Sis. He motioned to Kennedy, and they proceeded down the spiral staircase toward the lower ground floor. Many people were flooding out of the room that housed the Viking exhibition. A thick cloud of gray smoke billowed out behind them.

"Run!" a guy that looked like a Hollister model shouted in an American accent. "There's dudes with guns in there!"

Kennedy wavered, looking unsure. "Shouldn't we—"

Drake walked ahead to the door and took a brief look inside. Total chaos greeted him. He counted eight guys in camouflage gear, with face masks and machine guns, clambering into the biggest Viking longboat he'd ever seen. Behind them, in an act of unbelievable recklessness, a smoking hole had been blasted through the side of the museum.

These guys were crazy. What gave them their edge was that they possessed the shocking directness of fanaticism. Blowing entrances into buildings and firing rockets above crowds seemed to be their norm. No wonder they'd pursued Ben and him around Paris earlier. Car chases were probably just helped them wind down before sleep.

Kennedy put a hand on Drake's shoulder and peered inside. "I think you just convinced me."

"Proves we're on the right track. We just need to get close to their commander."

"I'm not getting close to any of those *wankers*," she swore with a surprisingly good English accent.

"Cute. But I gotta find a way to get us off their kill list or figure out what they're up to."

Drake noticed several more civilians milling around the room and then suddenly running toward the exit. The Germans weren't keeping tabs on everyone, just confidently executing their plan which, Drake had to assume, was to steal the artefact.

"Come on." Drake slipped around the doorframe into the room. He used the perimeter exhibits for cover, watching

Kennedy carefully, and padded his way as close to proceedings as was safe.

"*Beeilen euch!*" someone shouted urgently.

"Something about 'hurry'," Drake said. "They'll have to be quick. An incident at the Louvre will get a pretty fast response from the French."

"I saw armed guards back there at the entrance," Kennedy pointed out.

Then, another of the Germans yelled, and held up a slab of stone the size of a dinner tray. It looked heavy. The soldier was asking for help unloading it over the lip of the longboat.

"Clearly not of the regiment," Drake commented.

"Or American," Kennedy noted. "I used to have a Marine boyfriend who could've tucked that trinket under his foreskin."

Drake choked. "Nice image. Thanks for contributing. Look." He nodded toward the gap in the wall where a white-suited masked man had just appeared. "Looks like the same guy that stole the shield in York."

The man briefly examined the sculpture before nodding in approval and turning to his commander. "Very good. Time to—"

Gunfire erupted. The Germans froze for a second, staring at each other in confusion. Bullets ripped through the room and everyone dived for cover.

More masked men appeared in the newly blasted entrance. A new force, dressed differently to the Germans.

Drake's immediate thought was, *French police? Armed guards?*

"*The Cultists!*" one of the Germans shouted in disdain. "Kill! Kill!"

Drake covered his ears as a dozen machine guns opened fire. Bullets ricocheted from human body to wooden exhibit and then to plaster wall. Glass shattered and priceless displays were ripped to shreds before being sent crashing to the floor. Kennedy swore loudly, which Drake was starting to realize was not exactly fresh ground for her. "Where are the fucking *French* for fuck's sake?"

Drake's head was spinning. *Cultists?* What kind of twisted hell had they stumbled into here?

The exhibit beside them exploded into a thousand pieces. Glass and bits of wood rained down on their backs. Drake started to crawl backwards, dragging Kennedy with him. The longboat was being riddled with lead. The cultists had advanced into the room by now and several of the Germans lay dead or twitching. As Drake watched, one of the cultists fired point-blank into a wounded German, spraying blood all over a three-thousand-year-old Egyptian terracotta vase.

"No love lost between loony relic hunters." Drake winced. "And all that time I spent playing *Tomb Raider*—it was never like this."

One of the Germans tried to escape. He ran right up to Drake without noticing him, then gave a start of surprise when his path was blocked. "*Bewegen!*" He raised his gun.

"Yeah, up yours too," but Drake raised his hands.

The man's finger tightened on the trigger.

Kennedy made a sudden movement to the side, drawing the German's attention. Drake moved in and elbowed him in the face. A fist came swinging toward Drake's head, which he side-stepped even as he kicked out the soldier's knee. A shriek barely covered the sound of snapping bone. Drake was on him in a second, knees pressing hard on his heaving chest. With a quick wrench he ripped away the soldier's mask and grunted.

"Don't know what I was really expecting."

Blond hair. Blue eyes. Solid features. Confused expression.

"Laters." Drake rendered him unconscious with a choke hold, trusting Kennedy to keep an eye out for his comrades. When Drake looked up, the battle still raged on. In that moment, another German came barreling around a falling exhibit. Drake shoulder-charged him to the side, and Kennedy kneed him in the solar plexus. The man went down hard.

One of the cultists was dragging the Odinic sculpture away from the dead and bloody fingers of his dying enemy. A German soldier outflanked him and attacked from the side, but the cult member was good, twisting and delivering three deadly strikes, then heaving the limp body over his shoulder and smashing it to the ground. The cultist fired three close shots for good measure then calmly continued dragging the sculpture toward the exit.

Drake was impressed with his skills. When the cultist reached his comrades, they laid down a hail of fire as they retreated over the still-smoking rubble.

"We win!" the cultist cried in an English accent, and raised a fist at the surviving Germans. Drake detected arrogance in her words. Yes, definitely a woman under the mask. But there was something else, something familiar about her..

The woman paused and removed her mask in a gesture of absolute disdain. She laughed at the Germans. "*Ha!* You think we can't follow you anywhere? You think we don't know what you're up to? We were *waiting* for you. We know where you're going next – we're all on the same quest. I'd keep *away* from Uppsala if you want to survive."

Drake might have collapsed if he hadn't already been on his knees. The shock of the moment was like being hit by a bullet. He recognized this so-called cultist. He knew her well. It was Alicia Myles, a Londoner, who used to be his equal in the British SRT.

The Special Reconnaissance Team: a secret regiment within the SAS, inside the covert British entity known as the Ninth Division. They were the best of the best. Patriots. Hand-picked by those who themselves had been hand-picked.

"I know her," he whispered without thinking. "We were in the regiment together."

Wells' earlier comment had unearthed memories that should have stayed buried forever. *You were* more *than SAS. Why would you want to forget that?*

Because once, we were something other than soldiers.

Those times, those battles, those live-or-die moments of combat and comradeship, were the moments that had shaped him.

Alicia Myles was one of the best he'd ever seen. Women had to be better than men in the Special Forces to get even half as far. And Alicia had gone right to the top, the first female member of the SAS.

What was *she* doing mixed up in this, and sounding like the fanatic he knew she certainly was not? Only one thing motivated Alicia—money.

Could that be why she was working for the cultists?

Drake started crawling toward the room's real exit. "So, far from getting us taken off the kill list and unmasking our enemies," he panted, "we've now got more enemies, and achieved nothing except to confuse ourselves even further."

Kennedy, crawling after him, said, "My life...in a nutshell."

SEVEN

PARIS, FRANCE

Kennedy's hotel suite was a palace compared to the one Drake and Ben had spent a couple of hours in earlier.

"Thought all you cops were broke," Drake grumbled as he checked ingress and egress points.

"We are. But when your vacation time is pretty much non-existent for ten years, your checking account really stacks up."

"Hey, can I use that?" Ben asked, reaching for the laptop that sat on a coffee table by the window. They had found him hiding in the shadow of the buildings near the glass pyramid after they had finally made their way out of the museum. In the chaos, it had been easy to pretend they were a couple of frightened tourists.

"Why aren't we alerting the French authorities to what we know?" Kennedy asked as Ben opened up her laptop.

"Because they're *French*," Drake said with a laugh, then sobered when no one joined in. He perched on the edge of Kennedy's bed, watching his friend work. "Sorry. The French won't know anything. Going through this with them now will only slow us down. It's the Swedes we should contact. Alicia said something about keeping away from Uppsala. She has to know that's only going to make everyone more interested. The Swedes are our best bet if we want to follow this lead."

"Know anyone in the Swedish Secret Service?" Kennedy raised an eyebrow at him.

"No, but I do have a call in to my old commander."

"When did you quit the SAS?"

45

"You never quit the SAS." When Ben looked up, he added, "I read that somewhere."

"Three heads should be better than two." Ben stared at Kennedy for a second. "That's if you're still in?"

A pause and then a slight nod. "I'll help you. For now." Kennedy's hair fell over her eyes, and she spent a minute tying it back. "These nine pieces of Odin...my first question is *why do they want them?* Second question is—what are they?"

"We were just figuring that out back at the cafe." Ben was tapping furiously at the keyboard. "There's a legend, which Mr. Crusty here disapproves of, alleging that there's an actual tomb of the gods—literally, a place where all the ancient gods are buried, which ties in to Euhermistic theory. Or maybe—" Ben allowed, "this tomb is simply full of *tributes* to the old gods, we don't know. But it's not just a dusty old legend either—a number of academics have debated it, with many papers being published over the years. Problem is," added Ben, rubbing his eyes, "it's tough reading. Old legends aren't renowned for their prosaic language."

"*Prosaic?*" Kennedy echoed with a smile. "You go to college yourself?"

"On occasion, but he's also in a band," Drake shot back, deadpan. "Lead singer."

Kennedy raised an eyebrow but didn't bite. "So you have a tomb of the gods that should never have existed. Okay. So what?"

"If the tomb's ever desecrated, the world will drown in fire...etc....etc."

"I see. And the nine pieces?"

"Once assembled at Ragnarok, they point the way to the tomb."

"Where's Ragnarok?"

Drake kicked at the carpet. "Nothing more than another red herring. It's not a place. It's actually a series of events, a great battle, the world cleansed by a flood of fire. Natural disasters. Pretty much Armageddon."

Kennedy frowned. "So even the hard-assed Vikings feared the apocalypse."

Looking down, Drake noticed on the floor a recent but very creased copy of *USA Today*. It had been folded around the headline: FREED SERIAL KILLER CLAIMS TWO MORE.

Nasty, but not unusual for the front page of a newspaper. The thing that made him snatch a further look, as if his eyes had been seared, was the picture of Kennedy, in her cop's uniform, within the body of the text. And the smaller headline beside her photo: COP CAN'T TAKE IT—GOES AWOL.

He linked the headlines to the almost empty bottle of vodka on the dresser, the painkillers on the bedside table, and the absence of luggage, tourist maps, souvenirs and an itinerary.

Shit.

Is she helping us to avoid her own problems? Distracting herself?

Kennedy was saying, "So the Germans and the cultists want to find this non-existent tomb for the glory and the riches maybe? And to do this they have to assemble Odin's Nine Pieces in a place that's not a place. That about right?"

Ben pulled a face. "Well, 'A song's not a song till it's been pressed into vinyl'—as my dad used to say. In English—we still have a lot of work to do."

"It's a stretch."

"This is more like it." Ben turned the laptop screen around. "Odin's Nine Pieces are listed: Eyes, Wolves, Valkyries, Horse, Shield and Spear."

Drake counted. "That's only six, kiddo."

"*Two* Eyes. *Two* Wolves. *Two* Valkyries."

"Which one's in Uppsala?" Drake winked at Kennedy.

Ben scrolled for a while, then said, "It says here that a spear was thrust through Odin's side while he hung fasting on the World Tree, revealing all his many secrets to his volva—his seeress. Listen to another quote—'*Near the Temple at Uppsala is a large tree with widespread branches that are always green both in winter and summer. What kind of tree it is nobody knows, for no others like it have ever been found*'. That's from a text hundreds of years old. The World Tree is—or *was*—in Uppsala and is central to Norse mythology. Medieval Scandinavians revered old Uppsala as one of the most important locations in the area. The Danish chronicler, Grammaticus, held Odin himself to have resided in Gamla Uppsala way back in ancient times. It was known as a residence of Swedish kings and says nine worlds exist around the World Tree. Oh, another reference to Uppsala, quote: 'Odin used to sojourn there, near an immense ash called Yggdrasil', considered holy by the locals. It's gone now, though.'

He read on. 'Scandinavian chroniclers have long held Gamla Uppsala to be one of the oldest and most important locations in Nordic history.'

"And this is all out there?" Kennedy said. "Where anyone can find it?"

"Well," Ben said, "it all needs linking together. Don't underestimate my powers, miss. I'm good at what I do."

Drake nodded in appreciation. "He is, believe me. He's helped me blag my way through a photographic career for the last six months."

"You have to piece together lots of different poems and historical sagas. A saga is a Viking poem of high adventure. There's also something called the *Poetic Edda*, written by descendants of people who knew people who knew the chroniclers of that time. There's a lot of information to sift through."

"And we know nothing about the Germans or their intentions. Not to mention the cultists. Or why Alicia Myles is—" but Drake's cellphone started to ring. "Sorry...yes?"

"Me," the voice on the other end belonged to his old commander.

"Hello, Wells."

"Sit down for this, Drake." Wells gave him a moment. This was clearly something big. "The SGG—the Swedish Special Forces, *and* elements of the Swedish Army have been recalled from all over the world."

Drake was momentarily speechless. "You're kidding?"

"I don't joke about work, Drake. Only women."

"Has this ever *happened* before?"

"Not that I recall."

"Do they give a reason?"

"Usual bollocks, I'm afraid. Nothing definitive."

"Anything else?"

There was a sigh. "Drake, you really owe me some Mai-time stories here, pal. Is Ben still there?"

"Yes. And do you remember Alicia Myles?"

"Jesus. Who wouldn't? You lucky bastard. She's with you?"

"As a matter of fact, no. I just saw her in the Louvre, about an hour ago."

Ten seconds of silence, then, "She was part of *that?* Impossible. She would never betray her own."

"We were *never* 'her own', or so it would seem."

"Are you saying she helped rob the museum?"

"That I am, sir. That I am." Drake walked to the window and stared out at the car lights whipping by below. "Hard to digest isn't it? Looks like she's made money her new vocation."

"Initial reports say that two enemies fought at the museum?"

"Yes. By the sound of it, these cultists who appeared knew the Germans' movements in advance."

Behind him he could hear Ben and Kennedy making notes about the famous and the more obscure locations of the Nine Pieces of Odin.

Wells was breathing heavily. "Alicia fucking Myles! Riding with the enemy? I just can't believe it, Drake."

"I saw her face, sir. It was her."

"Unbelievable. What's your plan?"

Drake closed his eyes and shook his head. "I'm not part of the team anymore, Wells. I don't have a friggin' plan. I shouldn't need to have a plan."

"I know. I'll assemble a team, pal, and start strategizing it from this end. Keep in touch."

The line went dead. Drake turned. Of course he had a plan, but Wells didn't need to know. In his experience the only way to deal with an enemy that wanted to kill you was to take them out first. He needed help for that, which was why Wells would prove useful. He was also becoming increasingly intrigued with the hunt for Odin's artefacts and now that Alicia Myles was involved. . .that took matters to a whole new level.

Wells had been correct. She shouldn't be working for the enemy. Was she also in trouble? Self-preservation and practicality told Drake that he should stop pursuing this madness. Seven years on and he thought he'd quelled the old fire but the flame still flickered, burning low but rising steadily, more imperative, forcing him to remember the thrill of it all. And now with the appearance of an old comrade the buzz of expectancy was back.

Both Ben and Kennedy were staring at him. "Don't worry," he said. "I'm not cracking up. What have you got?"

Kennedy used a spoon to whack a few sheets of paper she'd covered in cop shorthand. "Spear—Uppsala. Wolves—New York. After that, not a clue."

Drake shrugged. "We can only deal with what we know."

Kennedy gave him an odd smile. "A man after my own heart."

"What we know," Ben repeated, "is that Uppsala's next."

"Yeah," Drake muttered, "but I'm not sure my Gold Card can handle it."

EIGHT

UPPSALA, SWEDEN

During the flight to Stockholm, Drake decided to find out exactly what was going on with Kennedy.

Following a series of furious hand signals between Drake and Ben, the New York cop ended up sitting by the window with Drake next to her. Less chance of escape that way.

"So," he said as the plane finally leveled off and Ben flipped open Kennedy's laptop. "I'm picking up a vibe. I'm not being nosey, Kennedy, I just have a rule: I need to know about the people I work with."

"You think I'm working with you?"

"Either that, or you're using us as a means of getting distance." Drake shrugged. "I should know. I've done it myself twice before. Events got twisted to hell. I lost control. Things happened that should never have happened. I couldn't take back my mistakes and. . .well. . ."

Kennedy tapped the bulkhead beside her. "I should have known...always a price to pay for the window seat. Tell me first, how'd that vibe of yours work with this Alicia Myles that you seem so shocked to have seen?"

"That girl's a law unto herself. Crazy as all hell and as loyal as a bulldog." Drake made a face. "Wild and beautiful."

"Know her that well do you?"

"I did. Met her in Africa, which is quite fitting, whilst working for the Ninth Division." The words were out of his mouth before he could stop them, proving he still had a long way to go.

"The what?"

"Doesn't matter. Pretend I didn't blurt out a secret and tell me why you're running."

"Why do you wanna know?"

"If it's a personal problem—nothing you don't want to talk about. If it's work—a short synopsis."

"And if it's both?"

"Shit. I'm not trying to pry, but I have to put Ben first. I promised him we'd survive this, and I'd say the same to you. We have a *kill* order against us. They won't stop unless we make them, and we don't even know who *they* are or what their final agenda is, yet. One thing you're *not* is stupid, Kennedy, so you know I need to be able to trust you to work with me on this."

A flight attendant leaned over, offering a paper cup brimming with hot coffee.

"Caffeine." Kennedy accepted the drink gratefully. She had to reach past Drake. Her hand brushed against his cheek, they were in such close quarters.. He noticed she was wearing the third nondescript trouser suit since he'd met her. It told him she was a woman that received attention for the wrong reasons; a woman dressing down to fit in where she seriously wanted to belong.

Drake snagged a coffee for himself. Kennedy drank for a minute, then slipped a strand of hair behind her ear with a gentle gesture that Drake found himself drawn to.

She turned to him. "Maybe I am running further away, and it's none of your business, but I bagged a dirty forensic scientist. Caught him pocketing a fistful of dollars at a crime scene, and told IA about it. Ended up he got a stretch. A few years."

"Nothing wrong with that. His colleagues giving you shit?"

"Man, shit I can take. I've been taking it since I was five. What isn't right, what messes with my brain like a fucking power drill, is the reality you *don't* think about—that *every single one* of the bastard's previous cases is then brought into question. Every. Single. One."

"Officially? By whom?"

"By shit-eating lawyers. By shit-eating politicians. By campaigning mayors. By fame-seeking publicity nuts, too blinded by their own ignorance to tell right from wrong. By *bureaucrats*."

"Not your fault."

"Oh yeah? Tell that to the families of the victims of the worst serial killer New York State has ever known. He killed all those men and women and now, because of one crooked scientist's mistakes, he's been set free."

Drake clenched his fists in anger. "You said they *released* this guy?"

Kennedy's eyes were dead pits. "Two months ago. He's killed again since, and has now disappeared."

"No."

"All on me."

"No. It's on the system."

"I *am* the system. I work for the system. It's my life."

"So they sent you on holiday?"

Kennedy wiped her eyes. "Forced leave. My mind isn't...what it was. The job requires clarity every minute of every day. A clarity I can't achieve anymore."

She turned her abrasive attitude up full. "So? You happy now? Can you *work* with me now?"

But Drake didn't respond. He understood her pain. His own worst encounter with harsh blind bureaucratic response was the primary reason he'd quit the Army. The other...was Alyson.

They heard the captain's voice explain that they were thirty minutes from their destination.

Ben said, "Crazy. I just read that Odin's Valkyries are part of a private collection, whereabouts unknown." He broke out a notebook. "I'm gonna start taking notes. Some of this information is only mentioned briefly in museum archives."

Drake barely heard any of it. Kennedy's story was tragic, and not what he needed to hear. He buried his reservations, and didn't hesitate to cover her shaking hand with his own.

"We need your help on this," he whispered so Ben wouldn't hear and quiz him later. "*I* do. A good backup is essential to any operation."

Kennedy couldn't speak, but her brief smile was enough. Distance from her job and a new focus was exactly what she needed right now.

*

A plane change and a fast train later, and they were nearing Uppsala. Drake attempted to fight through the miasma of travel weariness that sought to fog his brain.

Outside, a late afternoon chill brought him round. They flagged down a cab and climbed in. Ben consulted his notebook. "Gamla Uppsala is basically *old* Uppsala. This place," he indicated Uppsala in general, "was built after a cathedral burned down in Gamla Uppsala. This is, essentially, new Uppsala, though it's hundreds of years old."

"Wow," Kennedy drawled. "How old does that make *old* Uppsala?"

"My thoughts exactly."

The cab hadn't moved. The driver now turned half around. "To the mounds?"

"'S'cuse me?" Kennedy asked.

"See the mounds? The royal mounds? All tourists go there." The halting English didn't help.

"Yes." Ben nodded. "The royal burial mounds. It's in the right area."

They ended up taking a mini-tour of Uppsala. Playing tourist, Drake couldn't really make sense of the circuitous route. On the bright side, the Saab was comfy and the city impressive. Uppsala was a university city these days, and the roads were crammed with bikes. At one point their chatty, though hard to decipher, driver explained that a bicycle wouldn't stop for anyone on the road. It would ride them down without thought.

"Accidents." He waved his hands at flowers adorning the pavements. "Many accidents."

Old buildings passed by on either side. Eventually, the city relented, and some verdant countryside started to brighten the landscape.

"Okay, so Gamla Uppsala is now a small village, but was a big thing back in the early ADs," Ben continued. "And Odin is said to have sacrificed himself on the World Tree whilst his seeress looked on, and listened to every secret he'd ever kept. She must have meant a lot to him." He frowned, clearly thinking, "They must have been incredibly close."

"It all sounds like a Christian confessional," Drake ventured.

"But Odin didn't *die* here?" Kennedy asked.

"No. He died fighting at Ragnarok, along with his sons—Thor and Freyr. So goes the legend."

The cab swung around a wide parking area before stopping. To the right, a well-worn dirt path led off through sparse trees. "To the mounds," their driver said.

They thanked him, and exited the Saab into bright sunlight and a crisp breeze. Drake's idea was to reconnoiter the immediate area and the village itself first, to see if anything caught their eye. After all, with so many international concerns applying their well-stroked egos to what could only be described as a global free-for-all, something may well have jumped out.

Beyond the trees, the landscape became a flat expanse of open field, interrupted only by dozens of small hillocks and three large mounds that lay dead ahead. Beyond this, in the distance, they spied a pale-colored roof and another building to its right, which marked the start of the village.

Kennedy paused. "No trees over there, guys."

Ben was engrossed in his notebook. "They're not gonna hang a sign out are they?"

"You have an idea?" Drake watched the wide-open fields for any signs of activity.

"I remember reading there were up to three thousand burial mounds here once. Today, there's a few hundred. Do you know what that means?"

"They didn't build 'em very well?" Kennedy smiled.

"Lots of *underground* activity in ancient days. And then these three 'royal' mounds. In the nineteenth century they were named after three legendary kings of the House of Yngling—Aun, Adil and Egil—one of Scandinavia's most renowned royal families. But—" he paused, enjoying himself, "it *also* claims that the earliest mythology and folklore had the royal mounds *already there*, and that they were ancient tributes to the earliest— *original*—three kings, or *gods,* as we would know them now. That's Freyr, Thor and *Odin.*"

"Random input here," Kennedy said. "But have you noticed how many references to biblical stories we keep getting from all these ancient stories? Three *kings.*"

"They're *sagas*." Ben corrected. "Poems. Academic scribblings. Something that might be important—the mounds are referenced many times with the Swedish word falla, and manga fallor—not sure what that means. And, Kennedy, didn't I read somewhere that Christ's story was very similar to one involving Zeus?"

Drake nodded. "And the Egyptian god, Horus, was another forerunner. Both were gods that supposedly never existed." Drake nodded toward the three royal mounds standing prominent against the flat landscape. "Freyr, Thor and Odin, eh? So who's who then, Blakey?"

"Not a clue, mate."

"Worry not, munchkin. We can torture the information out of those villagers if need be."

They proceeded past the burial mounds, playing the part of three weary tourists for the benefit of watching eyes. The sun beat down hard on their heads and Drake saw Kennedy break her sunglasses out.

Ben's phone rang. Kennedy smirked, already bemused by the frequency of family contact. Drake playfully met her eyes.

"Karin!" Ben said happily. "How's my big sister?"

Kennedy tapped Drake on the shoulder. "Lead singer in a band?" she inquired. "He doesn't seem the sort."

Drake shrugged. "Heart of gold, that's all. He'd put himself out to help you without complaint. How many friends or colleagues have *you* got like that?"

Kennedy fixed him with a stare. "I'm a cop. So, *a lot*. But not as many now as I used to."

The village of Gamla Uppsala was picturesque and clean, a few streets of land-locked, high-roofed buildings, all hundreds of years old, well-preserved and sparsely populated. The occasional villager regarded them with curiosity.

Drake headed for the church. "Local vicars are always helpful."

As they approached the porch, an old man wearing ecclesiastic robes all but ran them down. He paused in surprise.

"*Hej. Kan jag hjalpa dig?*"

"Not sure about that, mate." Drake gave his best Yorkshire accent. "But which one of them mounds over there belongs to Odin?"

"So you are English?" The priest spoke the language well, it seemed, but struggled to understand. "Vad? What? Odin?"

Ben stepped forward and drew the vicar's attention to the royal mounds. "We're looking for Odin."

"See." The old man nodded. "Yes. Umm. *Storsta...*" He struggled to find the word. "Big."

"The biggest?" Ben held his hands wide apart.

Drake studied the mounds.

"Figures." Kennedy started to turn away, but Ben had one last question.

"*Falla?*" he mouthed wonderingly at the vicar, and exaggerated a shrug. "*Or manga fallor?*"

It took a while but the answer, when it came, chilled Drake to the bone.

"Traps...many traps."

NINE

GAMLA UPPSALA, SWEDEN

Drake followed Ben and Kennedy toward the largest of the royal mounds, making a play of struggling to adjust the straps on his backpack so he could calmly survey the area. The only cover was about a mile beyond the smallest barrow, and for a second he thought he saw movement there. Quick movement. But further scrutiny revealed nothing more.

They paused at the foot of Odin's barrow. Ben set off in a hurry. Drake followed more serenely, and smiled at Kennedy walking just that little bit faster than him.

Underneath, he started to grow more and more agitated. This did not sit well with him. They were hopelessly exposed. Were other enemies already here, searching for this part of the Nine Pieces of Odin? Did Ragnarok and the world ending in fire carry any weight in real life today? If it did, even just slightly, then there was another reason Drake wanted to be involved.

Any number of high-powered rifles could be tracking them, crosshairs steady, awaiting the order. The wind whistled loudly and snapped around his ears, increasing his sense of exposure as he drifted past the other two over to the unprotected side.

It took about twenty minutes to gain the top of the grassy knoll. When Drake reached it, Ben was already sitting down in the grass.

"Forgot the picnic hamper, crusty?"

"Left it on your buggy." He looked around. Up here, the view was breathtaking, endless green rolling fields, hills and streams everywhere, and purple mountains in the distance. They could see the village of Gamla Uppsala spreading out to the city boundaries of new Uppsala.

Kennedy stated the obvious. "So I'm just gonna say something that's been bothering me for a while. If this *is* Odin's mound, and it hides the World Tree—which would be a killer discovery—why hasn't anyone ever found it before?"

"That one's easy." Ben was tying back his unruly locks. "No one has really known where to *look* before. It seems that until the discovery of the shield a month ago, this was all thought to be a dusty old legend. A myth. And it wasn't easy connecting the spear to the World Tree—now called Yggdrasil almost universally—and then to Odin's brief nine days there."

"And—" Drake interjected, "this tree isn't gonna be easy to find, if it exists. They won't have wanted any old fruitcake just stumbling onto it."

Now Drake's cellphone started to ring. He glanced at Ben in mock seriousness as he picked it out of his backpack. "Jesus. I'm starting to feel like *you*."

"Wells?"

"Ten-man team at your disposal. Just say the word."

Drake swallowed his surprise. "*Ten* men. That's a big team.".

"Big stakes, so I hear. This thing's escalating by the hour."

"It is?"

"Governments never change, Drake. Slow to start, then eager to bulldoze their way in and scared to finish. If it's any consolation, though, it's not the biggest thing going on in your neck of the woods at the moment."

Wells's statement surprised him. "It isn't?"

"That bloody volcano, you know the one that keeps erupting every month or so? They say it might be about to blow again."

"*What?*"

"And tell me the first thing you think of when you hear about an erupting volcano."

"Rivers of fire. Which reminds me of Ragnarok," Drake said, his throat suddenly dry. He had now heard references to that phrase twice in as many days, the first being back in Paris where Ben had found references to Odin's legend. He watched Ben and Kennedy tracing the mound's circumference, kicking grass, and felt a deep-rooted fear like nothing he'd ever experienced.

"Where is it? Iceland?" he asked.

Wells coughed. "Yes. Near where they found that shield of yours."

Drake was about to bite for the second time when Ben called him over. "This place is bigger than we thought. If the World Tree is here, it's not going to be an easy find."

Drake told Wells he'd call him back, then studied Ben. "Are we sure we're on the right track?"

"Where else could it be? What we need is some ground penetrating radar. A complete scan of this area."

"No time," Drake cut him off. "What else are you looking for?"

"Runic inscriptions," Ben said. "It was written that they showed the way to Yggdrasil, though I don't see any."

Kennedy snorted. "Like it would be that easy."

Drake eyed the skies. "It's going to be dark soon. I know we're in a hurry, but without more info we could be barking up the wrong tree, so to speak."

Kennedy gave him wide eyes. "I have no idea what you just said."

"Only that this may be a red herring. I mean, look around." He gestured at the general area. "There's nothing here."

"But..." Ben kicked at the ground as if the World Tree might somehow miraculously appear.

"It's cold. It's getting dark. Let's find a bed, a meal, and gather up some more intelligence. Odin's not going anywhere."

Kennedy lowered her head. "You know, sat here, for the first time I actually feel as though the eyes of the world aren't judging me."

Drake pushed his plate away. The pair were waiting for Ben to return with one of the laptops. The lodging they'd found offered only a hard-wired Internet, and that only in the dining room. "I can't say I'm not grateful for your help, Kennedy, but is hiding really the best thing at this time?"

"You did it. You ran."

Drake shook his head. "Funny thing. I was the...model soldier. The young man with no living family, desperate to see action and better myself. I wanted to do good. Help people. What eventually happened to me, what made me run, turned me into the man I am today. Suspicious. Wary. I question everything."

"What happened to you?" Kennedy's voice was soft, curious.

Drake didn't answer, replaying tragic events in his head that had no place being repeated aloud here, to someone he had really only just met.

Kennedy let it go. "But you still help people. You put the welfare of others before your own. That's the kind of quality people recognize and makes them trust you, y'know? It's one of the reasons I'm here."

"Yes."

"Are you glad that you ran?"

Drake gave her a knowing look. "Yes."

Kennedy looked away. "Then maybe I will be too."

"Don't use *me* against me."

"I didn't mean it that way. I just..." Kennedy stared at the nearby wall as if she might see through it, all the way to New York and beyond, into the distant future. "What I imagined my life to be? It all just came crashing down."

Drake laid a gentle hand on hers. "I know. But was it really your fault?"

Kennedy stared at the hand, but didn't make any attempt to remove it. "Does it matter?" She regarded him with tired, perceptive eyes. "The papers are involved. The politicians. The bosses. Everyone has an opinion and it generally revolves around their own agenda. So—does it really matter that it wasn't my fault?"

Drake squeezed her fingers. "When you put it that way—"

Ben raced through the door, almost tripping in his haste and then pulling up suddenly when he saw the pair holding hands. Drake pulled away self-consciously. Kennedy just smiled.

Ben dropped the laptop heavily onto the white plastic table. "All right. I started without you. Look at this. You remember the runic inscriptions they found on Odin's Shield?"

"Yes." Drake recalled the animal symbols quite clearly. He'd taken dozens of pictures of them.

"They're also Viking symbols, yes? *Odinic* symbols. Scientists have matched them to ancient treasures found around the world, dating back to Viking times. And if the symbols are on the shield—"

"Then they should also be on, or around, the World Tree," Kennedy finished.

"Right."

"We looked." Drake reminded him. "Didn't find any."

"We didn't look hard enough." Ben shrugged. "They're buried."

"So we look again. But carefully. It makes me nervous that none of the other teams have arrived here yet."

Kennedy gestured toward the room's only window where wraiths of dark and shadow clustered as if eavesdropping on their conversation. "They're out there," she said. "Just waiting."

The new dawn found them ascending once again to the summit of Odin's barrow. Drake had managed to secure a rusty old spade from the hotel's handyman—after parting for twice its value—and looked to Ben for guidance.

"Any ideas?"

"Nope."

Drake studied their surroundings. "I feel a little exposed up here. The only thing we've found out so far is that they don't want us dead. Yet. Let's get on with it." He slammed the edge of the spade hard into the earth, encountering no resistance. After a few minutes of aimless observation Ben and Kennedy wandered off to poke around other areas. Drake's face was bathed in orange and red, lit by the colors of the rising sun.

As the morning wore on, Drake's enthusiasm and belief waned. He called Ben over. "We could be standing on top of the bloody tree and never know it."

"At least we still haven't been attacked," Kennedy pointed out. "That's something."

"And it could mean we're in the wrong place entirely."

By lunchtime, Drake had had enough. He sat down amidst the faded clumps of grass, gazing at the faraway stands of trees and barrow mounds. From the rucksack he produced a bottle of water. "Time for a rethink. We're off the mark."

Kennedy was close and hunched down beside him. "Why,

Matt?" she asked. "Why does it matter so much? If we're wrong then we're pretty safe, don't you think?"

Drake knew she was right, but couldn't suppress the urge that was a part of him. "I guess when I start something I bloody well need to finish it," he admitted. "I want to know what this is all about. Don't you?"

"Sure. But not if it puts us all in more danger." Kennedy took the bottle off him and put her lips to the neck, touching the lingering ghost of his own.

"Steady on, lass. That's the only bottle I brought."

"Friggin' soldier boys."

Just then, Ben shouted, *"Found something!"*

"Gotta go." Drake raced over to Ben, casting about as best he could. Kennedy was also looking around, but the only activity she seemed to see was back at the village.

"Keep it down, mate. Whatcha got?"

"These." Ben dropped to his knees and scooped out tufts of soil and mud and tangles of grass to reveal a stone slab about the size of an A4 piece of paper. "I found three in a line."

Drake peered closer. The stone's face was badly weathered, but had been partially protected by the overgrowing grass. Its surface bore some kind of marking.

"Runic inscriptions," Ben said in excitement. "Viking symbols."

"If the kid's right, there could be dozens," Kennedy drawled, looking around the steep, grassy hillside. "So what? Doesn't help."

"*Kid* says it might do," Ben said. "If they're on the shield *and* on this mound then they're important. I think we should find the runes associated with what we're looking for. The rune for spear. The rune for tree. And the rune for—"

"Odin," Kennedy finished.

Drake had an idea. "I'm betting we can use line of sight. We all need to see each other to know it's worked, right?"

"Soldier's logic," Kennedy laughed. "But worth a try, I guess."

Drake itched to ask her about "cop's logic" but time was slipping away. Other factions were coming and were surprisingly absent, even now. They kicked the grass from each stone as they investigated the area around the green knoll. At first it was a thankless task, the stones long since buried and the grass thick and resistant. Drake made out symbols that looked like shields, crossbows, a donkey, a longboat, then—*a spear!*

"Got one." His low-pitched voice carried to the other two, and no further. He sat down with his backpack and organized the rest of the supplies they'd bought during their cab ride through Uppsala. Flashlights—including a supersized one—matches, water, a couple of knives he'd told Ben were for clearing debris. He'd received an I'm-not-that-bloody-gullible look, but their need was more imperative than Ben's unease right now.

"Tree." Kennedy fell to her knees, scraping at the stone she'd found. "These runes are surprisingly accessible once you get the top layer off. Almost as if..." She paused.

Drake scooped out more loose soil. "They've been recently uncovered and reburied." He nodded. "Keep going. Nothing we can do about it now."

It took Ben ten more stressful minutes to find something. He paused, then retraced his recent steps. "Remember what I said about how Tolkien based Gandalf on Odin?" He tapped the stone with his foot. "Well, that's Gandalf. Even has a staff. Hey!"

Drake watched him carefully. He'd heard a grinding sound, like heavy shutters rasping open.

"Did you cause that by stepping on the stone?" he asked.

"Think so."

They all looked at each other, expressions flickering from excitement to worry, to fear, and then, as one, they stepped forward.

Drake's stone gave slightly. He heard the same grinding sound. The earth in front of the stone sank, then the depression ran quickly away around the mound like a turbo-charged snake.

Ben shouted, "There's something here."

Drake and Kennedy tracked the sunken earth to where he stood. He crouched down and peered into a crack in the ground. "Some kind of tunnel."

Drake brandished his flashlight. "Follow me," he said.

The moment they were out of sight, two radically different forces started to mobilize. The Germans had been laying low in the wooded environs around the sleepy town of Gamla Uppsala, and now geared up and followed in Drake's footsteps.

The other force, a contingent of troops from the Swedish Army's Elite Forces, that had been quietly observing this place for days, continued to watch the Germans and discussed the odd complication posed by the three unknown civilians that had just descended into the pit.

They would need to be fully interrogated and debriefed. By any means necessary.

That is, if they survived what was about to come.

TEN

THE PIT OF THE WORLD TREE, SWEDEN

Drake stooped low. The dark passageway had started as a crawl-hole, and was now less than six feet high. The ceiling was made of rock and dirt, and riddled with big, dangling loops of overgrowing grass that they were forced to chop out of the way.

Like tackling a jungle, Drake mused. *Only underground.* It brought back memories of operations he'd undertaken in the SAS. Old days, mostly good, long gone now.

Some of the tougher vines, he noticed, had already been hacked apart. Another shiver of unease ran through him.

They came to a section where the roots were so dense they were forced to crawl again. The going was tough and filthy, but Drake put elbow before elbow, knee before knee, and encouraged the others to follow. When even coaxing failed for Ben, Drake had to physically push the young man through, and found himself using his old drill sergeant's voice to urge Ben to greater efforts.

"At least the temperature's dropping," Kennedy muttered, wiping away sweat. "We must be heading further down."

Drake's eye was now caught by something revealed in the glow of his flashlight.

"Look at that."

He pointed to runes, carved into the wall. Odd symbols that closely resembled those that decorated Odin's Shield. Ben's choked voice echoed up the passage.

"High five, mate. Nordic runes. Good omen."

Drake shone his light away from them with regret. It would

have been nice to be able to translate them on site. Now. *The regiment and Wells,* he thought briefly, *have far better resources. Maybe it is time to bring them in.*

Another fifty feet, and the sweat poured off him. He could hear Kennedy breathing heavily and cursing that she'd worn her best suit. He resisted the urge to ask how it was any different to the other half dozen or so. He heard nothing from Ben at all.

"You okay, Ben? Got your long hair tangled on a root?"

"Har-bloody-har."

Drake continued crawling through the dirt. "Another thing that worries me," he said between breaths, "is the translation of 'many traps'. The Egyptians used to build traps, elaborate ones, to protect their treasures. Why not the Norsemen?"

"Can't imagine a Viking thinking too hard over a trap," Kennedy puffed back.

"Don't pre-judge," Ben shouted along the line. "The Vikings had great thinkers too, you know. Just like the Greeks and the Romans. They weren't all barbarians."

A few turns, and the passage started to widen. Another ten feet, and the roof vanished above them. At this point they stretched and took a breather. Drake's flashlight picked out the passageway ahead. When he shone it on Kennedy and Ben, he laughed.

"Shit, you two look like you've just risen from the grave!"

"And I guess you're used to this crap?" Kennedy waved an arm. "Being SAS and all?"

Not SAS, poisonous words that Drake couldn't shake. "Used to be," he said, and quickly walked on.

Another abrupt turn and Drake felt a breeze on his face. A sense of vertigo hit him like an unexpected clap of thunder, and it was a second before he realized he was standing on a ledge with a cavernous drop below him.

An unbelievable sight greeted his eyes.

He stopped so suddenly that both Kennedy and Ben walked into him. Then they too beheld the sight.

The World Tree stood before them in all its glory. It had *never* been above ground. The tree was vast; its solid roots delved into the foundations of the earth below them, held fast by age and surrounding rock formations, its branches golden brown, its leaves a perennial green, fed by something as yet unnamable. Its trunk disappeared a hundred feet down into the depths of a gargantuan pit.

Their path wended away to become a narrow staircase, cut into the rock walls around it.

"Traps," Ben breathed. "Don't forget the traps."

"Screw the traps," Kennedy voiced Drake's very thought. "Where's the *light* coming from?"

Ben looked from side to side. "It's *orange.*"

"Glow sticks and amber flares," Drake said. "Some part of this place has been prepped."

He used to send men in to prepare an area such as this; a team to assess the danger and neutralize and catalogue it before returning to base. Sometimes, if an enemy was expected, the team would lie in wait.

"We don't have long," he said. His faith in Kennedy had just risen another notch. "Come on."

They descended worn and crumbling steps, the sheer drop always to their right. Ten feet down, and the staircase started to slope sharply. Drake stopped as a three-foot gap opened up. Nothing spectacular, but enough to give him pause—because the yawning drop below became all the more apparent.

"Here we go."

He jumped. Three feet wasn't much of a gap. But it was the drop that worried him. One wrong move and it was a long plunge to certain death.

He landed true and turned immediately, sensing Ben would be more than a little apprehensive. "Don't worry." He ignored Kennedy and concentrated on his friend. "Trust me, Ben. *Ben.* I will catch you."

He saw the faith in Ben's eyes. The absolute trust. It was time to earn it again, and when Ben jumped, then tottered, Drake steadied him with a hand on the elbow.

Drake winked. "Easy."

Kennedy jumped. Drake watched closely whilst pretending not to. She landed with no problem, saw his concern, and frowned.

"It's three feet, Drake. Not the Grand Canyon."

Drake rolled his eyes at Ben. "Ready, mate?"

Twenty feet more and the next gap in the staircase was wider—this time thirty feet. Luckily it was spanned by a thick, freshly-laid wooden plank – more evidence that this place had already been prepped - that rocked as Drake padded across. Kennedy followed, and then an uneasy Ben compelled by Drake to keep his eyes up, to look ahead and not down, to study his destination and not his feet. The young man was panting hard by the time he reached solid ground, and Drake called for a brief break.

As they paused, Drake saw that the World Tree had spread so wide here that its thick limbs almost touched the staircase. Ben reached out reverently to stroke a limb that shivered at his touch.

"This is...this is mind-boggling," he whispered.

Kennedy used the time to retie her hair and study the entrance above them. "So far, all clear," she said. "I gotta say, on current form, it sure wasn't the Germans that prepped this place. They woulda ransacked it and turned the tree into kindling with flamethrowers."

Drake looked across. "So who?"

A few more gaps and they'd descended fifty feet, almost halfway. Drake wondered if the old Vikings weren't the equal of the Egyptians after all, or maybe this place was so old that some of the steps had simply fallen away with time. That was when he stepped on a rock stair that was in fact a cleverly fashioned section of hemp, twine and pigment. He fell, saw the endless drop, and tried to twist his body in mid-air.

Kennedy dived headlong, but missed catching his jacket.

Drake flailed. An empty death snapped at his heels. With a last, desperate lunge he caught himself by the fingertips.

Kennedy hauled him up. "Ass swaying in the breeze?"

He scrambled back onto solid ground and flexed his bruised fingers. "Thanks."

They proceeded carefully, testing each step, now more than halfway down. Beyond the empty expanse to their right the massive tree stood in perpetuity, untouched by breeze and sunlight, a forgotten wonder of olden days. A miraculous, living creation of the gods.

Ben studied the tree and remarked on some of the history he

had retained. "A sacred tree—not Yggdrasil—was located near the temple at Uppsala above," he said. "They say it was a Yew tree and scholars suggested it had widespread branches that were always green through winter and summer, and that it stood next to a spring and a well. The descriptions are reminiscent of the Yggdrasil legend and it was thought that the Swedes had purposefully created a copy of the world of the Norse gods at Uppsala. It stands up that Yggdrasil itself would be here."

"It's all just guesswork, though, isn't it?" Kennedy asked with an arched eyebrow.

Ben shrugged. "It's actually worse than that. Norse cosmology and legend, every myth, has direct parallels in Asian cosmology and myth. Legends from Siberia to Germany and many more pay tribute to the world tree. Christianity parallels Norse and Egyptian and even Greek mythology. It's as if...all the gods came from one source, one time and place, and later branched away."

They passed more and more Viking symbols. Ben guessed at some of the markings. "It's like a primordial wall of graffiti," he said. "People just carving their names and leaving messages— early versions of 'John was 'ere!'"

"The cavern makers' signatures?" Kennedy asked.

"Yes." Ben nodded.

Drake tested another step, clinging to the cold rock wall, and a deep grinding roar echoed across the cavern. A river of rubble cascaded upon them from above.

"Run!" Drake cried. "Now!"

They pelted down the staircase, heedless of other traps. A gigantic boulder fell with a mighty roar, chipping off more ancient stones as it clattered down. Drake covered Ben's body with his own as the boulder smashed through the staircase where they had stood, taking about eight feet of precious stone steps with it.

Kennedy flicked stone chips off her shoulder, and regarded Drake with a dry smile. "Thanks for the help."

"Hey, I knew the woman that saved this guy's ass could outrun a mere *boulder*."

"Funny, man. So funny."

But it wasn't over yet. There was a sharp *twang* and a thin but solid length of twine snapped across the step that separated Ben and Kennedy.

"*Shit!*" Kennedy shouted. The length of twine had shot out with so much force it could easily have separated her ankle from the rest of her body.

Another snap two steps further down, and Drake danced in place.

Another roar from above signified the next falling rock.

"It's a replicating trap," Ben told them. "Same thing keeps happening over and over. We need to get below this section."

Drake couldn't tell which steps were snared and which weren't, so he trusted to luck and speed. They pounded headlong down twenty steps, trying to stay airborne as much as possible. Parts of the staircase crumbled as they traversed the ancient pathway, disintegrating into the depths of the rocky cavern.

The sound of rubble hitting the bottom grew louder.

The snapping of hard twine followed their flight.

Drake stepped on another false stair, but his momentum took him over the short void. Kennedy leapt it and him, graceful as a gazelle in full flight, but Ben tumbled in her wake, now rolling into the gap.

"Legs!" Drake shouted, then fell backward across the void, his shoulders braced on the far side, his body bridging the gap. Relief washed away a feeling of sick tension when Kennedy pinned his legs. He felt Ben hit his body, then tumble across his chest. Drake guided the kid's momentum as best he could, then gave him an extra push onto solid ground.

He then sat up quick, crunch style. "Keep going!"

The air was filled with bits of rock. A piece glanced off Kennedy's head, leaving a cut and a gush of blood in its wake. Another struck Drake's ankle. The agony made him grit his teeth, and spurred him to run faster.

Then bullets raked the wall above their heads. Drake ducked and took a momentary look up at the entrance.

He saw a familiar force gathered there—the Germans.

They ran at full pace now, beyond reckless. Drake allowed precious seconds to elapse as he fell to the rear. When another salvo of bullets pitted the stone next to his head, he dived forward, bouncing down the steps, rolling full circle with his arms tucked in, and coming back up to full height without losing an ounce of momentum.

Ah, the good old days were back.

More bullets. Then Ben and Kennedy collapsed in front of him. Horror sheared a hole through his heart until he realized they'd simply hit the bottom of the cavern at a sprint and, unprepared, had run themselves right into the ground.

Drake slowed. The bottom of the cavern was a thick mess of stone, dust and tree-debris. When they rose, Kennedy and Ben were a sight to behold. Not only were they covered in dirt and mud, but now with extra glued-on dust and leafy mold.

"Ah, for my trusty camera," he said. "Years of blackmail stands before me."

Drake picked up a glow stick and hugged the curve of the cavern that ran away from the gunmen. It took minutes to walk the outer limits of the tree, constantly overshadowed by its imposing stillness and outspread branches.

Drake clapped Ben on the shoulder. "Better than any Friday night groupie session, mate."

Kennedy glanced at the young lad with disbelief. "You have *groupies*? Your band has *groupies*? That's a conversation I'm looking forward to."

"Only two—" Ben began to stammer as they rounded a portion of the final curve, but then clammed up in shock.

They all stopped.

Ancient dreams of amazement stood before them, rendering them speechless for about half a minute.

Finally, Ben found his voice. "Now that's...that's..."

"*Gobsmacking*," Drake breathed.

A row of Viking longships stretched away from them, single file, stood end to end, as if stuck in the middle of an archaic traffic jam. Their sides were adorned with silver and gold, their sails festooned with silk and jewels.

"Longboats," Kennedy said numbly.

"*Longships*." Ben still had wits enough to correct her. "These things were considered great treasures of their time. There must be...what? I can't even see how many."

"Maybe they built these down here," Drake said, squinting in the low light of the glow stick. "Some kind of homage. But it's the spear we came for. Any ideas?"

Ben was now staring at the World Tree. "Wow, guys. Can you imagine? Odin hung in that tree. *Odin.*"

"So now you believe in gods, groupie-boy?" Kennedy sidled next to Ben.

Drake climbed onto a narrow ledge that ran the length of the longship traffic jam, level with their high sides, as if it might be used to climb aboard. The rock felt sturdy. He gripped a timber edge and leaned over. "These things are filled with loot. Safe to say, no one's ever been down here before the people who left these glow sticks."

He studied the line of ships again. A display of unimaginable riches, but where was the *real* treasure? At the end? Did the longships lined the way? The rough sides of the cavern were adorned with ancient drawings. He saw an enormous depiction of Odin hanging on the World Tree, a woman kneeling before him.

"What does this say?" He beckoned Ben over. "C'mon, hurry. Those guys aren't jamming Bratwurst down their throats up there. Let's move."

He indicated a rough swirl of text underneath the woman's supplicating figure. Ben shook his head. "Don't know. But technology, later, will find a way." He took a snap with his trusty iPhone that, thankfully for Drake and Kennedy, had proved to be out of signal down here. The last thing they wanted was a call from mom or dad interrupting their search.

Drake pointed out another depiction, the fourth out of five. It showed a line of longships that led toward a glittering object, something hidden inside a dark cavern. The only thing visible was its glow.

Drake took a moment to include Kennedy in the decision making. "I guess we should follow these longships," he said. "You okay with that?"

"Like the cheerleader said to the football team—I'm game, boys. Lead the way."

He forged ahead, aware that if this super-tunnel came to a

dead end they would be all but trapped. The Germans would be hard on their tail, not resting on their laurels.

Drake focused on the ledge that had been hewn into the rock. Every so often they came across another glow stick. Drake masked them or moved them to create a more shadowy environment, preparing for the conflict he knew was ahead. He scanned the longships below, and finally made out a tight path meandering between them—Plan B.

He counted two, four, and then ten longships as he went past. The glow sticks ran out. Drake's feet started to ache with the effort of negotiating the narrow path.

The faint noise of a tumbling boulder, and then a louder scream echoed through the gargantuan cavern, its meaning obvious. Without a sound they all bent even harder to their task.

Drake came at last to the end of the row. He'd counted fourteen ships, every one pristine and laden with loot. As they approached the back of the tunnel, darkness started to encroach.

"Guess the glow stick men never got this far," Kennedy remarked.

Drake rummaged for the big flashlight. "Risky," he said. "But we need to know."

He clicked it on and swept the beam from side to side. The passageway narrowed drastically, until it became a simple archway up ahead.

Beyond the archway lay a single set of stairs, leading into further blackness.

Ben then stage-whispered, "They're on the ledge!"

This was it. Drake took action. "We split up," he said. "I'll go for the stairs. You two get down there among the ships and head back the way we came."

Kennedy started to protest, but Drake shook his head. "No. Do it. *Ben* needs protection, I don't. And *we* need the spear."

"And when we reach the end of the ships?"

"I'll be back by then."

Drake sprang away without another word, leaping off the ledge and making for the blind staircase. He looked back once and saw shadows advancing along the ledge. Ben was following Kennedy down the rubble-strewn slope to the base of the last Viking ship.

Drake hit the stairs at a dead run, taking them two at a time. *Come on.* He climbed until his calves ached and his lungs burned, and came out onto a wide platform. Beyond this ran a narrow stream, rushing madly, and still further away stood a raised altar of rough-hewn rock, almost like an archaic barbecue.

But it was the massive symbol engraved into the wall behind it that caught Drake's attention: three triangles, overlaying one another. Some mineral within the carvings caught the artificial light and gleamed like sequins on a black dress.

No time to lose. He waded across the stream, sucking in air when the freezing water rose surprisingly to his thighs. As he approached the altar, he saw an object resting on its surface. A short, pointed artefact, not astonishing or impressive. Actually quite mundane...

...the Spear of Odin.

The weapon that had pierced the side of a god.

A surge of excitement and apprehension passed through him. *This* was the event that made it all real. Up until now it had been a bunch of *maybes,* just clever speculation. But now it was all frighteningly real.

Horrifyingly real.

ELEVEN

THE PIT OF THE WORLD TREE, SWEDEN

Drake didn't stand on ceremony. He grabbed the spear and headed back the way he'd come, through the freezing stream and down the crumbling stairs. He switched the flashlight off as he neared the bottom, and slowed when utter darkness enveloped him.

Faint beams of light swept the entrance below.

He kept going. It wasn't over yet. He'd long since learned that, more often than not, the man who stood and thought overlong in combat was the man who never made it home.

He stopped on the last step, then crept into the passageway's deeper darkness. The Germans were close now, almost at the end of the ledge, but their flashlights would only pick him out as another shadow at this range. He skipped across the passage, hugged the wall, and started for the slope that led to the base of the Viking ships.

A man's voice snapped, "See that! Look sharp up there!" The voice surprised him. It carried the deep twang of the American South. The Germans weren't working alone. Or else the man was a mercenary.

Bollocks. The eagle-eyed soldier had seen him. He ran faster. A shot rang out, striking rock close to where he'd just been.

A shadowy figure leaned out over the ledge—probably the American. "There's a path down there among the ships. Nap time's over, guys. Get your lazy asses movin'."

One of the Germans swore loudly in English "Why us, Milo? You think you are Captain America. *You* go first."

The German then yelled in surprise as Milo manhandled him bodily down the slope.

Drake thanked his lucky stars for the German's unruliness. He was on the man in a second, smashing his vocal chords and twisting his neck with an audible crack before anyone else could follow. The difference between soldiers and mercenaries consistently proved the saying: Mercs never get old.

Drake raised the German's gun—a Heckler and Koch MG4— and fired off a few rounds. One man flew back hard against the rock wall.

Ah, yes, he thought, *still better at shooting a gun than a camera.*

"It's the *Canadian* cult!" someone hissed.

Drake smiled at the furious whispers. Let them think that.

Without any more dalliance he sprinted along the path as fast as he dared. Ben and Kennedy were ahead, and needed his protection. He'd sworn to get them out of this alive, and he wouldn't let them down.

At his back, the Germans were proceeding down the slope with caution. He fired off a few more rounds to keep them busy, and started counting ships.

Four, six, nine.

The pathway grew precarious with sudden slopes and potholes, but finally leveled out. At one point it thinned so drastically that anyone over two hundred and fifty pounds or taking steroids would probably break a rib squeezing between the timbers, but it widened again as he counted the twelfth ship.

The vessels loomed over him, ancient, intimidating, smelling of old bark and mold. A fleeting movement behind caught his attention and he saw a figure that could only be this new guy, Milo, *sprinting* along the narrow ledge that ran at Drake's shoulder level, a ledge which most people could barely walk along. Drake didn't even have time to fire—the American was moving so fast.

Why'd he have to be so bloody good?

Landed myself in the middle of a Gladiator competition here...

He leapt forward, almost past the ships now, using his momentum to bounce from step to step, almost free-running from random mounds to deep clefts, and angling his leap off the inflexible walls; even using the ships' timbers to gain momentum between jumps. The deep burn of exertion returned like an old friend, to settle deep in his chest, reminding him of an old adage: *Pain is good! Pain is life! If you feel pain, it means you're still alive!*

"Slow down!"

The disembodied voice floated from ahead. He paused, seeing Kennedy's vague shape, relieved to hear her drawl. "Follow me," he cried, knowing he couldn't let the American, Milo, beat him to the end of the passage.

He broke past the final ship at breakneck pace, Ben and Kennedy lagging in his wake, just as Milo leapt off the ledge and cut past the front of the very same ship. Drake tackled him around the waist, making sure he landed heavily on his sternum.

He wasted a second flinging his gun toward Kennedy.

Whilst it was still in mid-flight, Milo scissor-kicked and twisted loose, flipped over onto his hands, and was then up, facing him.

He snarled. "Matt Drake, the one and only. Heard a lot about you. Been lookin' forward to this, *bud*."

He struck with elbows and fists. Drake caught multiple blows on his arms, wincing as he backed up. This guy knew him, but who the hell was he? An old enemy? A shadow-ghost from the dark days of his past? Milo was in close, and happy to stay there. Drake's peripheral vision noted the knife at the American's waistband.

He caught a vicious kick on his own instep.

Behind him he could hear the first clumsy movements of the advancing German force. They were just a few ships back.

Ben and Kennedy watched in amazement. Kennedy had the machine gun raised.

Drake feinted one way, then twisted the other, spinning away from Milo's vicious leg-breaker. Seven years of civilian ease had dulled his reactions and softened his body strikes. Then Kennedy fired a shot, kicking up dirt an inch from Milo's foot.

Drake grinned as he moved away, made as if to pet a dog. "Stay," he said mockingly. "There's a good boy."

Kennedy reversed her gun, moved in, and hit Milo with the

butt. It took two strikes before the American collapsed. Drake ran past them, caught Ben's arm, and pulled hard as the young man turned automatically toward the crumbling staircase.

"No!" Drake shouted. "They'll pick us off one by one."

Ben looked aghast. *"Then where else?"*

Drake shrugged disarmingly. "Where do you think?"

He headed straight for the World Tree.

TWELVE

THE WORLD TREE, SWEDEN

The World Tree was old but strong, its limbs plentiful and sturdy.

"Just like being a boy scout again," Drake urged Ben on gently, encouraging him to go faster without causing panic. "Shouldn't be a problem for you, Blakey. You okay, Kennedy?"

The New Yorker came last, keeping the gun trained below her. Luckily, the World Tree's extensive symmetry of branches and leaves helped conceal their progress.

"Easier than the Empire State," she said lightheartedly.

Ben laughed. Good sign. Drake thanked Kennedy inside, starting to feel better about having her along on this...

Crap, he thought, for he'd almost thought "on this *mission*". Back to the old vernacular in less than a week.

Drake climbed upward from branch to branch, sitting or standing astride one limb while reaching for the next. Their progress was quick, which meant their upper-body strength lasted longer than expected. Even so, about halfway up, Drake noticed that Ben was flagging.

"Tweenie getting tired?" he asked, and saw an immediate redoubling of effort.. Twice, they managed to make out the stone staircase rising beside them, and saw no sign of pursuers.

Voices echoed up to them. "Englishman—Matt Drake," a voice called, distorted by a thick German accent.

Another time he heard "SRT failure". The American drawl was Milo's, revealing that he knew about Drake's secret unit. Who *was* this guy?

Shots splintered the heavy boughs. Drake called a pause to resettle the shifting rucksack with its hidden treasure, then spied the wide branch he'd been aiming for—the one that almost touched the staircase.

"Out there," he motioned to Ben. "Straddle the branch and move—fast!"

They would be exposed for maybe a minute. Subtracting surprise and reaction time that still left almost half a minute of extreme danger.

Ben broke cover first, Drake and Kennedy a second after, all moving on their hands and haunches along the branch toward the staircase. When they were spotted, Kennedy bought them more precious seconds by unleashing a fusillade of lead, punching holes through at least one unlucky tomb raider.

And now they saw that Milo had indeed sent a team running up the staircase. Five men. And they were coming fast. They would reach the end of the branch before Ben got there.

Ben saw it too, and faltered. Drake shouted in his ear, "*Never give up! Never!*"

Kennedy squeezed the trigger again. Two men fell, one rebounding off the cavern wall and flying down into the pit, the other clutching his side and screaming. She squeezed it once more, and the mag ran dry.

But still two Germans remained and stood facing them, weapons ready. Drake felt his face set hard. They had lost the race.

"Shoot them down!" Milo's voice echoed up. "We'll pick through the scraps down here."

"*Nein!*" A different thick German accent rang out. "*Der Speer! Der Speer!*" Despite its panic the voice carried the note of authority.

One of the Germans taunted, "Crawl, little insects. Come here."

Ben moved slowly. Drake could see his shoulders shaking. "Trust me," he whispered into his friend's ear, and coiled every muscle. He would leap when Ben reached the end of the bough. His best play was to use his skill set.

"I still have a knife," Kennedy murmured.

Drake nodded.

Ben reached the end of the bough. The Germans now waited calmly.

Drake started to rise.

And then, in a blur, both Germans staggered backwards, as if hit by a torpedo. Their bodies, ragged and bloody with bullet holes, slammed off the wall and rebounded lifelessly down into the pit, cartwheeling.

A few meters above the bough, where the stairs curved, a small contingent of men stood, all holding AK-5 assault rifles.

"The Swedes." Drake whispered, recognizing their armament, but surprised to see them. *Maybe they had previously prepped the place, leaving the glow sticks.*

Louder, he said, "About bloody time."

THIRTEEN

MILITARY BASE, SWEDEN

The room they ended up in—a spartan twelve-by-twelve with a pitted desk and an ice-rimmed window—took Drake back a few years.

"Relax." Drake tapped Ben's white knuckles, which were clenched in anxiety. "Standard military bunker, this place. I've seen worse hotel rooms, mate, believe me."

"I've been in worse *apartments*." Kennedy seemed at ease, her cop training at work.

"Another boyfriend?" Drake raised an eyebrow.

"Sure. Why?"

"Oh, nothing." Drake counted past ten on his fingers, then looked down, as if to start using his toes.

Ben managed a thin smile.

"Listen, Ben," Drake said, "it was hairy there for a while, but you saw that Swedish guy make the calls. We're good. Anyway, we need to hang out a bit. We're all knackered."

The door opened, and their host, a well-built Swede with blonde hair and a hard-as-nails gaze, clipped across the concrete floor. When they'd been captured and Drake had explained who they were and what they were doing, this man had introduced himself as Torsten Dahl, and had then withdrawn to make a few calls.

"Matt Drake," he said. "Kennedy Moore. And Ben Blake. The Swedish government has no particular quarrel with you..."

Drake was disturbed by the accent that wasn't at all Swedish. "You go to one of those shiny-arse schools, Dahl? Eton, or some such?"

"Shiny-arse?"

"Schools that help promote officers through lineage, *money,* and *breeding.* Whilst ignoring skills, proficiency and enthusiasm."

"Well, then, I imagine I did." Dahl's tone was even. He wasn't rising to the bait.

"Great. Well...if that's all..." Drake rose.

Dahl held up a hand whilst Ben gave Drake an aggrieved look. "Stop being an idiot, Matt. Just because *you're* a coarse Yorkshire peasant doesn't mean the rest of us are all royal *inbreds,* does it?"

Drake blinked at his lodger in surprise. Kennedy made a roll-with-it motion. It occurred to him then that Ben may have found something in this mission that had truly hooked him and was wanting more.

Dahl said, "I'd appreciate a sharing of knowledge, friends. I really would."

Drake was all for sharing, but knowledge was power, as they say, and he was now trying to figure a way to enlist the Swedish Government's help.

Ben was already warming up to his tale of the Nine Pieces of Odin and the Tomb of the Gods when Drake interrupted.

"Look," he said. "Me and the kid here, and now maybe the gronk, are the headline attraction on some kind of kill list—"

"Kill list?"

"I'm no *gronk,* you English asshole." Kennedy half rose to her feet.

He studied his hands, scarred from tussling with Milo and climbing the World Tree, and thought about how his quick and deeply ingrained reactions had returned over the last few days.

How right Alyson had been.

"What's a gronk?" Ben asked.

Dahl sat on a hard metal chair and clomped his heavy boots down on the table. "A female that enjoys the company of servicemen," he said, diplomatically.

"My own description would have been a little *coarser.*" Drake glanced at Ben, then said, "Now, the kill list. The Germans want us dead for crimes uncommitted, Dahl. Talk about being in the right place at the wrong time. I made the mistake of point-blank photographing these guys. Maybe it's their figures on film – even ears and body movement can be uniquely identified these days – or I snapped something important, but they've been hunting us ever since." He shook his head. "We pursued this only to find out who tried to kill us three times in two days and then put an end to them. Now, we're arse-deep in some kind of international treasure hunt. So—your turn."

The Swede didn't answer for a while, just stared through the icy window into the snow-blanched landscape and beyond, toward crumbling cliffs that stood desolate and alone against a wild ocean.

Kennedy said, "Dahl, I'm a cop. I didn't know these two until a couple of days ago and I might not be with them tomorrow. But they have good hearts. Trust them."

Dahl nodded. "Your reputation precedes you, Drake. The good *and* the bad of it. We will help you, but first—" he nodded to Ben. "Continue."

Ben restarted, as if he'd never been interrupted. Drake sneaked a glance at Kennedy, and saw her smile. He looked away, shocked on two counts. First, by Dahl's reference to his reputation, and second, by Kennedy's seemingly heartfelt endorsement.

When Ben had finished, Dahl said, "It is fair to say the German crew are a new entity in this international fiasco. They had not engaged our attention before that business in York."

"New?" Drake said. "They're very well organized for newbies, controlled by fear and iron discipline. And they have a major asset in a guy called Milo—American Special Forces at a guess. Check the name. And, by the way, why aren't they in your custody?"

The Swede looked embarrassed and angry. "It seems they left a force on the *outside* to cover their retreat. I left a small contingent of men to keep them underground. My men," he shook his head regretfully, "were ambushed."

"And you didn't know they were there? You must have been spying on that cavern for days. It *was* you who left the glow sticks, right?"

"Yes. And no, we didn't know they were there. Like you say, they are led by at least one Special Forces soldier. They are clever." He paused for breath. "Now, the good news is that we *do* have intel on the cultists."

"Eyes on?"

"Yes, we have someone inside, but they're inexperienced, and alone." Dahl cast a surreptitious glance toward Kennedy. "The Swedish government's relationship with your new Obama regime isn't what I'd call *first-rate*."

"Sorry about that." Kennedy faked a smile, then made a show of looking around. "Look, dude, if we're gonna be here a while, do you think we could get something to eat?"

"Food's already being prepared to your taste by our sous chef." Dahl batted her false smile right back. "Seriously, though, there's burgers and chips on the way."

Drake's mouth started to water. He couldn't remember the last time he'd eaten.

"I'll tell you what I can. The Viking cult are nothing to do with the state. They call themselves the *Forn Sidr*, which means 'ancient custom', and relates to Paganism. The Vikings were originally pagans, of course. They began life as a secret cult, devoted to the Viking Erik the Red. Don't smile, these things are more popular than you would think. These people, through cosplay, act out events and battles, and even sea voyages on a regular basis."

"No real harm there." Ben sounded a little defensive. Drake stored that nugget away for later.

"Not at all, Mr. Blake. But the real damage starts when a billionaire businessman becomes the modern-day leader of a Viking cult, then throws millions of dollars into the ring."

"So lighthearted fun becomes—"

"Obsession," Dahl finished as the door opened. Drake almost moaned as a standard meal of burger and chips was placed before him. The smell of onions and cooked meat was divine.

Dahl continued, as they tucked in, "A Canadian businessman called Colby Taylor devoted all his spare time to Erik the Red who, as I'm sure you know, landed in Canada shortly after discovering Greenland. From out of this study was born a manic fascination for Nordic mythology resulting in endless explorations, digs, and discoveries. The man purchased his own library and tried to buy up every Nordic text in existence."

"Nut job," Kennedy said.

"Agreed. But a 'nut job' that funds his own 'security force'— read that as *army*. And he's reclusive enough to stay below most people's radar. His name has come up time and again with regard to the Nine Pieces of Odin, so, naturally, Swedish Intelligence has tagged him as a person of interest."

"He stole the horse from under the noses of the Germans," Drake said. "You know that, don't you?"

Dahl's wide eyes indicated he didn't. "We do now."

"Can't you get him arrested?" Kennedy asked. "On suspicion of theft or something?"

"Envision him as one of your US based Mafia or Triad leaders. He is untouchable—the man at the top and surrounded by muscle who carry out his dirty work—for now. We believe the current situation will bring him out."

Drake liked the implied sentiment. He told Dahl about Alicia Myles' involvement, and gave Dahl as much background on her as he was allowed to disclose.

"So," he said when he'd finished. "Are we helpful, or what?"

"Not bad," Dahl admitted, as the door opened again and an older man with a surprisingly thick mane of long hair and a lush beard walked in. To Drake he looked like a modern Viking.

Dahl nodded. "Ahh, I've been waiting for you. May I present Professor Roland Parnevik." He smiled. "*Our* expert in Nordic mythology."

Drake nodded, then saw Ben sizing the new man up as he would a rival. He understood now why Ben was secretly loving this mission. He patted his young friend on the shoulder.

"Well, our family guy here might not be a professor, but he sure knows his way around the Web—a kind of modern medicine versus old remedies, eh?"

"Or the best of both worlds." Kennedy pointed her fork at both parties in question.

The cynical side of Drake calculated that Kennedy Moore could be angling this mission in a way that might save her career. A surprising, softer side enjoyed watching the way the edges of her mouth turned up when she smiled.

Parnevik stumbled into the room, clutching an armful of scrolls and balancing several notebooks precariously on top of the pile. He looked around, stared at Dahl as if he couldn't remember the soldier's name, then dumped everything on the table.

"It's in there," he said, jabbing a finger at one of the scrolls. "That one. The legend is real...like I told you months ago."

Dahl plucked out the indicated scroll with a flourish. "You've been with us a week, Professor. Just a week."

"Are you sure?"

"Oh, I'm sure." Dahl's tone conveyed a prodigious amount of patience.

Another soldier walked in through the door. "Sir. This one's mobile" –he nodded toward Ben– "has been ringing incessantly. *Hela tiden*...non-stop." A smirk came next. "It's his mother."

Ben was up in a second, taking the proffered phone and hitting a speed dial button. Drake smiled with affection, and Kennedy looked mischievous. "Jeez, I can think of so many ways to corrupt that boy."

Dahl began to read from the scroll:

"I heard he died at Ragnarok, swallowed whole by his doom— the man-wolf, Fenrir, who was turned by the moon.

"And later, Thor and Loki lay cold by his side. The greatest of Gods among countless Gods, our rocks against the tide.

"Nine Pieces scattered to the wind along the One True Volva's ways. Bring not these pieces to Ragnarok or risk the end of days.

"Forever shall thou fear this, hear me sons of men, for to defile the Tomb of Gods is to start the Day of Reckoning."

Dahl shrugged. "And so on. And on. And on. Professor, I already got the gist of this from momma's boy over there. Seems the Web is indeed mightier than the scroll. And faster."

"You have? Well, like I said...months, Torsten, months. And I've been ignored for years. *Institutionalized,* even. The tomb has *always* existed, you know. It didn't just materialize in the last month. Agnetha gave me that scroll thirty years ago, and where are we now? Hmm? Anywhere?"

Dahl was struggling to stay calm. Drake stepped in. "You talk of Ragnarok, Professor Parnevik; a place that doesn't exist."

"Not anymore, sir. But once—yes. Once it *certainly* existed. It is a place. Otherwise—where did Odin, Thor and all the other gods die?"

"You believe they once lived, then?" He feigned disbelief, but of course he'd already held the spear in his hand.

"*Yes!*" Parnevik practically screamed.

Dahl's voice was lower. "For now," he said, "we've agreed to suspend our misgivings."

Ben was back at the table, pocketing his cellphone. "So you know about the Valkyries, then?" he asked cryptically, picking up his knife and fork. "You know why they're the jewel in Odin's crown?"

Dahl just looked exasperated. Parnevik blinked and stammered. "The...jewel in...what?"

FOURTEEN

MILITARY BASE, SWEDEN

Ben smiled as the room grew quiet. "This is our admittance ticket to officially join this treasure hunt," he said to Dahl. "I found it written time and again, whilst researching Norse mythology, that the Valkyries 'ride to the realms of the Gods'. Look it up—it's there."

Kennedy impatiently tapped her fork against her plate. "Meaning?"

"They show the way," Ben said. "You can assemble the Nine Pieces of Odin at Ragnarok all month long—but it's the *Valkyries* that show the way to the Tomb of the Gods."

Drake frowned. "And you've been keeping this to yourself?"

"It doesn't matter. No one knows where the Valkyries are, Matt. They're in a private collection somewhere. The wolves in New York are the last of the nine pieces we actually have a location for."

Dahl smiled as Parnevik attacked his scrolls. White tubes flew everywhere amidst a flurry of muttering. "Valkyries. Valkyries. Here—no. There—maybe. Ahh."

Drake caught Dahl's eye. "And the Apocalypse theory? Hellfire on earth and everything razed etc....etc."

"I'm sure Parnevik here could recite you a similar legend for almost every god in the pantheon. Shiva. Zeus. Seth. But if *Forn Sidr* find that tomb, they *will* desecrate it, never mind the consequences."

Drake's thoughts flashed upon the crazy Germans. "As would *our* new friends." He nodded and gave Dahl a slight smile. "Out of choices..."

"Balls to the wall," Dahl finished the military mantra, and the two shared a look.

Ben leaned across the table to catch Dahl's attention. "Excuse me, mate, but we're wasting time here. Give me a laptop. Let me surf. Or better still, get us en route to the Big Apple and we'll surf in the air."

Kennedy nodded. "He's right. I can help. The next logical target should be the National History Museum, and let's face it, the US isn't ready for that. Yet."

Dahl nodded. "Mobilization is already underway." He looked hard at Ben. "Are you offering to help, young man?"

Ben opened his mouth, but then paused, as if sensing the importance of his answer. "Well, we're still on the kill list, right? Look at what we've uncovered already. And Matt's ex-SAS. Kennedy's an NYC cop. We're practically the perfect team!"

Dahl's eyes narrowed, as if weighing his decision. Silently, he slid Drake's cellphone across the table and indicated the screen. "Where did you photograph the runes in that picture? The pit?"

"Yes. Alongside the longships, there was a wall full of carvings. This woman," he tapped the screen, "knelt by Odin's side as he suffered on the World Tree. Can you translate the inscription?"

"Roughly, yes. It says 'Odin and the volva Heidi entrusted with the god's secrets'. The professor is researching this now..." Dahl glanced at Parnevik as the man tried to collect all his scrolls at once.

"God's secrets?" Parnevik swung around like a hellhound had landed on his back. "Or *gods'* secrets. Hear the nuance? Understand what I'm saying? No? Let me through, fool." He spoke to the empty doorway and disappeared.

"We will take you," Dahl told them. "Talks with your government have begun. They are not enjoying being told they're way behind on this. Hopefully, it will all be taken care of during our flight. But for now we're heading to New York with a dozen Special Forces soldiers and no clearance. We're taking guns into the National History Museum." He paused. "Still want to come?"

"The SAS might help me," Drake said. "They have a team standing by and a commander that could grease some wheels."

"I guess I'll try the precinct captain." Kennedy's dark change of demeanor at the thought of going home was obvious. Drake promised himself there and then that he would help her if he could.

Trust me, he wanted to say. *I'll get you through this.* But the words froze in his throat.

Ben flexed his fingers. "Just gimme an iPad or something. Quick."

FIFTEEN

AIRSPACE

Their aircraft was equipped with a device called a picocell, a cell tower that allowed the use of all cellphones on planes. Essential for Government military forces, but Ben Blake had his own priorities.

"Yo, Sis, got a job for you. Don't ask. Listen, *Karin*, listen! I need info on the National History Museum. Exhibits, Viking stuff. Blueprints. Who runs the place. And..." his voice lowered several octaves, "*phone numbers.*"

Drake listened to a heartbeat of silence, then heard: "Yes, the one in New York! How many are there? Oh...really? Okay, Sis, I'll paypal you some dosh over to cover it. Love you."

As his friend broke the connection, Drake said, "She still out of work?"

"Sits at home all day, mate. Works lates in a dodgy bar. It's her way of punishing herself for something she didn't do."

Drake knew that Karin had struggled for seven years to attain a degree in computer programming, something that for her should have been child's play. Karin's IQ was off the charts, genius level. But when the Labour Government folded at the end of Blair's reign, she left Nottingham Uni to find that, in spite of her potential, she could now blame her procrastination and need to self-denigrate on the newly arrived recession.

"She still in that drug-den in Nottingham?"

"It's not a drug den," Ben sighed. "But some undesirables do rent the properties around her, I'll admit. She stays in during the day and takes cabs to work."

Drake remembered Ben telling him that the most terrifying moments of Karin's life were when she returned to her flat, darkness, stale sweat, and other nasty odors surrounding her. Despite her black-belts in martial arts, she remained a walking felony just waiting to happen.

In the land of the damned and the ignored, the man who lives in shadow is king.

"Do you really need your sister for this?" Dahl, who was seated on the other side of the plane, asked. "Or..."

"Look, it's not charity, mate. I have to concentrate on the Odin stuff. Karin can do the museum legwork. Makes total sense."

Drake made his own speed dial call. "Let him work, Dahl. Trust me. We're here to help."

Wells answered. "Been catching zees, Drake? What the hell's going on?"

Drake filled him in.

"Well, here's a solid gold nugget for you. We checked into Alicia Myles. You know the score, Matt. You're never *truly* out of the SAS." Wells paused. "Last known address—111 Hildegarde Strasse, Munich."

"Germany? But I saw her with the Canadian cultists."

"Uh huh. That's not all. She lived in Munich with her boyfriend—one Milo Noxon—a rather nasty citizen of Las Vegas, USA. And he's Ex-Marine Force Recon. The best the Americans have to offer."

Drake took a moment to consider this. "*That's* how he knew me then, through Myles. The question is—did she swap sides to spite him, or to help him?"

"Answer unknown. Maybe you could ask her."

"I'll try. Look, we're swinging by our balls up here, Wells. Think you could contact your old mates in the States? Dahl's already been in contact with the FBI, but they're stalling. He's going higher. We're seven hours out...and coming in blind."

"You trust them, or are you asking our guys to clean up the inevitable cluster-fuck?"

"Yes, I trust them. And yes, I also want our guys there if possible."

"Understood." Wells cut the connection.

Drake glanced around. The airplane was small, but roomy. Eleven Special Forces Marines sat in the back, lounging, snoozing, and mostly pumping each other up in Swedish. Across the aisle, Dahl snapped constantly into his phone, while in front of him the professor rolled out scroll after scroll, resting each one delicately on the seatback, scanning for the ancient differences between fact and fiction.

To his immediate left, Kennedy, back to wearing her number one formless trouser suit, made her first call. "Captain Lipkind there? Tell him it's Kennedy Moore."

Ten seconds passed, then, "No. Tell him he can't ring me back. This is *important*. Tell him it's about national security if you want, just *get him*."

Ten more seconds, then, "*Moore!*" Drake heard the bark, even from where he sat. "*Can't it wait?*"

"Listen to me, Captain, there's a situation. First, check with Officer Swane of the FBI. I'm here with Torsten Dahl of the Swedish SGG. The National History Museum is under direct threat. Check the details and call me back straight away. I need your help."

Kennedy closed her phone and let out a deep breath. "Bang goes my pension."

Drake checked his watch. Six hours until landing.

Ben's cellphone chirped, and he snatched it up. "Sis?"

Professor Parnevik was leaning out across the aisle, chasing an errant scroll with a veiny arm. "Kid knows his Valkyries," he said to no one in particular. "But where are they? And the eyes—yes, I will find the eyes."

Ben was saying, "Great stuff, Karin. E-mail me the blueprints of the museum, and highlight that room for me. Then send the curator's details by separate mail. Hey, Sis, say hi to Mum and Dad. Love ya."

Ben resumed his clicking, then started taking a few more notes. "Got the museum curator's number," he shouted. "Dahl? Want me to scare the crap out of him?"

Drake broke out into a relaxed smile as the Swedish intelligence officer waved a frantic *No!* without dropping a vowel. It was good to see Ben exhibiting this kind of confidence. The geek had withdrawn a little to allow the man inside some room to flourish. Drake should have had him out in the field years ago.

Kennedy's phone broke out into song. She flipped it open quickly and depressed the speakerphone button, mouthing the word, *Lipkind.*

"Moore."

"What the *crap* is going on? I'm first blocked by half a dozen shitheels, and then told, and not politely, to keep my nose in the gutter where it belongs. Something's got all the big dogs barking, Moore, and I'm betting it's you." He paused. "Not for the first time, I guess."

Kennedy gave him the abbreviated version that ended with a plane full of Swedish Marines and an unknown SAS team en route, now five hours from US soil.

Drake felt a flutter. *Five hours.*

At that moment Dahl shouted, "New intel from our insider! The Canadian cultists weren't even in Sweden. It seems they sacrificed the World Tree and the spear to concentrate on the *Valkyries.*" He sent a nod of praise toward Ben, pointedly excluding the grimacing professor. "Clearly, they agree with our young prodigy. But...they've come up empty-handed so far. We knew they were in a private collection, but this collector must be a real recluse. To keep such a prize off the grid means something...maybe he's one of those private collectors that comes by his treasures the wrong way." His lips compressed into a hard line.

"Or..." Drake shrugged, "he could be a criminal."

"Good suggestion. But either way, you have to ask: why do the *Forn Sidr* cult and the Germans want all this? The nine pieces? Surely not to destroy the world?" Dahl shook his head.

"Are you kidding?" Ben asked. "The Canadians are part of a Viking *cult.* Imagine how they would feel about finding and owning the pieces and then the bones of Odin. The Germans will reveal their true intentions."

Drake spoke into the silence. "Are they gearing up for New York? For the Wolves?"

"Yes," Dahl sighed. "Apparently so."

"Remember," Ben said. "The pieces, when assembled, show the

way to the tomb of the gods. *That's* the real treasure here. That's what they're looking for. And if we can't get all the pieces together, then we have to find another way."

Dahl shrugged. "This is where it gets ugly. The cultists are gearing up to hit the museum early morning, NYC time."

Kennedy's face took on a murderous look as she listened to both her boss and Dahl. "They're using the date," she hissed to both parties. "Those bastards—and the Germans, no doubt—are concealing their real intentions behind the date."

Ben looked up. "I've lost track."

Drake echoed him. "What date?"

"When we land in NYC," Dahl explained, "it'll be around 08:00 on September 11th. If they are rumbled and have to fight their way out of the museum they can hide their true intentions behind the premise of a date-significant, terrorist attack."

SIXTEEN

AIRSPACE

Four hours left. The aircraft droned on through the soupy sky.

Dahl said, "I'll try the FBI again. But I can't seem to get past this level of screening. It's a bloody stone wall. Ben—call the curator. Drake—get in touch with your old boss. Clock's ticking, and we're nowhere. This hour requires progress. Let's go."

Kennedy was pleading with her boss. "To hell with Thomas Kaleb, Lipkind," she said. "This has nothing to do with him, *or* my career. I'm telling you something the FBI, the CIA and all those other three-letter pricks don't know. I'm asking..." She paused. "I guess I'm asking you to trust me."

Drake wanted to slide up to Kennedy Moore and offer a few words of encouragement.

Then, Wells answered his call. "Speak now."

"Where we at, mate? You talked us into US airspace yet?"

"Well—yes...and no. I'm hitting reams of red tape, Drake, and that doesn't sit well on my lap—" He paused dramatically, then grunted in disappointment. "That was a *Mai Kitano* reference, pal. Try to keep up."

Drake smiled despite himself. " Look, Wells, keep your head together for this mission—help us out—and I'll regale you with stories about Mai's undercover work in Hong Kong."

"That does sound intriguing. You're on, my man and a shame Mai can't be with us on this. Look, we're en route, tooled up, and *my* people across the pond don't seem to have a problem with that."

Drake sensed the "but". "Yes?"

"Someone in authority is denying landing privileges and no one's *ever heard* of your plane, and that, my friend, smacks of insider corruption."

Drake heard him. "Okay, keep me posted." The press of a button ended the call.

He heard Kennedy say, "Low level is perfect, Captain. I'm overhearing chatter here that speaks of a conspiracy. Be careful."

She closed her phone. "Well, he's prickly, but he's taking me at my word. He's sending as many black-and-whites to the scene as he can, low key. And he knows someone in the local Homeland Security field office," she said, smoothing her limp blouse. "Beans are being spilled."

Drake thought: *There's a major arsenal heading for that museum. Enough to start a bloody war.* He didn't say anything out loud, but he did check his watch.

Three hours left.

Ben was still involved with the curator. "We're not talking about a major rearrangement here, sir, just moving the exhibit. I don't need to tell you how large the museum is. Just shift it, and all will be well. Yes...the SGG...Swedish Special Forces. The FBI are being informed as we speak...no! Don't wait for them to call. You can't afford to delay."

Fifteen seconds of silence, then, "You never heard of SGG? Well, *Google it, then!*" Ben jabbed at his phone in frustration. "He's stalling," Ben said. "I just know it. He sounded cagey, like he was trying to come up with excuses."

"More red tape." Drake gestured to Dahl. "We're drowning here."

A heavy silence followed, then Dahl's cellphone rang. "Oh, my," he said. "*Den Statsministern.*"

Drake made a face at Kennedy and Ben. "His prime minister."

Some respectful, but nevertheless candid words were passed that increased Drake's respect for Torsten Dahl. The Special Forces officer gave it to his boss exactly the way it was. Drake was gloomily convinced he was going to end up liking this guy.

Dahl ended the call, then spent a moment gathering his thoughts. At last he looked up and addressed the plane.

"Straight from a member of the President's cabinet, his closest advisors," Dahl told them. "This flight will not be cleared to land."

Three hours to go.

"They wouldn't inform the President," Dahl said. "Washington DC and Capitol Hill is deeply immersed in this, my friends. I'm not saying *illegally*" –he held up a palm toward Kennedy– "but it's more of an ass-covering exercise. The Statsministern says it has gone global now, a conspiracy of international proportions where nobody knows who supports who. That alone," he said, "speaks to the gravity of our mission."

"Cluster-fuck," Drake said. "It's what we used to call a disaster on a massive scale."

Ben, in the meantime, had tried the curator of the National History Museum again. All he got was voicemail. "Not right," he said. "He should have checked on *something* by now." Ben's dexterous fingers immediately began flying over the virtual keyboard.

"Got an idea," he said loudly. "Hope to hell I'm wrong."

Then Wells rang back, explaining that his SAS team had sneaked a landing at an abandoned New Jersey airfield, sanctioned by high-ranking US army personnel. The team was inbound toward central New York, travelling by any means necessary.

Drake checked the time. Two hours to landing.

And then Ben cried out, "Nailed it!" Everyone jumped. Even the Swedish Marines gave him their full attention.

"It's here!" he shouted. "Plastered all over the Internet, if you have the time to look." He jabbed at the screen angrily.

"Colby Taylor," he said. "The Canadian billionaire is the National History Museum's biggest contributor and one of New York's major financiers. Whatcha bet he made a few calls?"

Dahl grimaced. "That's our blockage," he groaned. "Taylor owns more people than the Mafia." For the first time, the Swedish officer appeared to slump in his seat.

Kennedy couldn't hide the disappointment. "Fat cat suits win again," she hissed.

"Maybe, maybe not," Drake said. "I always have a Plan B."

One hour to go and they still needed landing clearance.

SEVENTEEN

NEW YORK CITY, USA

The Port Authority Police Department of New York was arguably best known for its humbling bravery and loss during the events of September 11th. What it was less known for was its covert handling of most SAS flights originating out of Europe. Whilst not employing a dedicated team to police this element of its work, the intercontinental personnel involved were in such a small minority that, over the years, many of them had become close friends.

Drake made one more call. "Coming in hot tonight," he told Jack Schwarz, PAPD Inspector. "You missed me, pal?"

"Jeez, Drake, been...what? Two years?"

"Three. New Year's Eve, '07."

"Wife okay?"

"Alyson died, mate, which you know. That enough chitchat to mark my identity?"

"Thought you left the Service."

"I did. Wells called me back for one last job. He call you?"

"He did. Said you promised him some Mai-time."

"Schwarz, listen to me. This is your call. You should know that the shit *will* hit the fan, and that our entry *will* be traced back to you, eventually. I'm sure, by then, we'll all be heroes and this will be considered a favorable act, but..."

"Wells filled me in," Schwarz said, but Drake heard the undertone of unease in his voice. "Don't worry, bud. I still have enough juice with the right people to swing landing permission."

Drake thanked him and ended the call. Dahl studied him,

worried but determined. "We have stealth capabilities on this plane. We have radar jamming. But in light of the date and the country we're entering, I'm somewhat loath to engage them."

Drake took a deep breath. "Don't engage 'em, mate. Don't go near it. Schwarz will get us through. He's done it before."

Their plane glided into US airspace.

The plane landed in weak daylight and taxied up to an indistinct terminal building. The minute the door cracked open, twelve fully loaded members of the Swedish SGG jogged double time down the rickety metal stairs and piled into three waiting vehicles. Drake, Ben, Kennedy and the professor followed.

A minute later, the cars shot down an empty runway, picking up speed, aiming for a concealed exit at the back of the airfield that, after a few turns, emptied onto a discreet slip road to join one of Manhattan's main tributaries.

New York City stretched out before them in all its splendor. Modern skyscrapers, old bridges, classic architecture. Their convoy of vehicles cut directly to the heart of the city, taking chances, using every wily shortcut known to their native drivers. Horns blared at them, curses curdled the air, curbs and trash cans were clipped. On one occasion, a one-way street was employed that cut seven minutes off their journey and caused three fender benders.

Inside the cars, the action was almost as hectic. Dahl, at last, got the call from the Swedish prime minister, who had finally reached a friendly high-ranking FBI agent and received clearance and code words to enter the museum, but only *if* they got there first.

Dahl turned to their driver. "*Faster!*"

"Impossible," the man answered. "This is New York."

Ben handed Dahl a map of the museum, complete with the wolves' location.

More information filtered through. Black-and-whites had arrived. Rapid Response teams were being notified. Dahl worked even faster, making a point of liaising with the responding SWAT captain and other converging entities. Judging from his deep sighs, his efforts weren't always met with the best response.

Drake reached Wells. "You got a sit-rep?"

"We're outside. Cop-cavalry arrived two minutes ago. You?"

"Twenty away. Give us a shout if anything happens." Something caught his eye as it flashed by the window. An intense feeling of *déjà vu* sent shivers dancing across his ribs as he saw a huge billboard proclaiming the arrival of Abel Frey, in New York, along with his stunning catwalk show.

That's mad, Drake thought. *Truly insane.*

Ben had woken his sister in the UK and enrolled her in *Project Valkyrie* as he called it. "Saves time," he told Dahl. "She can continue the research whilst we're in there looking for those wolves. Don't worry, she thinks I want to photograph them for my degree."

"Lying to Sis?" Drake frowned.

"He's growing up." Kennedy patted Blake's arm. "Give the kid some space."

"What do we need to know about the wolves?" Drake asked. "Anything important?"

Ben considered the question. "Geri and Freki, meaning ravenous in Old Norse, were two wolves said to walk alongside Odin. They are confirmed both on the *Poetic Edda* and the *Prose Edda*, both thirteenth-century texts by acclaimed scholars of their day. Of course, as we keep finding, they can be compared to similar figures found in Greek, Roman and Vedic mythology. Remember that—everything's connected. Their likenesses have been found on bronze plates, illustrations and more. Of course, this piece of Odin is a sculpture, probably fashioned like most of the other pieces to fit together at Ragnarok."

Drake's cellphone chirped. He didn't have to check the caller ID to know it was Wells. "Don't tell me, mate. Is it *Forn Sidr*?"

Wells laughed softly. "You wish."

"Sorry?"

"*Both* the cultists *and* the Germans, using separate routes. This war's about to start without you. "

Dahl said, "A Rapid Response SWAT team is three minutes away. Frequency is 68."

Drake glanced out of the wide window. "We're here."

*

"Central Park West entrance," Ben said as they exited the cars. "Leads to the only two sets of staircases that ascend from the lower level, all the way to the fourth floor."

Kennedy jumped out into the morning heat. "Which floor houses the wolves?"

"Fourth."

"Figures." Kennedy shrugged, and patted her midriff. "Knew I'd end up regretting those holiday pastries."

Drake hung back as the Swedish soldiers ran hard at the museum steps. Dahl spoke quickly to someone in US authority as he ran. Once there, they unslung their weapons. Dahl stopped them in the shadow of the high entrance, the team flanked by circular pillars.

"Tweeters *on*."

A dozen "Checks!" sounded out. "We go first." He looked hard at Drake. "Our American friends are a minute or so away. Drake, you follow. Grab these."

He handed Drake two cylindrical objects the size of lighters, and two earpieces. Drake twisted the cylindrical barrels to "68" and waited until both started emitting a green light from their bases. He handed one to Kennedy and kept the other for himself.

"Tweeters," he said to her blank look. "It's the new 'friendly fire' aid. Friendlies are all tuned to the same frequency. Look at a colleague and you get an annoying chirp in your ear, look at a bad guy and you hear nothing..." He fitted his earpiece. "Not foolproof, I know, but it helps in situations where you've got a lot going on. Like this."

Ben said, "What if the frequency clashes with another?"

"It won't. It's adaptive spread spectrum frequency hopping. The devices 'hop' through seventy-nine randomly chosen frequencies within pre-assigned ranges—*together*. Has a range of around two hundred feet."

"Cool," Ben said. "Where's mine?"

Kennedy fiddled with the barrel. "And you know this how?"

Drake gave her dead eyes. "Being out of the game doesn't mean I don't have friends that keep me up to date." He was thinking of Sam and Jo, his old teammates from the Ninth Division.

"You and Professor Parnevik get to spend some time in Central

Park," Drake told Ben. "Tourist stuff. Chill, mate, this is gonna get hairy."

"Hope he doesn't want to go jogging. Guy told me he runs two hours a day, every day."

Without another word, Drake spun to follow the last of the Swedish soldiers through a high archway into the museum's murky innards. Kennedy followed closely.

"Could do with a gun," she mumbled.

"*Americans,*" Drake intoned, but then smiled quickly. "Relax. The Swedes should mop up *Forn Sidr*, double quick, and the Germans are even less professional."

They reached a Y-shaped staircase overseen by arched windows and a vaulted ceiling, and hurried up without pause. Normally this staircase would have been crammed with wide-eyed tourists, but today the whole place was eerily silent.

Drake paced himself, and stayed vigilant. Scores of dangerous men were racing through this vast old space right now. It was only a matter of time until they converged.

Up they ran, their boots echoing loudly off the high walls, squeaks of static from their throat-mics resonating with the building's natural acoustics. Drake was concentrating hard, recalling his training, but also trying to keep a surreptitious eye on Kennedy. The civilian and the soldier continued to clash inside him.

Approaching the third floor, Dahl motioned an "ahead-slow". Kennedy moved close to Drake. "Where are your SAS buddies?"

"Hanging back," Drake said. "After all, we don't wanna commit overkill now, do we?"

Kennedy stifled a laugh. "You're a comedian, Drake. A real funny guy."

"You should see me on a date."

Kennedy missed a beat then said, "Don't presume I'd accept." Her right hand went habitually to smooth out the front of her shirt.

"Don't *assume* I was asking."

They started up the final staircase. As the lead soldier approached the last curve, a shot rang out. A chunk of plaster exploded an inch away from his head.

"Down!"

A fusillade of bullets peppered the walls. Dahl crawled forward on his stomach, making a series of motions with his hands.

Drake translated, "The scarecrow method."

One soldier fired off a quick volley to keep their enemy busy. Another took off his helmet, hooked his rifle into the strap, and inched it forward, into the line of fire. They heard a faint rustle of movement. A third soldier popped up from cover below the staircase and nailed the sentry between the eyes. The man fell dead without getting a shot off.

"Nice." Drake liked the well-planned movements.

They ploughed on up the stairs, weapons ready, and fanned out around the arched entrance to the fourth floor before peering cautiously into the chamber beyond.

Drake read the signs. This was the hall of Saurischian dinosaurs. *Bollocks*, he thought. Wasn't the T-Rex kept in here?

He sneaked a glance inside the room. Several professional-looking dudes in civvies were looking busy, all equipped with some kind of heavy machine pistol, most likely a "spray and pray" Mac-10. Even then the T-Rex still commanded his attention, rearing in terrible majesty, an enduring epitome of nightmare even millions of years after its extinction.

And walking right past it—clipping smartly past its very jaws—was Alicia Myles. "Keep it on the clock, boys! One mistake here and I'll personally gut every one of you! Hurry it up!"

"Now *there's* a lady," Kennedy whispered mockingly from a millimeter away. Drake was aware of her understated perfume and slight breathing. "Your old friend, Drake?"

"Taught her everything she knows," he said. "Literally, at first. Then she went way past me. And she's never been a lady, that's for sure."

"Four on the left," a soldier reported. "Five on the right. Plus the woman. The Odin exhibit must be near the back of the room, maybe in its own alcove, I don't know."

Dahl took a breath. "Time to move."

EIGHTEEN

NEW YORK NATIONAL HISTORY MUSEUM

The Swedes burst out of hiding, firing with precision. Four cultists dropped, and then another. Three of them flew back into a glass exhibit that, in turn, toppled and crashed to the floor with a noise like an explosion.

The remaining cultists spun and fired in place. Two Swedes screamed. One fell, leaking blood. The other collapsed in a writhing heap, clutching his thigh.

Drake slithered into the room across the polished floor, then crawled behind a display of giant armadillos. After checking Kennedy was safe, he raised his head to peer through the glass.

And saw Alicia kill two sprinting Swedes with perfect shots.

From beyond the T-Rex now appeared another four member of the *Forn Sidr*. They must have been in the alcove where the sculpture of the wolves was on display. They had odd leather harnesses strapped to their bodies and heavy-duty rucksacks on their backs.

And more Mac-10s. They sprayed the room with bullets.

The Swedes dived for cover. Drake hit the floor, snaking an arm around Kennedy's head to keep her as low as possible. The glass above him shattered, fragments spraying the area and pattering down on them. Armadillo fossils and replicas burst and disintegrated around them.

"Mop up quick, huh?" Kennedy muttered. "Yeah, right."

Drake shook himself, scattering glass shards everywhere, and looked for the outer wall of the museum, where one of the cultists had fallen.

"Already on it."

Using the shattered display unit as cover, he shuffled over to the prone soldier. As he pulled at the machine pistol, the man's eyes snapped wide open.

"Hey!" Drake's heart hammered. "Thought you were a goner."

The man grunted, eyes wide in pain. Drake recovered quickly, wrestled the weapon away, and clubbed him into oblivion. "Bloody zombie, coming back from the dead!"

He spun on one knee, but the cultists had retreated beyond the ribbed belly of the T-Rex. All he could see from behind the display unit were their legs.

Kennedy scooted next to him, sliding to a stop by his side.

"Nice slide," he said, bobbing left and right, trying to see what the cultists were up to.

At last, Drake saw movement between three of the Rex's cracked ribs and gasped in disbelief. "They have the wolves," he breathed. "And they're smashing them to pieces!"

Kennedy shook her head. "No. They're *breaking them into bits*." She pointed. "Look. See the rucksacks. No one said the Pieces of Odin had to be intact, did they?"

"And it's easier to carry them out like that." Drake nodded. "And put them back together later."

He was about to move to the cover of the next exhibit when all hell broke loose. From the far corner of the room a dozen screaming banshees stormed. They whooped, they fired wildly, they laughed like geeks overdosing on multiple Jager Bombs at spring break.

"Looks like the Germans are here," Drake said drily before hitting the floor.

The T-Rex shook madly as a lead fusillade smashed through it. Its head drooped, teeth gnashing as if the violence had enraged it enough to come back to life. A cult member flew backwards amidst a cloud of gore. Blood sprayed all over the dinosaur's jawbone.

The Germans piled in, manic.

From outside a nearby window Drake heard the familiar *whump whump* of helicopter rotor blades approaching.

Not again.

THE BONES OF ODIN

At the edge of his peripheral vision, a creeping team of SWAT figures stole toward him, all darkly dressed. When Drake glanced that way, the tweeters went crazy in his ear.

Then the cultists went for it too, causing mayhem. They burst from underneath the giant belly of the T-Rex, firing frantically. Drake grabbed Kennedy's shoulder.

"Move!" They were in the line of flight. He pushed Kennedy away, just as Alicia Myles ran into view. Drake raised his weapon, then saw the massive German, Milo, barreling in from the left.

In one mutual second of pause, all three lowered their weapons.

Alicia looked surprised. "I *knew* you'd get into this, Drakey, you old git!"

Milo stopped dead. Drake glanced between the two. "Shoulda stayed in Sweden, mate."

Bullets laced the air around them, not penetrating their tense cocoon.

"Your time will come," Milo whispered thickly. "Like Parnevik's. Like your little boyfriend Ben Blake, and his *sister*."

Drake didn't have time to respond. Out of the corner of his eye he saw Alicia drop to the ground. He turned around and saw an RPG missile blasting through the belly of the T-Rex. He dived for the floor as knives of bone scythed in all directions. The grenade swept across the hall, straight through one of the side windows. After a heavy pause there was a gigantic explosion that shook the room, then a tortured sound of ruined metal and shrieking joints.

Metallic death crashed into the side of the National History Museum.

Drake flattened himself on top of Kennedy as the helicopter's momentum sent it crashing into the museum's wall, causing a cave-in of heavy debris. The nose smashed right through, sending rubble forward in undulating heaps and the cockpit hit the collapsing wall almost vertically. The pilot yanked on the cyclic stick in mad panic before disappearing beneath his own windshield.

Then the rotor blades struck...and sheared off.

Spears of flying metal created a kill zone inside the room. A six-foot-long spike made a whickering noise as it flew toward Drake and Kennedy. The Yorkshireman flattened himself as much as possible against a wall and felt a rush of air as the scythe sliced past Kennedy's scalp, embedding itself three feet deep into the furthest wall.

He lay stunned for a moment, then whipped his head around. The helicopter lost all momentum. In another moment it slipped down the side of the Museum like Wile E. Coyote slid down the side of a mountain.

Drake counted four seconds before the resounding crunch of heavy metal rang out. He took time to survey the room. The cultists hadn't broken stride. They'd reached the side of the room, four guys with heavy rucksacks plus Alicia and one covering fighter. They deployed what looked like abseiling units.

Most of the Germans were looking towards the downed helicopter, as though they couldn't believe what had happened. Drake didn't spot the man in white, and wondered if this mission had been too risky for him. He saw SWAT approaching them in a sweeping pattern, the Swedes having surrendered authority when the Americans arrived.

The cultists were escaping with the wolves. Drake attempted to rise. Kennedy helped out by elbowing him hard before wriggling out from underneath, sitting up, and wiping a tiny smear of blood from her scalp.

"Perv," she muttered, in mock anger.

Drake watched three of the five remaining Swedish Special Forces troops try to head off the cultists as the first used his rappel unit to leap out the destroyed window.

But Alicia spun around, her face sporting the playful smile that made Drake cringe inside. She skipped forward and darted through them, bending highly trained soldiers in a way that made them scream, taking less than twelve seconds to incapacitate the team.

It took Drake less than a second to realize she hadn't actually killed anyone.

By then, three cult members had jumped soundlessly and expertly out of the building.

The remaining soldier sprayed cover fire.

The New York SWAT team assaulted the Germans, driving them toward the rear of the room, dropping all but three of them where they stood. The remaining three, including Milo, flung their weapons and ran.

Drake flinched as the T-Rex finally gave up the ghost and collapsed in a pile of old bones and dust.

The fourth cultist jumped, quickly followed by Alicia. The final soldier tripped as he prepared to leap. He fell back into the room to sprawl amidst the burning rubble, just another casualty of a madman's war.

NINETEEN

NEW YORK

Almost immediately, Drake began to evaluate and analyze. More than anything, it was clear that Milo had possessed some kind of unpleasant knowledge about Ben, his sister and Professor Parnevik.

He fished his cellphone out quickly and checked it for damage before hitting speed dial.

The phone rang and rang, unanswered. Ben wouldn't leave it this long, not Ben...

His heart started to beat fast, quicker than it had under fire. He'd tried to protect Ben, promised him he'd be alright. Instinct had made him chase the terrorists instead of protecting his friend. He was battling two distinct men here, the one he'd once been and surely had to become again, the other a persona he'd taken on to obliterate that past and all the horrors it continued to foster. If anything happened to–

A voice whispered, "Yes?"

"Ben? You okay? Why are you whispering?"

"Matt, I got a call from Dad, wandered off to talk, then looked back and saw these two goons attacking the prof. I started to run toward them and they took off on motorbikes with a few others."

"They took Parnevik?"

"Sorry, mate. I would've helped him if I could."

"*No!*" Drake's heart was still recovering. "It's not your fault, Blakey. Not at all. Did these bikers have rucksacks strapped to their backs?"

"Some did."

"Okay. Stay there."

Drake breathed deeply and tried to calm his sudden urge to give chase. The cultists would have been in a hurry. They must have had eyes on the crowd when Drake and the teams arrived. Ben had dodged a nasty one, thanks to his dad's call, but the professor was in terrible trouble. "Their plan was to abseil out of the museum onto waiting bikes," he told Kennedy, then looked around the demolished room. "We need to find Dahl. We have a problem."

"Only one?"

Drake surveyed the devastation they had made of the museum. "This thing just exploded, big time."

Drake exited the museum amongst an assortment of government personnel. They were setting up a staging post outside the Central Park West entrance, which he deliberately ignored when he spotted Ben sitting on a bench opposite. The kid was crying uncontrollably. What now? Kennedy sprinted beside him across the stretch of grass.

"It's Karin," Ben's eyes were overflowing. "I e-mailed her to ask how she'd been getting on with the Valkyries, but this MPEG bounced back."

He spun his laptop around so they could see. The screen showed a tiny video file playing on repeat. The clip lasted about thirty seconds.

In black-and-white stop-motion it showed fuzzy images of Ben's sister hanging limply in the grip of two heavy-set masked men. Dark patches that could only be blood were smeared around her forehead and mouth. A third man had his face up to the camera, shouting in a thick German accent.

"She put up a fight this one!" The man wagged his finger mockingly. "Stop helping them, little boy. We can track all web traffic, so stop asisting them. If you do, you'll get her back in one piece—" a nasty laugh. "More or less."

The fragment restarted from the beginning.

"She's a second dan black belt," Ben was babbling. "I didn't think anyone could b-beat her, my-my big sister."

Drake put an arm around Ben as his young friend broke down. His expression, seen by, but not meant for, Kennedy was pure battlefield hatred.

TWENTY

NEW YORK

Abel Frey, world renowned German fashion designer, multi-millionaire, and owner of the infamous twenty-four-hour party chateau—La Verein—sat backstage at Madison Square Garden and watched his minions scuttle about like the freeloading vermin they really were.

During solstice or periods of hiatus, he housed his staff comfortably in the confines of his extensive home in the Alps—everyone from world-famous models and pop stars he used, all the way down to lighting techs and security staff— where the parties never stopped for weeks on end. But when the tour was on, and the name of Frey graced the spotlight, they scurried and worried and catered to his every whim. If he wished to stage a show in York, UK, one day and New York the next—then his people made sure it happened.

The stage was taking shape. The catwalk was half erected. His lighting designer was interfacing with the Garden's crew, trying to come up with a mutually respectful Magic Sheet—a synchronized light and sound schedule—for the two-hour-long show.

Frey intended to hate their first effort and make the bastards sweat and start again.

Supermodels strutted back and forth in varying stages of undress. The backstage area of a fashion show was the opposite of a stage show—less material was needed rather than more—and these models, at least the ones who lived with him at La Verein, knew he'd seen it all before.

Fear reined them in, these cattle. Fear, greed, gluttony, and those other wonderful sins that led through the gates of hell, that chained ordinary men and women to those who wielded power and wealth—from the Victoria's Secret catwalk queens to the East European ice sculptures, and right down to the true dregs of his fortunate staff—every last sniveling bloodsucker.

But it was all an elaborate sham, this public persona. A multi-million dollar mock-up to hide his one true obsession. An open face to hide the one he'd cultivated and built with blood and corpses so carefully and for so long.

Frey noticed Milo enter the room. The American didn't look pleased. "Back there!" He nodded toward Frey's makeshift office.

Frey's face hardened as they sat in private. "What happened?"

"What *didn't?* We lost the chopper. I squeaked my ass out of there with two guys. They had SWAT, the SGG, Drake, and some woman. It was hell in there, man." Milo's inflections literally wounded Frey's cultured ears. The brute had just addressed him as *man.*

"The piece?"

"Lost to Myles." Milo was grinning.

"*The* Forn Sidr *got it?*" Frey gripped the arms of his chair in anger, causing them to distort.

Milo pretended not to notice, betraying an inner unease. Frey's ego made his chest swell. "*Pathetic!*" he screamed so loudly Milo flinched. "*You useless morons lost out to a bunch of Mounties!*"

Spittle flew from Frey's lips, spattering the table that separated them. "*Do you know how long I've been waiting for this moment? This* time*? Do you?*"

Unable to control himself, he slapped the American Special Forces man across the face. Milo's head whipped around and his cheek colored, but he gave no other reaction.

Frey forced a superior cocoon of calm to envelop him. "My life," he said with a supreme effort that he knew only those with high breeding could pull off, "has been dedicated—no, devoted— to finding this tomb...this Tomb of the Gods. But we need the Nine Pieces! The fashion house means nothing in comparison. I will transport the tomb—piece by piece—to my chateau. I will own the very bones of the gods. I am a ruler," he said, waving a hand toward the door, "and I do not mean a ruler of those idiots. I can force a good man to fight to the death in my battle arena, but that doesn't make me a ruler. Do you understand?"

Frey's voice dripped with intellectual superiority. Milo nodded along, but his eyes were blank. Frey read it, quite wrongly, as stupidity. He sighed.

"Well, what else do you have for me?"

"This." Milo stood up and tapped on the keyboard of Frey's laptop for a few seconds. A live feed came up, focused closely on an area near the National History Museum.

"We have men posing as a TV crew, though they won't be able to pass it off for too long. They have eyes on Drake and his cohorts. Also SWAT and whatever SGG remain and, look, I believe *that*—" he tapped the screen lightly, leaving unwanted smears of sweat and God knew what else behind, "—is an SAS team."

"You believe...?" Frey said. "You're trying to tell me that we now have a multi-international race on our hands? And we no longer have the greatest resources." He sighed. "Not that it's helped us thus far."

Milo shared a secret smile with his boss. "You know it has."

"Yes. Your girlfriend, Alicia Myles. She is our best placed asset in the camp of these cultists, and her time is approaching. Let us hope she remembers who she answers to."

"It's more the *money* she'll remember," Milo said, with great vision.

Frey's eyes lit up. "I'll not forget that."

"We also have Ben Blake's sister, the one we piggybacked onto as she sniffed around the Web."

"Good. Send her to the chateau. We will return there soon." He paused. "And check them all out. I want to know their backgrounds, starting with that woman. She seems familiar. Who is she?"

Milo studied the face and shrugged. "No clue."

"Well, *find out!*"

Milo placed a call to the "TV crew". "Use the facial recognition software on Drake's woman," he growled.

Four silent minutes later, he received an answer. "Kennedy

Moore," he told Frey. "A New York cop."

"Yes. *Yes.* I never forget a depravity and she was central to that serial killer travesty in New York. Move aside, Milo. Let me work."

Frey googled the name and followed a few links. In less than ten minutes he knew everything, and his smile grew broader and even more twisted. The beginnings of a superlative idea grew past puberty in his mind.

"Kennedy Moore," he couldn't resist explaining to the grunt, "was one of New York's finest. She is currently on forced leave. She arrested a dirty cop and got him sent to prison. His conviction led to the release of some of the people *he'd* helped convict, something to do with a broken chain of evidence." Frey paused. "A wonderful lawyer got a man called Thomas Kaleb released—the 'worst serial killer in Northern United States history' it says here. My, my. This is gross."

Milo grimaced. "He's an indiscriminate killer," he said.

Frey smiled at him. "You have dispatched more than your share of innocents have you not?"

"Only in the execution of my job. I'm a soldier."

"You *were* a soldier. And it's a thin line, yes? Never mind. Back to the job at hand. This man Kaleb has murdered *two more innocents* since his release. The clear result of an ethical doctrine and a bunch of moral values I'd say, eh Milo? Anyway, this Kaleb has now disappeared."

Milo's head swerved toward the laptop screen, toward Kennedy Moore. "Two more? She will blame herself."

Frey laughed now. "You're not so dense that you don't get it, are you? Imagine her grief. Imagine her torture! Imagine...if we found Kaleb first."

Milo caught on and, despite himself, gave the grin of a demented circus clown.

"I have a plan." Frey giggled with delight. "Oh, do I have a plan."

TWENTY-ONE

NEW YORK

Inside the mobile HQ, chaos reigned. Drake, Kennedy and Ben followed Torsten Dahl and the furious SWAT commander up the steps and through the commotion. They negotiated two compartments before stopping in the relative quiet afforded by an alcove at the end of the big metal shed.

"We got a call." The SWAT commander threw his weapon down in anger. "We got a call and fifteen minutes later three of my men are dead! What the...?"

"Three?" Dahl asked. "We lost six. Respect requires we take a moment for–"

"Screw respect." The SWAT guy was furious. "*You* invaded *my* turf, you English asshole. You're as bad as the terrorists!"

Drake held up a hand. "Actually, *I'm* the English asshole. This prick's Swedish."

The American looked bewildered. Drake gripped Ben's shoulders tighter. He could feel the lad shaking. "We helped," he told the SWAT guy. "*They* helped. It could've been much worse."

And then fate dropped its ironic hammer. Bullets started peppering the HQ. Everyone hit the floor. Metallic pings bounced off the wall. Before the firing had ended, the SWAT commander had stood up. "It's bulletproof," he said with some embarrassment.

"We need to go." Drake looked for Kennedy, but failed to spot her.

"*Into* the line of fire?" the SWAT guy said. "Who the hell *are* you?"

"It's not the company or the bullets that bother me," Drake said. "It's the rocket-propelled grenade that might soon follow."

Drake exited in time to see black-and-whites screaming off in the direction the bullets had come from. A hard perimeter formed around the walking group of men and women.

He looked around for Kennedy again, but she seemed to have vanished.

Then a new face was suddenly amongst them. A bureau chief, judging by his three-star insignia and, as if that weren't enough, pushing in behind him was a man sporting the rare five stars of a police commissioner. Drake knew immediately that this was the guy they should be talking to. Police commissioners handled counterterrorism.

The SWAT commander's walkie squawked, "All clear. Got a weapon on the roof here, controlled by remote. It's diversionary."

"Of course it is." Drake thought about the cultists and the Germans getting further away with their captives.

Torsten Dahl addressed the newcomer. "You really should speak to my Statsministern."

"It's done," the commissioner said. "You're outta here."

"No, wait," Drake began, physically restraining Ben from rushing forward. "You don't understand..."

"No, no," the commissioner said through gritted teeth. "I don't. And what I mean is you're outta here, *on your way to Washington DC*. Capitol Hill wants a piece of you guys, and I hope they take it in *big* slices."

The flight lasted ninety minutes. Drake had worried about Kennedy's mysterious disappearance right up until the time she reappeared, which was when the jet was about to set off.

She came running up the aisle, breathless.

"Thought we'd lost you," said Drake, feeling enormous relief, but trying to keep their reunion lighthearted.

Kennedy didn't answer. Instead, she threw herself down in a window seat, out of chatting distance. Drake got up to investigate, but stopped when she flinched away from him, her face as white as alabaster.

Where had she been, and what had happened there?

No calls or e-mail communications were allowed during the flight. No television. They flew in silence; a few guards watched them without interfering.

Drake could have let it all flow over him. The old training called for hours, days, and months of waiting. Of prepping. Of surveilling. For him, an hour could pass in a millisecond. At one point they were offered plastic bottles of alcohol, and Drake hesitated for more than a moment.

The whisky gleamed, the amber charm of disaster, his weapon of choice the last time things got tough—when Alyson died. He recalled the pain, the desperation, all too well, and still his eyes lingered.

"Not here, thanks." Ben was alert enough to motion the hostess away. "Once in the US, we're Mountain Dew boys. Bring that."

Ben even tried to snap Drake out of it by doing the geek thing. He leaned into the aisle, watching the hostess sway back to her station.

His face reddened when the hostess looked back and caught him staring. After a second she said, "This ain't *Hooters Air,* kid."

Ben shrank back into his seat. "Oh, dear."

Drake shook his head. "Cheers, mate. Your constant humiliation serves as a happy reminder that even in my early years of life I was never at your level of immaturity."

"Bollocks."

"Seriously—thanks."

"No worries."

"And Karin—she will be okay. I promise."

"How can you promise that, Matt?"

Drake paused. His inbuilt obligation to help the needy had spoken, not his clear-cut judgment. The new façade he was trying to maintain would never be able to save Karin...the old soldier, though—he just might.

One more reason to stop the struggle and just let it happen.

"They won't hurt her yet," he said. "And soon we're going to have more help than you can imagine."

"How do you *know* they won't hurt her?"

Drake sighed. "It's an educated guess, based on experience. If they wanted her dead they'd have killed her straight away, right? No messing. But they didn't. So..."

"Yes?"

"The Germans want her for something. They'll keep her alive." Drake thought they might have taken her for isolated interrogation.

Ben managed a strained smile. Drake felt the plane begin its descent, and started to review the facts in his head. With his little team falling apart, he had to step up and protect them more than ever now.

Within two minutes of disembarking, Drake, Ben, Kennedy and Dahl were ushered through several sets of doors, up a quiet escalator, along a plush corridor lined with dark blue paneling, and finally through a heavy door that, Drake observed, was discreetly locked behind them.

They found themselves in a premier first-class lounge, empty except for themselves and eight other people: five armed guards and three suits—two women and an older man.

The man stepped forward. "Jonathan Gates," he said softly. "Secretary of Defense."

Drake was genuinely shocked. The Secretary was maybe fifth or sixth in line for the presidency. He took a breath and stepped forward, noting the offensive movements from the guards, then spread his hands.

"All friends here," he said. "At least...I think so."

"I believe you are right." The Secretary of Defense came forward and offered his own hand. "To save time, I have already been apprised of events. The United States is willing, and able, to help. I'm here to... *facilitate* that help, since this crisis comes with a more international slant than most we've had to face of late."

One of the women offered soft drinks all round. The drinks broke the ice a little. Drake and Ben stayed near Gates, sipping diet Dew. Kennedy went over to the window to stare out at the taxiing planes, seemingly lost in her own thoughts. Torsten Dahl sank into a comfy seat with an Evian, body language tailored to pose no threat.

"My sister," Ben spoke up first. "Can you help her?"

"The CIA has contacted Interpol, but we have no leads on the Germans yet." After a moment, noting Ben's distress and what effort it took to address a member of Congress, the Secretary added, "We *are* trying, son. We *will* find them."

"My parents don't know yet." Ben glanced involuntarily down at his cellphone. "But it won't be long—"

Now the other woman stepped forward—vivacious, self-assured, much younger, and with the look of the future ex-Mrs. Secretary all over her, a true carnivore or, as Drake said to himself, a *political* version of Alicia Myles.

"My country is nothing if not realistic, Mr. Dahl, Mr. Drake. We know we are way behind in this, and we know the stakes. Your SAS team has been cleared to operate. The Swedish SGG also. We have a Delta team standing by ready to assist. Not normally the best of bedfellows, I agree, but united through necessity, I think. And not without precedent. The International Security Assistance Force is currently operating in Afghanistan and comprised of US, UK, many NATO countries and others. And, despite the differences, it runs very well. Now, right here right now, all we need to do is add numbers..." she waggled her fingers. "Coordinates."

"And Professor Parnevik?" Dahl asked, speaking for the first time since the meeting had begun. "What news on the *Forn Sidr*"

"Warrants are being issued for known cult members," the Secretary said a little stiffly. "It's a diplomatic situa—"

"No!" Drake shouted. Everyone stared at him. He exhaled to calm himself. "No, sir. That's the wrong approach. This thing kicked off...what?...three days ago? Time is everything here, especially now. The next few days," he said, "will be where we win or lose."

Secretary Gates gave him an amused look. "I heard you still had some *soldier* in you, Drake. But not by that reaction."

"I'm switching between soldier and civilian when it suits." Drake shrugged, trying to compartmentalize the struggle. "Benefits of being *ex*-Army."

"Uh, huh. Well, if it makes you feel any better, the warrants won't help. Colby Taylor has disappeared from his Canadian mansion, along with the majority of his staff. My guess is he's been planning this for some time and has switched to a pre-arranged contingency. Essentially—he's off the grid."

Drake closed his eyes. "Any *good* news?"

The younger woman spoke up. "We *are* offering you the full resources of the Library of Congress to help your research." Her eyes twinkled. "The *largest* library in the world. Thirty-two *million* books. Rare prints. And a World Digital Library."

Ben looked at her as if she'd just agreed to enter a Princess Leia cosplay contest. "Full resources? So—theoretically—you could find out which German is insanely obsessed by Norse mythology? You could find old texts on Odin and this Tomb of the Gods. Stuff that's not on the Internet?"

"Technically, yes, and at the touch of a button," the woman said. "And, failing that, we have some *very* old librarians."

Ben's eyes lit with hope as he glanced at Matt. "Take us there."

The Library of Congress was unlocked for them in the very early hours of Sunday morning. Lights on, staff attentive, the world's largest library was certainly impressive. At first the architecture and feel of the place reminded Drake of a museum, but when he got a look at the endless ranks of bookcases and the curved reading balconies, he soon adapted to the respectful ambience, and his mood changed to match his environment.

Whilst Drake spent some time stalking the halls, Ben wasted no time initiating research mode. He sidled into a balcony, booted up a laptop, and sent their Swedish Special Forces commander in search of coffee and cookies.

"This is an awe-inspiring place," Drake said when he'd completed a circuit. "Makes a person respect history."

Ben gripped the bridge of his nose. "I don't know where to start," he confessed. "My head's a shed, mate."

Torsten Dahl tapped the rail that ran around the balcony. "If that means 'you're a little befuddled' in English, then start with something you know," he said in those learned Oxford tones. "Start with the legend."

Drake gave the Swede a bemused look as he handed over mugs of coffee and breakfast muffins, the careful procedure looking

wrong somehow when undertaken by a man he was slowly
coming to see as a highly capable soldier.

"Right." Ben eyed the screen. "Well, we know the poem. It
pretty much says that whoever desecrates the Tomb of the Gods
will bring hellfire to Earth. And that's *fire*, literally. Our planet
will burn. We also know this legend has unique parallels
throughout history, to legends written about most of the other
gods."

"What we *don't* know," Dahl said, "is why? Or how?"

"Fire," Drake said sharply. "The kid just said it."

Ben closed his eyes. Dahl turned to Drake with a tight smile.
"This is called *brainstorming*," he said. "Sifting through the facts
often helps reveal the truth. I meant—how the disaster is
triggered. Please either help, or go away."

Drake sipped coffee and kept quiet. Both these guys had lost
people and deserved space. He drifted to the railing and glanced
over, running his eyes around the circular room, noting the
positions of staff and American agents. Kennedy sat two floors
below, tapping away furiously at a laptop, isolated by her
own...*what?* Drake wondered. *Guilt? Fear? Depression?* He
knew all about that, and he wasn't about to start preaching.

The feeling took him back to when he first signed up for the
Army. His parents had died when he was young, and his uncle,
who looked after him, died on Drake's eighteenth birthday. With
fate and chance and choice arrayed like warriors against him he
had joined up the very next day, determined to make a difference
in any way he could. The decision had made the man, the Army
had molded it.

"The legend," Ben was saying, "indicates that it is the
desecration of Odin's tomb *alone* that will start the rivers of fire
flowing. In effect, it's saying 'keep your hands off'. But it doesn't
say *when,* or where the tomb lies.".

Drake frowned. *Rivers of fire?* He'd heard that phrase
somewhere recently. "Why did you say it that way?" he asked.
"Rivers of fire?"

"Dunno. Maybe 'cause I'm sick of saying 'hellfire spews forth'
and 'the end is nigh'. I feel like a Hollywood movie trailer."

"So you went for *rivers of fire?*" Dahl raised an eyebrow. "Like
lava?"

Drake snapped his fingers. "The Icelandic volcano, right?" He looked to the Swede for confirmation.

"Look, just because I'm Scandinavian doesn't mean I know all about—"

"Yes." The Secretary of Defense's assistant had materialized at that moment from a nearby rack of books. "On the southeastern side of Iceland. The entire world's aware of it. From reading new governmental research, I think it's on the brink of a small eruption."

Ben held his hands in the air. "Look, we're getting distracted here. The volcano can wait. What we need is loadsa crap on Odin." He highlighted several titles on the screen. "That, that, and *whoa*, definitely that. The Voluspa—where Odin tells of his visits with the seeress." Ben narrowed his eyes. "The legends speak of her an awful lot. It can't be just coincidence."

"Visits?" Drake made a face.

Ben shrugged. "The seeress shows up in the depictions, the carvings, the academic histories, the ancient Norse Sagas. She appeared in the pit and was the *only* one who learned all of Odin's secrets and was literally beside him as he hung on the World Tree. She's important to all this, Matt."

Gates' assistant leaned over Ben and clicked a few buttons, entered a password, and typed a line. Her trouser suit was the opposite of Kennedy's, designed tastefully to enhance her figure rather than conceal it. Ben's eyes went wide, his troubles momentarily forgotten.

Drake mouthed, *Put your eyes back in.*

Ben gave him the finger just as the assistant stood up. Luckily, she didn't see him. "They will be brought to you within five minutes," she said.

"Thank you, Miss." Drake hesitated. "Sorry, I don't know your name."

"Call me Hayden," she said. "Hayden Jaye. FBI liaison to Mr. Gates."

The books were deposited next to Ben a few minutes later, and he immediately chose the one titled Voluspa, the one relating to Odin's seeress. He leafed through the pages like a man possessed; like an animal smelling blood. Dahl chose another volume, Drake a third. Hayden sat close to Ben, studying the text with him.

And then Ben cried out, "I've got it! The missing link is Heidi! Bloody Heidi! This book follows—quote 'the travels of Odin's beloved seeress, *Heidi*'."

"Do you mean the children's book?" Dahl obviously remembered his school days.

Drake just looked blank. "Must say, I'm more of a Heidi Klum type of guy."

"Yes, the children's book! I suppose the legend of Heidi and the story of her travels must have integrated itself from Norse saga into Scandinavian myth through the years, and then a writer from Switzerland decided to use the fairy tale as the basis for a kid's book. Heidi was a seeress and first mentioned in the Poetic Edda, one of the best sources for studying Norse mythology. It's a prophecy mentioning everything from the gods of Asgard to the binding of Loki and even Ragnarok. Her travels are well documented in the prophecy, some of which later ended up in the book."

"Well, what does it say?" Drake felt his heart beat faster.

Ben read for a second. "Oh, it says a lot," he rushed on. "It says almost everything."

TWENTY-TWO

WASHINGTON DC

Kennedy Moore sat staring at her PC screen, seeing nothing at all, and thought about how much life could grind anyone under its heartless heel. One day could bring so much happiness that beauty could be found in almost everything, while the next could bring the weight of a cold, crushing world down.

She'd been feeling upbeat during the drive through New York. Feeling good about herself, and maybe even a little bit good about Matt Drake.

How perverse, she'd told herself. But didn't someone once say that out of great hardship comes great progress? Something like that.

Then the professor had been kidnapped, Ben Blake's sister abducted. And Kennedy had walked toward that mobile HQ with determination, head straight and once more fully invested in the game, her thoughts focused on making sense of the turmoil.

But, as she had started to climb the steps, Lipkind had materialized from the crowd and stopped her short.

"Captain?"

"Moore. We need to talk right now."

"Come inside," Kennedy motioned at the HQ, "we could do with the help."

"This is not about the museum, Moore. Cruiser's this way."

He moved off through the crowd, stiff back facing her like a silent accusation. Kennedy had to hurry to catch up.

"What's happened, Captain?"

"Get in."

The cruiser was empty except for the two of them. The street noise was dulled, the outside world with its earth-shattering events temporarily held in abeyance.

Kennedy half-turned in her seat to face Lipkind. "Don't tell me...please don't tell me..." The catch in her throat made Lipkind's stern expression slip, revealing the truth before the words fell out of his mouth.

But fall they did, and each word was another drop of venom landing on her already blackened soul.

"Kaleb struck again. It's his MO, down to a tee. We had a month's grace—then yesterday afternoon we got the call. Girl...ahh...girl from Nevada," his voice thickened. "New to the city. Student."

"No. Please... how do you know it was him and not some sick copycat?"

Lipkind narrowed his eyes. "He was overheard toward. . .toward the end. You know the noise he makes: that manic, terrible squealing. Like a pig being slaughtered. They heard it."

Kennedy felt tears prickling her eyes. It was a fact they'd never released about Kaleb – the horrifying screech he made as his victims died. "No. . ."

"I wanted you to know now, before you heard through the Media."

"No."

"I'm sorry, Moore."

"I want back in. Let me come back, Lipkind. *Let me in.*"

Lipkind was chewing his bottom lip, a sure sign of stress. "Not yet. Even if I wanted to, the Brass wouldn't approve. You know that."

"Do I? Does anyone know the thoughts of a politician? Since when did they do the right thing?"

"Ya got me." Lipkind's growl betrayed his heart. "But orders is orders. And mine haven't changed."

"Lipkind, this is...*ruining* me."

He swallowed drily. "Give it time. You'll be back."

"It's not *me* I care about! It's his fucking *victims!* Their *families!*"

"So do I, Moore. Believe me."

After a moment she said, "Where?" It was all she could do, all she could ask, all she could think about.

"Moore. You're not gonna pay no penance here. It's not your fault this psycho's a fuckin' *psycho*."

"Where?"

Lipkind knew what she needed and gave her the address.

Open building site. Three blocks south of Ground Zero. Developer by the name of Sanstone Holdings.

Kennedy arrived at the site in twenty minutes, noted the fluttering crime scene tape on the fourth floor of the open shell, and sent the cab away. She stood before the building, staring up with spiritless eyes. The place was deserted, still an active crime scene, but it was getting late on a Saturday and the incident was over twenty four hours old.

Kennedy kicked at the rubble, then let herself onto the construction site. She followed an open flight of rough stairs to the fourth floor, and walked out onto the concrete slab.

A strong breeze tugged at her loose shirt. If her hair hadn't been scraped back, it would have thrashed around as if possessed. From this vantage point, she could see in three different directions across the city, vistas that would ordinarily have taken her breath away but which felt wholly inadequate today.

She thought of the Odin case and of Matt Drake in particular. She wanted to return to the fray, to him, but wasn't sure she had the balls.

She ventured across the dusty slab, avoiding heaps of rubble and contractors' tools. The wind tugged at her sleeves, at her pants, making their excess material billow. She stopped near to where Lipkind had described the body's location. Contrary to popular TV, bodies were not normally marked out in chalk—they were photographed, before their exact location was measured from various fixed points.

Anyway, she just needed to be close. To bend down, to fall to her knees, close her eyes and pray. She felt...destroyed.

And the horror of it all rushed back, images flashing sickeningly through her mind—the moment she'd seen Chuck

Walker pocketing the slab of dirty money. The crash of the judge's gavel proclaiming his guilt. The dead stares of her colleagues, the terrible drawings that started appearing on her locker—attached to the hood of her car—fixed to her apartment door.

The letter she'd received from the serial killer, where he thanked her for all her help.

And now, what next? She needed to do penance for the new murder she felt responsible for helping Thomas Kaleb commit.

It wasn't her fault, but she needed to seek forgiveness from the dead and the grieving.

TWENTY-THREE

WASHINGTON DC

"This thing's brilliantly revealing." Ben was rushing his words in his excitement. "It says, 'Whilst he is still on the World Tree, a volva reveals to Odin that she knows many of his secrets—that he sacrificed himself on Yggdrasil and fasted for nine days and nine nights in pursuit of knowledge.' She tells him she knows where his eyes are hidden, and how he gave them up in exchange for even more knowledge."

"Odin the Wise," Dahl interrupted. "Parnevik said he was always considered to be the wisest of all gods."

Drake muttered, "Revealing your secrets to a woman is never wise."

Ben sent him an eye roll. "Odin fasted on the World Tree with a spear thrust through his side, like Christ on the cross. Heidi says that in his delirium Odin told her where his *companions* were hidden, and that he wanted her to scatter them—his *pieces*—and lay his body in the tomb to...to await the Day of Reckoning."

Ben grinned at Drake. "I may not have completed my quest for the fabled clitoris, my friend, but my work here is *done.*"

Then Ben remembered where he was, and the woman who stood beside him. He gripped the bridge of his nose. "Balls."

Dahl didn't bat an eyelid. "To my knowledge—which extends only to what I bothered listening to as Parnevik lectured—volvas, like Egyptian pharaohs, were always buried in the richest graves with many valuables beside them. Horses, wagons, gifts from faraway lands. They were considered royalty, I guess, since they were companions to the Norse gods."

Hayden was staring at Ben in a strange way. "If we follow your story logically through its entire course, Mr. Blake, then I guess the stories of Heidi's so-called *travels* are in fact an explanation of where all the Pieces of Odin were scattered...or hidden. By her."

"Call me...Ben. And yes, you're right."

Drake helped his friend out. "Not that it matters now. All the pieces have been found, except for the Valkyries and..." he paused.

"*The eyes,*" Ben said with an intense smile. "If we can find the eyes, we can stop this *and* grab ourselves a bargaining chip for Karin."

Drake, Dahl, and Hayden remained tight lipped. Drake eventually said, "The Valkyries are out there too, Blakey. Where were they discovered? There has to be some old newspaper account or something."

"Heidi *devised* the legend and the Ragnarok thing," Ben mused, still lost in research. "Odin must have tutored her before he died at Ragnarok."

Drake motioned Dahl and Hayden aside. "The Valkyries," he said to them. "Remember the complete lack of information about them, Dahl? And thus the possible criminal angle? Any chance Interpol can get together with the CIA and give it a shot?"

"I'll go authorize it now," Hayden said. "As you say, there has to be a starting point somewhere. And I'll follow up on the investigation our IT techs have been carrying out on the Germans. Like your cute little friend here *almost* says—electronic trails should lead us to them."

"Cute?" Drake smiled at her. "He's more than that. DIP in photography. Lead singer in a band. Family man, and"–he shrugged–"yes...my friend."

Hayden smiled and walked away. Drake started after her, both puzzled and pleasantly surprised. He'd been wrong about her. She was harder to read than Kennedy.

Drake prided himself on his judgment of character. Was he slipping? Had the civilian years made him go soft? Inside, he felt a subtle shift of perspective. Not forced, but natural. It was time to start admitting a few things to himself, truths he'd been hiding. The main one being that Alyson had always been right—he was truly a soldier, through and through.

A voice spoke in his ear, making his heart leap. "What's that?" *Kennedy!*

"Crap!" He jumped, and tried to disguise his little leap in the air as a routine stretching of his limbs.

The New York cop read him like a book. "I'd heard the SAS have never been ambushed in enemy territory. Guess you were never part of *that* team, huh?"

"What's what?" Ben asked distractedly.

"That." Kennedy leaned forward and tapped the side of the monitor, indicating a row of tiny icons hidden among a jumble of manuscript symbols.

Ben frowned. "They're picture icons. The search cross-references with some of the many pictures found here in books relating to Odin."

As Kennedy straightened, her hair came free of its bindings and fell across her shoulders. Drake watched it cascade down to the small of her back.

"Whoa. That's a lot of hair."

"Shut it, freak."

Ben double-clicked several picture icons. On each one, the screen transformed into vivid color, and text and bold titles leapt out at them. *Odin and Thor. Odin astride his Valkyries. Odin and the Seeress, arrayed at Ragnarok.* And beneath them all, a few lines of explanatory text.

Ben took time to pause on them and read aloud. Kennedy made him stop on the last one and re-read the blurb.

"This painting, by Lorenzo Bakke in 1795, impounded from the private collection of John Dillinger in 1934, is believed to be based on an older image and shows the Norse god Odin's companions laid out in peculiar order in the place where Odin died—the mythical battlefield of Ragnarok. His favored seeress looks on and weeps."

Kennedy said, "It could be a blueprint...of how to arrange the pieces."

TWENTY-FOUR

WASHINGTON DC

"Let's get some copies made." Ever cautious, Drake took some snaps with his phone. Ben had tutored him to keep a good, workable camera handy at all times and this was unforeseen pay dirt. "All we need now are the Valkyries, the eyes, and a map to Ragnarok." He stopped abruptly, jabbed by a splinter of memory.

Ben said, "What?"

"Not sure. A memory. Maybe something we've seen these last few days, but we've seen so much I can't narrow it down."

Dahl said, "Maybe you were right. It could be that a modern-day Dillinger has a very private collection of his own."

"Look here," Ben read on. "It says that this particular painting is unique, a fact not realized until the early '60s, whereupon it was included in a Norse mythology exhibition and sent on a short world tour. After that, and with waning interest, the painting was locked in the museum's vault and sadly forgotten. Until today."

"Good job we brought along a cop." Drake was making an attempt to boost Kennedy's self-esteem, still unsure where her thoughts were after returning to New York.

Kennedy began to tie her hair back, then hesitated. After a moment she jammed her hands in her pockets, as if trying to trap them. "Perseverance *is* best," she said. "Nine times out of ten it's grunt work that nails the case."

Drake tapped her on the shoulder. "How about you go get that painting and bring it here? There might be something we can't see from the photo. My old mate Dahl and I are gonna check out the shady side of art collecting. Shake a few trees." He paused, grinning. "*More* trees."

Kennedy groaned before walking away.

Dahl fixed him with narrow eyes. "Where do we start?"

"We start with the Valkyries," Drake said. "Once our friendly munchkin here tells us where and when they were discovered, we can track them."

"Detective work?" Dahl asked. "You just sent our best detective away."

"She needs physical distraction right now, not mental. She's frayed enough."

Ben spoke up. "The Valkyries were discovered, amongst other great riches, in the grave of a Viking seeress, a volva, in 1945, in Sweden."

"*Heidi's* grave?" Drake ventured.

"Had to have been. A good way to hide one of the pieces. Get your minions to bury it with you after you're dead. The Valkyries were said to be Odin's adopted daughters, and appear as beautiful warrior maidens on winged horses. They would visit battlefields and transport the most heroic of the slain to the halls of Valhalla. This was necessary because Odin needed only the best warriors to fight by his side at Ragnarok. The most famous Valkyrie is Brunhilde, mainly through Wagner's Ring Cycle."

"Fire that article across to the other computer." Drake and Dahl sat down next to each other with a brief air of uneasiness.

The clock was still ticking, Drake knew. For Karin. For Parnevik. For their enemies, and for the entire world. He pecked furiously at the machine, running through the Swedish museum's archives and trying to find out when the Valkyries disappeared from its inventory.

"You suspect an inside job?" Dahl said.

"Best guess—lowly paid museum guard or entrapped curator...something like that. They'd have waited until the Valkyries were demoted to the vault perhaps, and then quietly shipped them out. No one realizes for years, if at all."

"Or a robbery," Dahl shrugged. "We've got over sixty years to trawl through." He sighed and fingered the wedding band he'd slipped back on since they' entered the library. Drake paused for a second. "Wife?"

"And kids."

"Miss 'em?"

"Every second."

"Good. Maybe you're not quite the prick I thought you were."

"Fuck you, Drake."

"More like it. No robberies here that I can see. But look—the Valkyries went on *tour* in 1991, as part of the Swedish Heritage Trust's public relations campaign. *By 1992 they were missing from the Museum's catalogue.* What does that tell you?"

Dahl pursed his lips. "That someone connected with the tour decided to steal them?"

"Or...someone who *viewed* them on the tour decided to."

"Okay, that's more likely." Dahl's head was bobbing. "So, which places did the tour visit?" His fingers tapped four times on the screen. "England. New York. Hawaii. Australia."

"Bugger. That really narrows it down," Drake said, sarcastically.

"No, wait," Dahl said. "It does. The theft of the Valkyries had to be well-planned and well-executed. It had to be perfect. That still reeks of criminal involvement."

"If you were any sharper you'd—"

"*Listen.* Back in the early '90s, the Serbian Mafia started to dig its claws into Sweden's underbelly. They were into everything. In less than a decade extortion crimes doubled, and, as of now, there are dozens of organized gangs throughout the country. Some call themselves Bandidos. Others, like a chapter of the Hell's Angels, are just biker gangs."

"You're saying the Serbian Mafia have the Valkyries?"

"No. I'm saying they engineered their theft and subsequent sale, for money. Maybe even to fulfil an order. At the time, back then, it would have made sense. They're the only ones with the connections to pull it off, both at home in Sweden and here. These people are into *everything,* not just extortion. International smuggling wouldn't be above them."

"Okay. So how do we find out who bought them?"

Dahl unhooked his phone. "*We* don't. But at least three of the older kingpins now sit behind bars near Oslo." He moved off to make a call.

Drake rubbed his eyes and leaned back. He checked his watch and was shocked to see it was almost six in the morning. When had he last slept? It seemed only moments ago that he'd been carefully checking his camera equipment in preparation for the shield's major appearance. The rollercoaster of emotions he'd ridden since that night had, if nothing else, made him stop dwelling in a particular area of his past. It had put Alyson's memory firmly to the back of his mind, if only for now. He'd always been a doer, a decision-maker, until her death and his subsequent departure from the army. Maybe that was why his days as a civilian hadn't really moved him and he'd taken so long to find a career, or to find a new niche in life. A sudden noise pulled him from his reverie and he looked around as Hayden returned.

The Defense Secretary's assistant looked downcast. "Sorry, you guys. No luck with the Germans."

Ben's head whipped around, the strain of research and long days on the run now telling in his eyes and face. "*None?*"

"Not yet. I'm sorry."

"But *how?* This guy *has* to be somewhere." Tears filled his eyes and he locked them on Drake. "Doesn't he?"

"Yes, mate, he does. Trust me, we will find him." He patted his friend's arm, his eyes pleading with Hayden to make the breakthrough. "We need to take a breather and grab a butty, some proper scran," he said, his Yorkshire dialect shining through.

Hayden shook her head at him as if he'd just spoken Japanese. "Say again?"

TWENTY-FIVE

LAS VEGAS

Alicia Myles watched the multi-billionaire Colby Taylor as he sat on the expansive floor of one of the many apartments he owned through fake companies, this particular one twenty two flights above Las Vegas Boulevard. One entire wall was glass, giving a fantastic view of the Bellagio fountains and the golden lights of the Eiffel Tower.

Colby Taylor didn't give it a second glance. He was entranced by his latest acquisition, Odin's Wolves. They were thick, wooden carvings, the wolves themselves etched out in intricate detail. Each artefact broke down into four pieces. Colby just couldn't stop fitting them together.

"Part of my life's work," he whispered.

Alicia prowled over to him, stripped her clothes off one by one until she was naked, and then bent down until her eyes were level with his, a foot off the ground.

Money and danger were the two things that got her off. The money of Colby Taylor—megalomaniac extraordinaire—and the danger from the delicious knowledge that her boyfriend, Milo, that big, powerful bruiser from Vegas, actually loved her.

"You going to take a break, boss?" she asked breathily.

Taylor met her eyes. "I guess."

Alicia looked away, taking in the glittering lights of the Strip as they spread out before her. "Take your time. If you can."

"How's it going with Parnevik?" Taylor enunciated his question with grunts.

"Soon as you are done," Alicia answered in her clipped English tones. "I'm going to get everything we need."

"Information is power, Myles. We need to know what they

know. We're ahead, for now. But the Valkyries and the Eyes—they are the...real prizes."

Alicia tuned it out. The droning. The grunting. The obsessing. She might live for danger and money, but she had no real agenda save for constant stimulation. The journey was everything for her, not the destination. The present tuned out the past, made all the terrible noise of it go away. She had the skills and the charm to take whatever she wanted, which she did every day, without thought or regret. Her days as an elite member of the British Army had been mere preparation. Her missions in Afghanistan and Lebanon had been simple homework.

This was *her* play, her means to self-sufficiency. This time with Colby Taylor and his army was fun, but the Germans would offer a bigger pay day—Abel Frey represented real-world power, not Colby Taylor. Mix that with the heady danger of having Milo close by, and she saw nothing but fabulous fireworks on her horizon.

She gazed over the Strip, recognizing the ultimate power in those flashing lights and grand casinos, and took the small distractions Colby Taylor had to offer, all the while thinking about Matt Drake and the woman she'd seen him with.

She entered the guest bedroom of the apartment to find Professor Roland Parnevik tied spreadeagled to the bed, exactly as she'd left him. With a flush in her cheeks she cried *Geronimo!* and jumped onto the mattress, to land beside the old man.

She bounced on her knees and ripped the silver duct tape off his lips. "You ready to spill the beans, Prof?" She laughed like a maniac, and leapt off the bed. The professor's terrified eyes followed her every power-hungry move, firing her ego. She smiled, she twirled, she turned pensive.

But, ultimately, she sat herself on the old man's chest, causing his breathing to labor, and brandished a pair of rose cutters.

"Decision time," she said gaily. "Seriously, mate, I don't really care. I'm just here for the blood and the mayhem."

"What...what do you want to...know?" Parnevik's accent was thick with fear.

"Tell me about Matt Drake, and the woman who works with him."

"Drake? I...I don't understand...do you not want—Odin?"

"I don't care about all that Norse crap. I'm in this for the excitement." She clacked the rose cutters.

"Umm...Drake became involved by...accident."

Alicia felt ice envelop her. She shuffled carefully up Parnevik's body and displayed the blades.

"One last chance. I sense you stalling, old man."

"No! No! Please!" Now his accent was so thick and distorted she could barely understand the words. She frowned. "You sound like that chef from the TV. Blah, blah, bla-bla-bla."

"His wife—she died!" Parnevik blurted, and rolled his eyes in terror. "His friend has a sister that helps us! The woman—she is Kennedy Moore, police, from New York. She set free a serial killer!"

Alicia eased up on the blades. "Better. Much better, Prof. What else?"

"She...she is on...*forced* holiday. You see, this serial killer—he killed again."

"And?"

"Please. I can tell Drake is a good man!"

Alicia withdrew the rose cutters. "Well, he certainly comes across that way. But *I* got bloody every day with him in the SRT, not you. I know what haunts Matt Drake, and I know the answer he needs."

There was a shout and a bang, and then Colby Taylor thrust his head through the door. "Myles! I just got a call from our ally in the Swedish government. They've figured out where the Valkyries are. We need to hurry. *Now!*"

Alicia flipped the old man without effort and straddled his back. Whilst he whimpered she stuck him with a jet-injector, a needle-free syringe, delivering a miniscule tracker just under his skin.

Plan B, Alicia thought, her soldier training still running strong.

TWENTY-SIX

WASHINGTON DC

When Torsten Dahl's cellphone rang, Drake's mouth was full of crispy bacon. He gulped it down with fresh coffee, listening expectantly to hear who was on the other end of the line.

"Yes, Statsministern." Dahl's side of the conversation was a bland series of "I sees", affirmations and respectful silences. At the end there was an "I will not let you down, sir."

"Well?"

"My government has promised one of these Serbian scumbags an incredible reduction of their sentence in exchange for their help, but we do have confirmation." Drake could tell that under Dahl's conservative exterior there was a man wanting to rejoice.

"And?"

"Not yet. Let's get everyone together." In a few moments Ben had been dragged away from the laptop screen, Hayden was perched close by, and Kennedy was standing expectantly beside Drake, long hair still unfettered.

Dahl took a breath. "Short version: the leader of Sweden's Serbian Mafia in the nineties—a man currently in our custody—*gave* the Valkyries to his US counterpart as a gesture of goodwill. So, a man called Davor Davic received the Valkyries in 1994. In 1999 Davor stepped down as leader of the Mafia, passing control over to his son, Blanka, and retired to the place he loved more than anywhere in the world—even his homeland."

Dahl paused for a moment. "*Hawaii.*"

TWENTY-SEVEN

NEW YORK, USA

Abel Frey stared down from his penthouse apartment window at the millions of tiny ants scurrying along the pavements below. Unlike ants, though, these people were pointless, aimless, lacking the imagination to see beyond their miniscule lives. The term "headless chickens", he imagined, had been coined by a man standing at this very height, whilst he surveyed the disenchanted cesspool of humanity.

Frey had always indulged his fantasies. He had learned a long time ago that being able to do anything made everything *boring*. You had to come up with new, more diverse and entertaining pursuits.

Hence the battle arena. Hence the fashion business—a front for an international smuggling ring, now a way to conceal his interest in the Tomb of the Gods.

His life's work. But still one of the greatest mysteries of all time.

Whenever he felt close to finding the truth, he always discovered the mystery was much larger than he had previously imagined. Not possible, surely. The Tomb of the Gods wouldn't hold the answer to everything he'd ever imagined, would it?

The shield was flawless, a work of art and, in addition to the coded map carved into its surface, there was the cryptic sentence inscribed around its upper rim. His pet archaeologist was hard at work on it. And his pet scientist was trying to figure out another surprise—the shield was imbued with a curious material; undoubtedly a metal, but more substantial and yet startlingly light. Scientists had likened it to the mysterious Starlite material invented and then subsequently lost in the '70s. But why would a shield be made to withstand such great temperatures unless it was truly a weapon of the gods? Frey was both happy and frustrated to find there was even more to the mystery of Odin and the tomb than he had ever imagined.

He was not a man who liked to be rushed. He wanted to linger, to study the shield as it deserved. But the world marched on, and now there was an international race. How he longed to retire back to La Verein, and, whilst the improper socialites partied, he and a few select others would analyze the mysteries of the gods.

He grinned at the empty room. Maybe, once home, he would set a couple of male models against each other in the arena, offer them a way out. Better still, pit a few of his *captives* against each other. Their ignorance and desperation always offered up a better spectacle than spoiled slaves.

His e-mail pinged. A video feed appeared onscreen, showing the new prisoner, Karin Blake, sitting on her bed.

"At last." Frey got his first look at her. The Blake woman was quite dangerous, apparently. She had marked every one of the three mercenaries he'd sent to abduct her, one rather viciously. She was intelligent, maybe even a genius, and she'd just been locked up back at La Verein to await Frey's arrival.

From the blood of innocents—his eternal bliss. She sported short-cropped blond hair, a fringe, and a pair of wide eyes—though Frey couldn't be sure of the color at this pixel quality.

At that moment the door burst open and the brute Milo came through, cellphone brandished in one hand. "It's her," he cried. "Alicia!" There was a goofy grin on his idiotic face.

Frey kept his emotions hidden. "Ja? Hallo? Yes, tell me. That last piece in New York, it should have been *mine*." He didn't trust the English woman one bit for changing the plan.

He listened to her, smiling when she revealed the next location, frowning when he heard that the Swedes and their companions were already en route, and then he couldn't help but beam when she promised that soon she would deliver both of the Canadian's pieces to his eager hands.

Then he would have three pieces, and the upper hand.

Odin's tomb would be almost within reach.

"Hawaii?" Milo asked as he ended the call.

"Hawaii."

TWENTY-EIGHT

OAHU, HAWAII

On September 12th the midday sun over Hawaii was obscured by a dark rain of "jellyfish" parachutes—the signature chute of the American military. In a unique operation, Delta commandos landed, alongside Swedish SGG and British SAS—and one New York cop—on a remote beach at the north side of the island.

Drake hit the beach at a run – the sand cushioning his landing – clicked free of the dragging chute, and turned quickly to check Kennedy's progress. She landed amidst a couple of Delta boys, falling to one knee as she hit the ground, but soon regaining her feet.

Ben would stay with the aircraft, continuing his research with the help of Hayden, the young assistant to the Secretary of Defense, whom they had met at the library, and had been assigned as a US "advisor" to the mission.

In Drake's experience, advisors were usually better trained versions of their bosses—spies in sheep's clothing, so to speak, but with Hayden and her easy cooperation he was considering her a welcome exception.

They ran across the beach under the hot Hawaiian sun, thirty highly trained Special Forces soldiers, before hitting a gentle slope with the timely advantage of a tree-lined canopy.

Here Torsten Dahl stopped them. "You know the drill. Quiet and hard. Vault room's the target. Go!"

The decision had been made to hit the ex-Serbian Mafia leader's mansion with maximum force. Time was horribly against them—their rivals might already know the location of the

Valkyries, and establishing the upper hand in this race now was vital.

And during his term of leadership, Davor Davic had not been a forgiving man. There would be no mercy shown to the ex-mafia boss.

They topped the slope and ran across a road, straight up to Davic's private gate. Not even the breeze stirred against them. A charge was set, and in under a minute the high wrought-iron gates were tumbling pieces of metal. They charged through the opening and spread out through the grounds. Drake sheltered behind a thick palm tree, studying a sweeping lawn that led to some gleaming marble steps. At their summit was the entrance to Davic's mansion. To either side stood a bizarre array of statues and Hawaiian cultural treasures, even a moai figure from Easter Island.

No activity yet.

The Serbian Mafia retiree was fatally complacent.

An SAS man he recognized, his face half-hidden by a black balaclava, slid in beside Drake.

"Greetings, old pal. Nice day for it, eh? Love that direct sunlight on the lenses. Wells sends his regards."

"Sam? Bloody good to see you, mate." Drake hadn't seen his old friend in seven years, and Sam had been the best pal he'd had in the Ninth Division. The history and comradeship between them ran deeper than any ocean—it was the bond of men who fought alongside each other, men who looked death in the eye together, the bond only soldiers made. "Where's Wells, the old fool?" Drake stored away the fondness for later and didn't take his eyes off the garden.

"Says he'll get in touch soon. Something about you owing him some Mai-time."

"He just never lets up. I don't even know where Mai is these days."

"What's Mai-time?" Kennedy asked. She had scraped her hair back again, and wore a shapeless army uniform over her trouser suit. She carried a pair of Glocks.

Drake, as usual, carried no weapons, save for his Special Forces knife.

Sam said, "Mai Kitano is an old flame of Drake's. More importantly, who're you?"

"We need to focus. We're about to launch one of the biggest civilian assaults in history."

"Civilian?" Kennedy frowned. "If this Davic guy's a civilian then *I'm* Claudia Schiffer's ass."

The Delta team paused at the steps. Drake broke cover the moment they started climbing and raced across the open ground. When he was halfway, the shouting began.

Figures appeared at the top of the steps, variously dressed in suits and boxer-shorts and cut-off T-shirts.

Six brief shots rang out. Six bodies dropped lifelessly down the steps. The Delta team was halfway up, unmarked. Urgent shouting came from ahead. Drake reached the bottom of the steps and crabbed to the right where the curving stone banister afforded a bit more cover.

A shot rang out, loud, meaning it came from the Serbs. Drake turned to check on Kennedy once more, then double-stepped to the top.

Beyond, a short expanse of gravel led to the mansion's entrance, which lay between the two halves of an H-shaped building. Armed men were filing out of the open doors, and from the flapping French windows to either side of the entrance.

Dozens of them.

Caught napping—but quick to regroup. Maybe not so complacent after all. Drake saw what was coming and took cover among the statues. He ended up pulling Kennedy behind the Easter Island figure.

A second later, machine gunfire erupted. The guards fired curtains of lead in every direction. Drake dropped to his belly as several bullets hit the statue with dull thuds.

The guards came running forward. This was hired muscle, chosen more for their brawny stupidity than intellectual prowess. They ran straight into the Delta boys' carefully prepped lines of fire, and fell writhing amidst hails of blood.

Glass shattered behind them.

More shots were fired from the mansion's windows. A luckless Delta soldier caught a bullet in the head and fell, instantly dead.

Two of the guards had blundered amongst the statues, one of them slightly wounded. Drake unsheathed his blade in silence and waited for either of them to step around the statue.

The last thing the wounded Serb saw was his own spraying blood as Drake ended his life. Kennedy fired at the second Serb, missed, then dived for cover as he raised a weapon.

The hammer clicked on empty.

Kennedy rose. The guard swung a haymaker, muscles flexing.

Kennedy stepped out of range, then leapt forward as his momentum left him exposed. A swift kick to the groin and an elbow to the back of the neck sent him crashing to the ground. He rolled, a blade suddenly in his hand, slashing in a wide arc. Kennedy jerked back just enough to let the deadly tip pass her cheek before jabbing her stiffened fingers into his windpipe. She broke the soft cartilage in his throat. The man started to gasp and collapsed.

She turned away. He was done for. She had no wish to watch him die.

Drake stood watching. "Not bad."

"Maybe you'll stop mollycoddling me now."

"I wouldn't—" He stopped short. *Had he?* Either way, it wouldn't happen again. He covered his shame with manly bluster. "Nothing like watching a woman beating up a bad guy."

"Never mind." Kennedy crept behind a totem pole, another of the mansion's incongruous features, and surveyed the scene.

"We're splitting up," she told him. "You're going to find the vault room. I'm going around back."

He made a reasonable job of hiding his hesitation. "You sure?"

"Hey, bucko, I'm the cop here, remember? You're the civilian. Do as you're told."

Drake watched Kennedy creep off to the right, heading for the rear of the mansion where satellite surveillance had shown a helipad and several low-slung buildings. The SAS team had been deployed there already, and would be infiltrating it at this very moment.

He found his eyes lingering on her form, but then shock jarred him. Humility and uncertainty clashed in his head, creating a maelstrom of self-doubt. So many years since Alyson left. Thousands of days of instability, constant inebriation, bankruptcy, and then the slow rise back to normality.

Nowhere near there yet.

Plan B—the job at hand. He should try to embrace the returning military focus and leave the civilian stuff behind. He relieved both guards of their weapons and sneaked through the statues until he found the edge of the gravel driveway. He noted three targets at three different windows, and fired off three bursts in quick succession.

Two screams and a yell. Not bad. When the surviving man popped his head back out, searching for the assailant, Drake made him pay heavily.

Then he ran and skidded on his knees, coming to a halt up against the mansion's exterior, his head against the rough stonework. He glanced back at the Delta team as it rushed to catch up with him. He nodded at their leader.

"Straight through." Drake nodded at the door, then to the right. "Vault room."

They filed inside, Drake now last, hugging the curve of the wall. A wide, wrought-iron staircase spiraled up to the mansion's second level.

As they crept along the wall, more Serbs emerged along the upstairs balcony, directly above them. In an instant, the Delta team had made themselves sitting ducks.

With nowhere else to go, Drake fell to his knees and opened fire.

Kennedy sprinted to the high tree-line that masked the mansion's exterior wall. In no time she reached the back of the house, whereupon a faceless SAS soldier fell on his belly before her.

Like a rabbit she stood still, mesmerized by the barrel of the rifle. For the first time in months all thoughts of Thomas Kaleb deserted her.

"Shit!"

"It's okay," a voice said next to her ear. She sensed the cold blade only millimeters away. "It's Drake's bird."

The comment swept away her fear. "I am *not* Drake's bird. Whatever that means."

The man moved in front of her, smiling. "Well then, to use a time-honored Americanism, Miss Moore—*whatever*. I would prefer to properly introduce myself, but this is not the time or place. You can call me Wells."

Kennedy recognized the name, but said no more as a team of British soldiers materialized around her and began to move. The way they suddenly appeared without warning gave her the creeps. How the hell did they do that? The rear of Davic's property was comprised of an immense patio lined with Indian stone, an Olympic-size swimming pool surrounded by loungers and white pavilions, and several squat, ugly buildings out of keeping with the rest of the decor. Situated next to the largest building was a round helipad, complete with chopper.

After years of walking the New York beat, Kennedy had to question whether crime did, in fact, pay. It paid for these guys, and Kaleb. It would have paid for Chuck Walker if Kennedy hadn't seen him pocketing that wad.

The job's worth it, she thought. The people she saved, the lives she changed for the better, the children that grew up to be all that they could be...*that* alone was worth the heartache and grief.

The loungers had been occupied. Several men and women clad in swimwear now stood around in shock, clutching clothes and trying to cover excess flesh.

"Those people...let's call them *guests*...are probably not a part of the Serbian group," Wells said softly into a throat mic. "Move them away." He nodded to the three lead men. "The rest of you head for the seaward side of those buildings."

As the group split, several things happened at once. The chopper's blades started rotating; the sounds of its engines immediately overpowered the shouts of people nearby. Then a deep rumbling, like the sound of a roller-shutter door, preceded the sudden scream of a powerful automobile. From around the far side of a low building came a white streak of metal, an Audi R8 accelerating at top speed.

By the time it reached the patio area it was a lethal bullet—one that weighed a ton. It ploughed past the stunned SAS men, sending them sprawling through the air. Behind it came another car, this one black and larger.

The chopper's blades began to rotate faster, its engines screaming. The whole machine shook as it prepared to take off.

Kennedy, dazed, could only listen as Wells barked orders. She winced as the remaining SAS soldiers opened fire.

Pandemonium reigned in the garden.

Soldiers fired on the speeding Audi. Bullets struck through its metal casing, penetrating the wing and door skins. The car raced for the corner of the house, slewing at the last minute to make the tight turn.

Gravel shot from under its tires like tiny missiles.

A bullet smashed the windshield, obliterating it. The car literally died in mid-flight, its engine quieting as the driver slumped behind the wheel.

Kennedy ran forward, gun up. *"Don't move!"*

Before she reached the car it was obvious that the driver was its lone occupant. He wasn't anyone important.

A decoy.

The helicopter was two feet off the ground, spinning slowly. An SAS soldier shouted, but without any real venom in his voice. The second car, a black four-door Cadillac, was now barreling through the shallows of the huge pool, its tires spewing tidal waves of water in all directions. The windows were blacked out. No way to tell who was inside.

A third motor started up, this one currently out of sight.

Soldiers fired on the Caddy, taking out its tires and the driver. The car skidded, its rear end crashing into the pool. Wells and three other soldiers ran toward it, shouting. Kennedy kept an eye on the chopper, but, like the Caddy, its windows were opaque.

This was all part of some elaborate escape plan, Kennedy guessed. But where was the real Davor Davic?

The chopper started to rise. The SAS finally got tired of warnings, and shot out the rear rotary propeller. The monstrous machine started to spin. A soldier carefully aimed his grenade launcher.

Wells reached the Caddy and fired. Kennedy heard on the mic that Davic was still at large. Now the third car shot around the corner, engine screaming like an expensive supercar, but this thing was a Bentley, big and brash, its entire presence screaming *get the hell outta my way!*

Kennedy leapt into the trees. Several soldiers followed her. Wells spun and fired three quick shots that bounced right off the side windows.

Bulletproof glass!

"That's the wanker!" Wells cried. "That's Davic in the car."

The words were uttered a split second too late to save the chopper—the grenade had been fired—its explosive charge detonating against the chopper's underbelly. The chopper burst apart, sending shards of metal blasting everywhere. The mangled chunk of wrecked steel crashed straight down into the pool, displacing thousands of gallons of water with immense force.

Kennedy waited until the monster Bentley shot past her, then took off in pursuit. Swift deduction told her there was but a single chance to catch the fleeing Serb.

Wells saw it at the same time, and leapt into action. The R8 was totaled, but the Caddy was still serviceable, its wheels only an inch underwater on the pool's marble steps.

Wells and two of his soldiers ran for the Caddy. Kennedy increased her hot pursuit, determined to get a seat. At that moment there was an uncanny fizz of air as if a whirlwind had blown by and suddenly the corner of Davic's house exploded.

"*Crap!*" Wells hit the dirt. Rubble burst in all directions, raining down into the pool and onto the patio. Kennedy staggered. She turned her head toward the cliffs.

A newly arrived black helicopter hovered there, a figure waving through its open door.

"Did you like that?"

Wells raised his head. "Alicia Myles? What the hell are you doing?"

"*Could've taken your head off with that shot, you old dickhead. You owe me.*" Alicia laughed as the chopper rose for a moment before swinging around in pursuit of the Bentley.

The cultists – the *Forn Sidr* - were here.

*

Drake rolled forward an instant before the wall behind him turned into Swiss cheese. At least one bullet passed so close he recognized its sonic whine. He gained the ground underneath the balcony at the same time as most of the Delta team. Once there, he aimed upwards and opened fire.

As expected, the balcony floor was relatively weak. The firing stopped up there as bullets found targets and the screams began.

The Delta commander signaled to move out toward the vault. They ran quickly through two grandly furnished rooms, and then the commander motioned a halt. Satellite surveillance had forewarned them about a hidden, underground room.

Flashbangs were thrown inside. The American soldiers followed, shouting to enhance the disorientation effect. Immediately, though, there were half a dozen Serb guards grappling at close quarters with them. Drake took a breath and stepped inside. Chaos and confusion filled the room from end to end. He found himself confronted by a huge guard who grinned and belched, and then lunged forward for a bear hug.

Drake sidestepped hurriedly, delivered a blow to the kidneys and a stiff dagger-hand to the solar plexus. The man-beast didn't even flinch.

Drake backed off, warily circling his unmoving enemy. The Serb was huge: lazy fat over solid muscle, with a forehead big enough to break six-inch-thick concrete blocks. The man lumbered forward, arms wide. One slip up and Drake would be crushed to death, squeezed and popped like a grape. He quickstepped away, feinted right, and came forward with three instant jabs.

Eye. Ear. Throat.

All three jabs connected with their targets. The Serb squeezed his eyes shut in pain. Drake executed a risky dummy roll into a flying kick that generated enough momentum to knock even this brontosaurus off its wide feet.

The man crashed to the ground with a sound like a mountain collapsing. Pictures fell off the wall. His head slammed against the floor, knocking him unconscious.

Drake ventured further into the room. Two Delta guys were down, but all the Serbs had been neutralized. A wide door in the eastern wall had swung open and most of the Americans had been standing around the opening, but were now backing slowly away, cursing in fear.

Drake hurried to join them, unable to imagine what could make a Delta soldier panic. The first thing he saw was a set of stone steps descending into a well-lit underground chamber.

The second was the black panther stalking slowly up the steps, its wide snarl revealing a razor-sharp set of fangs.

"*Fuuuuuuck...*" one of the Americans drawled. Drake couldn't have agreed more.

The panther hissed as it crouched to strike. Drake backed off as the beast leapt through the air, a hundred pounds of lethal muscle in a rage. It landed on the top step and scrabbled for purchase, all the time pinning its hypnotic green eyes on the retreating soldiers.

"Hate to do this," the Delta commander said, as he sighted down his rifle.

"Wait!" Drake saw something glinting under the lights. "Just wait. Don't move."

The panther prowled forward. The Delta team kept it in their sights as it passed between them and sniffed disdainfully at the incapacitated Serb guards on its way out of the room.

"What the—?" one of the Americans frowned at Drake.

"Didn't you see? It was wearing a diamond-studded necklace. Cat like that, living in a house such as this, I'm *guessing*, is trained to attack only when it hears its master's voice."

"Nice call. I would've hated to kill an animal like that." The Delta commander waved at the Serbs. "These assholes, though, I'd waste all day just for fun."

"All the same," Drake added, "keep an eye on it."

They descended the steps, leaving two men on guard. Drake was third to reach the vault floor and what he saw made him shake his head in amazement.

"How twisted are these people?"

The room was jam-packed with what could only be described as personal trophies. Items Davor Davic considered valuable because—in his perversions—they were valuable to *other people*. Cabinets stood everywhere, large and small, haphazardly arrayed.

A jawbone from a T-Rex. An inscription beside it read: *From the collection of Edgar Fillion—Life reward*. Next to that, and resting in a grisly manner atop a bronze pedestal—a mummified hand, identified as *District Attorney No. 3*.

And many more. As Drake skirted the display cases, trying to reel in his morbid fascination and focus, he finally spotted the fantastic items they were looking for.

The Valkyries: a pair of pure-white statues mounted on a thick circular block. Both sculptures were about five feet in height but it was the striking detail in them that took Drake's breath away. Two buxom women, nude and, like the mighty Amazons of old, both with legs apart as if sitting astride something. Probably a winged horse, Drake mused. Ben would know more, but he recalled that the Valkyries used them to fly from battle to battle. He took in the muscled limbs, the classically boned features and the bewildering horned helmets.

"Sheeyit!" a Delta guy exclaimed. "Wish I had me a set of six-packs like that."

More revealingly, both Valkyries were pointing upwards at some unknown wonder with their left hands. Pointing, Drake thought now, straight at the entrance to the Tomb of the Gods.

Somewhere near Ragnarok.

At that moment one of the soldiers tried to remove an item from its display case. A loud buzzer sounded and a set of steel gates came crashing down at the base of the steps, blocking their exit.

The Americans reached immediately for gas masks. Drake shook his head. "Don't worry. Something tells me Davic is the kind of scum that would prefer his thieves caught live and kicking."

The Delta commander eyed the still-vibrating bars. "Blast those sticks apart."

Kennedy stared after the chopper and the fleeing Bentley in amazement. Wells, it seemed, was also at a loss as he gaped at the sky.

"Bitch," Kennedy heard him breathe. "I bloody well trained her. How *dare* she turn into a traitor?"

"It's a good thing she's gone then." Kennedy made sure her hair was still tied back after all the diving around, and looked away when she noticed a couple of the soldiers assessing her. "She had the higher ground. Now, if Drake and the Delta team have secured the Valkyries, we might be able to slip away while Alicia's occupied with Davic."

Wells looked like he was torn between two meaningful choices, but said nothing as they raced around the house. They saw Alicia's chopper spin around to confront the Bentley head on. Shots were fired that bounced off the fleeing car. Then the car suddenly braked hard and stopped in a cloud of gravel.

An object was thrust out of a window.

The chopper plummeted out of the sky, its operator possessed of almost supernatural instinct, as the RPG fired and whistled overhead. As its skids touched the ground, Canadian cultists spewed out of the doors. A firefight erupted.

Kennedy thought she saw Alicia Myles, a lithe figure clad in body armor, jump into the fray like the proverbial lion. A beast made for the fight, lost in the violence and fury of it all. Despite herself, Kennedy felt her blood running cold.

Was that *fear* she was feeling?

A thin figure collapsed out of the opposite side of the chopper. A figure she recognized in an instant.

Professor Parnevik!

He limped along, at first faltering but then showing renewed determination and finally crawling, as bullets laced the air above his head, one of them passing within a hand's width of his skull.

Parnevik at last inched close enough for the SAS and Kennedy to pull him to safety. The cultists, fully engaged in battle, didn't appear to notice.

"Right," said Wells, motioning to the house. "Let's get this done."

Drake helped haul the Valkyries out of the trophy room, as a couple of guys fixed a small amount of explosives to the bars. They threaded a narrow path through the appalling exhibits, trying not to look too closely. One of the Delta guys had come back from a morbid inspection a few minutes before to report a black coffin sitting at the rear of the room, its lid nailed shut.

The air of expectation had lasted an entire ten seconds. It took a soldier's logic to shut it down. The less one knows...

Not Drake's logic anymore. But even then, he seriously didn't want to know why an ex-Mafia boss would keep a black coffin in a personal display room. He was actually gratified when he flinched like a regular civilian as the bars were blown apart.

They moved toward the exit.

Gunfire erupted from above. The two Delta guards clattered down the steps, dead, full of ragged holes. In another second, a dozen men armed with sub-machine guns appeared at the top of the steps.

Outflanked and outgunned, covered from a higher vantage point, the rest of the Delta team had had the tables turned on them, and were now vulnerable. Drake inched toward a cabinet and its relative safety, trying not to think about the stupidity of getting caught like this, that it *wouldn't* have happened to the SAS, and trusting to luck that these new enemies wouldn't be foolish enough to shoot at the Valkyries.

There were a few moments of unrelieved tension suffered in a stifling silence until a figure came down the steps—a figure dressed in white and wearing a full-face mask.

Drake recognized him instantly. The same man who had received the shield on the catwalk in York. The man he'd then seen in Uppsala.

"I *know* you," he breathed to himself, then louder. "The bloody *Germans* are here."

The man raised a .45 and waved it around. "All of you, fools, drop your weapons."

An arrogant voice. A voice that belonged to smooth hands, its owner possessed of real-world power, the kind that's written on paper and granted in members-only clubs. The kind of man who had no clue about true toil and drudgery.

The Delta men held their weapons steady in menacing silence.

Again the man shouted, his breeding keeping him ignorant of the danger.

"Are you deaf? I said *now!*"

A Texan voice drawled, "Not happening, asshole."

"But...but..." the man stammered in astonishment, then abruptly ripped his mask off. "You *will!*"

Drake felt a rush of surprise as he recognized Abel Frey, the German designer. A poisoned tide of shock swept through Drake. It wasn't rational. It was like seeing Taylor Swift or Miley Cyrus up there, cackling about taking over the world.

Frey locked eyes with Drake. "And you, Matt Drake!" His gun arm trembled. "You cost me almost *everything!* I'll take that cop from you. *I will!* And she'll pay. Oh, how she'll pay!"

Before he could assimilate that, Frey aimed the gun between Drake's eyes and fired.

Kennedy raced into the room to see the SAS soldiers fall to their knees, motioning for silence. She saw before her a group of masked men, clad in body armor, angling their weapons toward what she could only think was Davor Davic's secret vault.

Luckily, the men were too busy to notice them.

Wells looked back at her and mouthed, "Who?"

Kennedy made a confused face. She could hear someone ranting, she could see his side profile, the .45 he held, waving inexpertly. When she heard him scream the name *Matt Drake*, she knew, and Wells knew, and a few seconds later the soldiers opened fire.

During the sixty seconds of gunfire that followed, Kennedy watched in helpless slow motion. The man in white fired his pistol. Her own shot arrived a split-second later, tugging the side of his coat as it passed through the hanging material. His face fell into shock as he turned, exaggerating its puffy slackness.

A pampered man.

Then the masked men fired. SAS soldiers squeezed off well-placed shots with precision and composure. More fire came from inside the vault. She heard American voices. German voices. English voices.

It was sluggish chaos. She hit two Germans—others fell. The guy in white screamed and waved his arms, and made his crew beat a hasty retreat. Kennedy saw them covering him and dying in the process, falling like decay from a wound, but the wound lingered on. In the end he escaped into a back room, his entourage decimated, barely escaping with their lives.

Kennedy raced down the corridor, a strange lump in her throat, an ice pick in her heart, not realizing how worried she was until she saw Drake alive and felt a cooling flood of elation.

Drake picked himself up off the floor, thankful that Abel Frey's aim had been every bit as shaky as his grasp on reality. The first thing he saw was Kennedy rushing down the steps; the second was her face as she rushed up to him.

"I'm so glad you're alright!" she cried, and gave him a hug before remembering her reserve.

Drake stared into Wells' knowing eyes before closing his own. He held her for a moment, feeling her slim body, her powerful frame, her fragile heart beating against his own. Her head was nestled against his neck, the sensation wonderful enough to send tingles across his synapses.

"Ay-up, I'm good. You?"

She pulled away, smiling.

Wells came up to them. "Drake. Strange place to meet up again, old mate. There are a few things you need to know. Things about Mai."

Drake was momentarily thrown. Wells had said the very last thing he had expected. After a second he noticed Kennedy's fading smile, and took control. "The Valkyries." He pointed. "C'mon, while we have the chance. Are we chasing the Germans?"

"It's utter chaos out there, man. We'll take what we can get out of this."

"Understood."

The Delta commander was already organizing and beckoned them over. "This isn't Sleepytown, England, guys. Let's haul ass. I've had about all the Hawaii I can handle on this vacation."

TWENTY-NINE

HAWAII

Drake, Kennedy, and the rest of the assault team rendezvoused with Ben and Hayden several hours later at a military base near Honolulu.

Time passed. Red tape was cut, mostly by Hayden. Bumpy roads were smoothed over. Governments bickered, then sulked, then finally started discussions. Jumped up bureaucrats were appeased with the political equivalent of milk and honey.

And the time of reckoning drew inexorably nearer.

The real players talked and worried and reasoned, and slept in a badly air-conditioned series of buildings near Pearl Harbor. When Drake returned, Ben's pensive greeting meant they'd made little progress on the hunt for the next piece of Odin—the eyes. Drake concealed his surprise; he had truly believed that Ben's expertise and motivation would have cracked the clues by now.

Hayden, the Secretary of Defense's sharp-witted assistant, had been helping him, but so far they had nothing.

Their single hope was that the other contestants—the Canadian *Forn Sidr* and the Germans—were faring little better.

Ben's attention had initially been broken by Drake's revelation.

"*Abel Frey?* The German designer is a criminal mastermind? Bog off, dickhead."

"Seriously, mate. Would I lie?"

"Don't part-quote DinoRock and especially Whitesnake at me, Matt. You know our band has a problem playing their music, and it's not funny. I just can't believe...Abel Frey?"

Drake sighed. "Here we go again. Yes. Abel Frey."

Kennedy backed him up. "Sounds like bullshit, but it's true. The guy's a recluse. Has a place in the German Alps called the Party Chateau. Supermodels. Money. A superstar life."

"In a way," Ben mused, "it's the perfect cover."

"Easy to fool outsiders when you're famous," Drake agreed. "You can choose your own destination. Smuggling must be relatively easy for these people."

Torsten Dahl came over at that moment. "This Abel Frey thing...it's been decided to keep it low-key for now. We watch and we wait, put surveillance around his chateau, but give him free rein, in case he ends up knowing something we don't."

"On the surface that's sound," Drake began, "but—"

"But he has my sister," Ben hissed. Hayden held up a hand to calm him. "Dahl is right, Ben. Karin's safe...for now."

Drake narrowed his eyes, but held his tongue. To protest would achieve nothing except to distract his friend even more. Again, he had trouble fathoming Hayden out. Was she thinking about Ben with best intentions, or was she thinking about her government's best interests?

Either way, the answer was the same. Wait.

Drake changed the subject. He probed another one close to Ben's heart. "How are your mum and dad?" he asked carefully. "They cottoned on yet?"

Ben gave an anguished sigh. "No, mate. Last call, they mentioned her, but I said she'd snagged a second job. It'll help, Matt, but not for long."

"I know." Drake eyed Wells and Hayden. "As leaders here, you two should help." Then, without waiting for a reply, he said, "So, what news on Heidi and Odin's Eyes?"

Ben shook his head in disgust. "Plenty," he complained. "There're snippets everywhere. Here—listen to this, to drink from Mimir's Well—the Well of Wisdom in Valhalla—everyone must offer up a critical sacrifice. Odin sacrificed his *eyes*, symbolizing his willingness to gain knowledge of events both current and future. Something like time travel. He may have been able to jump through time. Maybe all the gods could. Upon drinking, Odin foresaw all the trials that would affect men and gods throughout eternity. He saw the future. Maybe he visited it?

Maybe that has something to do with why all the gods died. Anyway, it says here that Mimir accepted Odin's eyes, and they lie there still, a symbol of what even a god must pay for a glimpse of ultimate wisdom."

"Okay," Drake shrugged. "Standard historical stuff, yeah?"

"True. But it's *all* like that. The *Poetic Edda,* the *Saga of Flenrich,* another I have translated as *The Many Traveled Paths of Heidi.* They explain what happened, but they don't tell us where the eyes are now, only that they have a link to Valhalla. The eyes are purported to be there but we also know Odin gave all his companions to Heidi."

"They're *in* Valhalla." Kennedy made a face.

"That's the Norse word for Heaven."

"Not a chance *I'll* ever find 'em, then."

"Whose Heaven?" Dahl ventured. "There are many. Supposedly."

Drake considered it all. "And there's nothing else? C'mon, mate, this is the last piece and all we have is a reference to Valhalla!"

"I've followed Heidi's path—her travels. She visits the places we know of, and then returns to her home. This isn't PlayStation. No side trips, no hidden achievements, no alternate paths, zilch."

Kennedy took a seat beside Ben and shook her hair out. "Could she have deposited two pieces in one location?"

"It's possible, but that theory doesn't play well with what we know so far. The other clues all point to each piece being hidden in a separate place."

"So you're saying *that's* our clue?"

"The clue has to be Valhalla," Drake said quickly. "It's the only phrase that hints to a place. And I remember you said something earlier about Heidi telling Odin she knew where his 'eyes were hidden', because he spilled all his secrets whilst hanging on the cross."

"Tree," Torsten Dahl spoke up. The Swede was looking worn, more battle weary from the administrative side of his job than the physical. "Odin hung on the World Tree."

"Whoops," Drake muttered. "Same story." He looked over at what Ben was drinking. "Is that coffee?"

"Kona," and Dahl looked smug. "The best Hawaii has to offer."

"Thought that was Spam," said Kennedy, demonstrating a piece of condescension.

"Spam is widely loved in Hawaii," Dahl said. "But coffee rules all. And Kona Macadamia Nut is king, at least for me."

"So you're saying that Heidi knew where Valhalla was?" Hayden tried her best to look confused rather than skeptical as Drake signaled someone to bring them more coffee.

"Yes, but Heidi was human. Not a god. So what she would have experienced was a *worldly* Heaven?"

"Sorry, dude," Kennedy joked. "Vegas wasn't founded till 1905."

"To a Norsewoman," Drake added, trying not to smile.

Silence followed. Drake watched Ben mentally clicking through everything he'd scrutinized so far. Kennedy pursed her lips. Hayden accepted a tray of coffee mugs. Wells had long since retired to a corner, feigning sleep. Drake remembered his intriguing words—*I have a few things to tell you. Things about Mai.*

Time for that later, if at all.

Ben laughed as he shook his head. "It's easy. A person's heaven is...their home."

"The place she lived? Her village. Her hut," Drake affirmed.

"Mimir's well lies *inside* Heidi's village!" Kennedy looked around, excitement shining in her eyes, then gave Drake a playful punch. "Not bad for a grunt."

"I've grown some real brain since I quit." Drake watched Wells flinch a bit. "Best move of my life."

Torsten Dahl rose to his feet. "To Sweden then, for the final piece." He looked pleased to be heading back to his homeland. "Umm...where was Heidi's home?"

"Ostergotland," Ben said, without checking. "Also home to Beowulf and Grendel—the place where they still talk of monsters roaming the lands at night."

THIRTY

LA VEREIN, GERMANY

La Verein, the party chateau, was located south of Munich, near the Bavarian border.

Like a fortress, it hunched halfway up a gentle mountain, its walls crenulated and even pocked with tiny arrow loops in various places. Round turrets perched at either side of the arched gate, and a wide sweeping drive allowed expensive motor cars to arrive in style and discard the latest sensations, just as handpicked paparazzi knelt down to snap their photos.

Abel Frey took a turn through the party, glad-handing several of the more important guests and ensuring his models behaved themselves. A frown here, a murmur there, even a rare joke, kept them all performing to his expectations.

Inside the private alcoves he pretended not to notice the thin white trails laid out on knee-high glass tables, the executives bending with straws up their nostrils, and the famous young actors and actresses, many of whom were doing the same. The heady scent of rising lust pervaded the room. Fifty-inch plasmas were tuned to music and fashion channels, and sport. Live music pumped through the chateau.

The fashion designer left without being noticed, and headed up a grand staircase for a quieter sealed-off wing. Another flight and his guards closed a secure door behind him, accessible only through key combination and voice recognition. He entered a room bristling with communications equipment and a bank of HD TV screens.

One of his most trusted geeks said, "Good timing, sir. Alicia Myles is on satphone."

"Excellent. Is she encrypted?"

"Of course, sir."

Frey accepted the proffered device, curling his lip at being forced to put his mouth so close to where his lackey had already sprayed spittle.

"Myles, this better be good. I have a house full of guests to attend to." The lie of convenience didn't register as a fabrication to him. It was simply what these lowlifes needed to hear.

"It's good. Even worth a bonus I'd say," the well-bred English voice said. "I have the Web address and password to Parnevik's locator."

"All part of the deal, Myles. All part of the deal."

"Sadly, I have to be quick. Log on to www dot locate the pro dot co dot uk, and type the lowercase password, *bonusmyles007*." A laugh. "A standard tracker format should appear. Parnevik is programmed in as number four. You should be able to track him anywhere."

Abel Frey saluted in silence. Alicia Myles was the best operative he'd ever used. "Good enough, Myles. When the eyes are secured, you're off the leash. Come back to us then, and bring us the *Forn Sidr's* pieces. Then we'll...talk."

The line disconnected. Frey put the cellphone down, content for now. "Okay." he said. "Get the machine rolling. We'll follow them to the final piece." It was finally within his grasp, as were all the other pieces, if the endgame played out the way it was supposed to. "Milo knows what to do."

He squinted at the tiny the row of TV monitors.

"Which one is captive six—Karin Blake?"

The geek scratched at his beard before waving a hand. Frey leaned forward to study the blond girl sitting on her bed with legs tucked up to her chin.

She belonged to him now.

"Send the video feed to my room immediately. Then tell Chef to send dinner there. Ten minutes after that I want my martial arts expert..." He paused to think.

"Sean Thomas?"

"Yes, that one. I want him to go in there and find out how good she really is."

"And captive number seven, the *special* one?"

"Treat him like a king! The best of everything. His time to impress us is coming..."

THIRTY-ONE

AIRSPACE OVER SWEDEN

The plane lurched. Kennedy Moore started awake, relieved she'd been jolted to consciousness by the turbulence, the new day chasing away her very own haunter of the dark.

Kaleb existed in her dreams exactly as he existed in the real world, but at night he killed her repeatedly whilst studying the torment and horror in her eyes, until the last spark died.

Suddenly awake and snatched from the underbelly of hell, she stared around the cabin with wild eyes. It was quiet; civilians and soldiers were napping or talking quietly. Even Ben Blake had fallen asleep, clutching his laptop, the worry lines not smoothed out by sleep, and tragically out of place on his boyish face.

Then she saw Drake, and he was gazing at her. Now *his* worry lines simply improved an already striking face. His honesty and selflessness shone plainly, impossible to hide, but the hurt concealed behind the composure made her want to comfort him...all night long.

She smiled inwardly. More DinoRock references. Drake's apparent pastime was a great diversion. It was a moment before she realized that her inner smile might have touched her eyes, because he smiled back at her.

And then, for the first time in all the years since she'd started at the Academy, she regretted that her vocation required her to de-sexualize her personality. She wished she knew how to flip her hair in just *that* way. She wished she had a bit more Selma Blair in her and a bit less Sandra Bullock.

Having said all that, it was quite apparent that Drake liked her.

She returned his smile, but at that moment the plane lurched again and everyone came awake. The pilot announced they were an hour out from their destination. Ben shook himself and walked zombie-like to grab some of the remaining Kona coffee. Torsten Dahl stood up and looked around.

"Time to break out the GPR," he said with half a smile.

They were routed to fly over Ostergotland, targeting several areas where both Professor Parnevik and Ben agreed Heidi's village may have stood. The poor professor was clearly still in pain from Alicia Myles's treatment, but gleeful as a puppy when he told them what he'd overheard about a map engraved into Odin's Shield.

Supposedly, the way to Ragnarok.

So far, no one had been able to translate or make sense of the actual map itself. Or was that just more misdirection from Alicia Myles and her fanatical crew?

Once the plane broke through Dahl's rough perimeter, he pointed out an image that appeared on the plane's TV. The Ground Penetrating Radar sent short pulses of radio waves into the earth. When it hit a buried object, boundary or void, it reflected the image back to the screen. Difficult to pick out at first, but simple with experience.

Kennedy shook her head at Dahl. "A GPR? Does the Swedish Army have everything on hand?"

"This device is essential," Dahl told her, seriously. "We have a hybrid version of this machine that detects landmines and hidden pipes. Very high-tech."

The dawn had broken over the horizon and then been chased away by tattered gray clouds, when Parnevik gave a shout. "There! That image could be an old Viking settlement. It has the right characteristics. You see the circular outer rim—that's the protective wall—and the rectangular objects within? They're small dwellings."

"So let's pinpoint the largest house..." Ben began hurriedly.

"No," Parnevik said. "That would be the community longhouse—the meeting place or feasting place. Heidi, if she *was* indeed here, would have the second largest house."

Clearer images were coming through as the plane descended

slowly. The settlement was soon plainly mapped out several feet below ground, and the second largest building became evident.

"You see that?" Dahl pointed to a deeper color, so faint it might have been overlooked if someone wasn't searching for it. "That means there's a *void*, and it's right under Heidi's house." He turned around. "She built her home right over Mimir's Well."

THIRTY-TWO

OSTERGOTLAND, SWEDEN

Once they were on the ground and had trekked across several miles of damp grassland, Dahl called for a halt.

Drake cast around at what he could only describe as a motley crew. The Swedes and SGG were represented by Torsten Dahl and three of his men, the SAS by Wells and ten soldiers. One had been left in Hawaii, wounded. The Delta team was down to six; then there were Ben, Parnevik, Kennedy and himself. Hayden had stayed with the plane.

Not a person among them appeared untroubled. The fact that the plane was waiting, fully fueled and armed and with their pieces on board—the spear and the Valkyries—ready to fly them anywhere in the world, only brought their grave situation into bolder relief.

"If it helps," Dahl said when everyone looked expectantly at him, "I don't see how they can follow us this time. But they'll be getting desperate. Abel Frey only has the shield. The cultists have the horse and the wolves." He pointed ahead. "So get to work. Start by using the light explosives to clear a few feet down, then it's shovel time."

"Be careful." Parnevik was wringing his hands. "We don't want a cave-in."

"Don't worry, Professor," Dahl said with good cheer. "Between the various forces collected here, I think we've mustered an experienced crew."

There was some grumpy laughter. Drake scanned their surroundings. They'd set up a wide perimeter, leaving men atop several hills that ringed the place where the GPR system indicated old guardhouses had once stood. If it was good enough for the Vikings...

The flatlands were calm, the gentle breeze barely ruffling a stand of trees that stood to the east of their position. A slight drizzle began and then gave up before trying again.

Ben's cellphone rang. "Dad? Just busy. I'll ring you back later." He closed the device with a look at Drake. "I'm out of time," he mumbled. "They already know something's up, just not what."

Drake nodded, and watched the first explosion without flinching. Grass sods and dirt plumed into the air. It was immediately followed by another slightly deeper *thump,* and a second cloud rose skyward.

Several men clattered forward, holding shovels the way they held weapons. A surreal scene.

"Be careful," Parnevik twittered. "We wouldn't want anyone to get their feet wet." He cackled, as if it were the greatest joke in history.

A clearer survey picture had shown a narrow void beneath Heidi's house, possibly the well, that led to an extensive cavern. Obviously, something more than a mere well lay down there and the team were erring on the side of caution. It took an hour of careful digging and several pauses whilst Parnevik crowed and studied unearthed artefacts before they struck thin air.

Ben, who hadn't yet had time to research the significance of Odin's eyes, asked the professor about their relevance. Parnevik looked glad to be of use. "On Odin's quest for all wisdom he sought council from one who, at that time, was said to be the wisest of all beings—Mimir. But there was a price to be paid for Mimir's council, a terrible price. So dreadful that Odin almost gave up his quest for the ultimate wisdom—the power to see into the past and the future—and turned back to Asgard. But he went on, met Mimir, and drank from a great horn filled with water from the well, despite Mimir's warnings and assurances that *All who have come to drink here have shunned from paying the price.* But Odin was on a quest, a quest to save the world. He did not shrink away. He drank and the future rolled out in front of him, clear as a stream. He beheld all the trials and troubles that would befall men and gods. But he also saw why the troubles had to fall—that they would make men stronger and more able to cope with what was to come. After that the great god put his hand to his face and plucked out his eyes, enduring a terrible pain. But he made no sound. The Father of all Gods bowed his head and took his leave, now wiser than any being could ever be...and blind."

Drake used the time to organize his thoughts. To date, it felt like he'd been on a rollercoaster ride without brakes. Sleep and rest were things of the past. Recently, he'd grown accustomed to following orders rather than carrying out a proactive course of action. But, over the last few days, he had begun to feel calmer and more focused than at any time since leaving the army. Clarity had returned. He missed York, he missed his new work, but everything seemed simpler when you were fighting a known enemy. He was starting to understand that he missed the Army more than he'd realized.

He knew two things for certain—they'd been on the back foot since the beginning, and they'd been forced by their enemies to *react* to situations, rather than create them; a result of entering the race in second place.

It was now time to start winning. Especially as they seemed to be the only faction dedicated to *saving* the tomb of the gods, rather than ransacking it.

So you believe in ghost stories? An old voice whispered in his brain. Gods. Odin. Ancient tombs.

No, he answered. *But I do believe in old horror stories...*

But the most terrible parts of his past were not stories. During one of his final missions as a member of the secretive SRT, he and three other members of his team—including Alicia Myles— had stumbled across a remote village in Northern Iraq, its male inhabitants tortured and massacred. Assuming the obvious, they'd investigated...only to find standard British and French soldiers, still in the throes of conducting an interrogation.

What followed had blighted the rest of Matt Drake's days in the army. Blind with rage, he and two other team members had reported their findings.

Only to be told to carry on with the mission at hand. To ignore the chaos.

Drake had overheard someone saying, "Shadow Elite."

Alicia Myles – they had been friends, then – had stood and watched, not tarring herself with any brush one way or the other. She couldn't stop the torture and she couldn't assist in the demise of the torturers. But she did follow the orders of her commanding officer.

Matt Drake had been told to move on. *Let's go.*

After that, the soldier's life was over for him. Yes, the interrogations may have been for the greater good, but how could slaughter ever stop more slaughter? And then, just prior to the next and, for him, final mission—a search around a secret society's house in Vienna—Alyson had met her death. Drake hadn't even found the right time to tell her he'd decided to quit the regiment. But leaving the service didn't mean the hideous memories receded in any way.

Still, was a good decision made years ago always going to be the best decision? Times and views changed and so did people.

Now he noticed Kennedy standing across from him, smiling as she had on the plane. Her hair hung free, her face turned lively and mischievous by a grin.

He grinned back. Torsten Dahl shouted, "Take a depth reading! We need a guide for the descenders."

When Ben asked him what a descender was, he just grinned. "Imagine a bungee jump where you don't bounce back. The descender is what stops you breaking your face on the ground."

"Cool."

Drake noticed his old commander inching his way around, and accepted the proffered flask of coffee. This chat had been coming awhile. Drake wanted it over with.

"Any news on Mai?" he asked, holding a cup in front of his lips so that no one saw his question.

"Hmm?"

"Just tell me."

"Hey, man, after the marked lack of information *you* hand out in regards to your *Miss Kitano,* you should hardly expect me to hand out freebies now, should you?"

Drake resisted the smile. "You are an old pain in the arse, you know that?"

"It's what keeps me at the top of my game. Now, tell me a story from one of her undercover missions—any of them."

"Well...I could waste your chance here and give you something tame," Drake said. "Or you could wait until this is all over, and I'll give you the gold...you know the one."

"Tokyo CosCon?"

"Tokyo CosCon. The day Mai Kitano officially became a legend. When she went undercover at Japan's biggest Cosplay convention to infiltrate and detain the Fuchu triads that ran the whole shebang at the time."

Wells looked like he was about to have a seizure. "Oh, hell, Drake. Alright, but you owe me now." He took a breath. "We've heard that the Japanese have just pulled her out of Hong Kong without warning, totally blowing the cover she's been crafting for *two years*."

Drake gave him a look of open-mouthed incredulity. "The Japanese did that to Mai? Why?

"Isn't it obvious?"

Drake thought about it. "No way would a soldier of Mai's status allow that. It would only happen if she arranged it herself. For personal reasons. She's the best they've got. The best they've ever had."

"We've been fielding calls from their justice department for about fifteen hours now, as have the Americans. They're coming clean with *us*—they've sent scouts to La Verein because it's the only connection they've found to this mess. It's only a matter of hours before we're forced to come clean with them. But, *they don't know where Mai is*."

Drake frowned. "A shame. Mai would be a fantastic asset right now."

"Agreed, mate, but governments are governments and, world in peril or not, they love to play their little games, don't they?"

Drake indicated the hole in the ground. "You wanna get dirty? Now's your chance."

Drake's descender was set to 126 feet. A quick-release muzzle was thrust into his hand, and a backpack given to him. He crammed a firefighter's helmet with an integral flashlight onto his head, and rummaged through the pack. A big flashlight, an oxygen tank, weapons, food, water, radio, first-aid—all his spelunking needs. He tugged on a heavy-duty pair of gloves and approached the rim of the hole.

"Geronimo?" he asked Kennedy, who was staying topside with Ben and the professor.

"Or grab your ankles, stick out your ass and hope," she said.

Drake gave her a wicked grin, "Hopefully, we'll get to that later," he said and leapt into darkness.

Immediately, he felt the Blue Diamond Descender working, its little wheel ticking a hundred times a second. As he continued to descend, his velocity lessened. The sides of the well—now dry, thankfully—flashed past in kaleidoscopic glimpses, like an old black-and-white movie. At last the descender slowed to a crawl, and Drake felt his boots gently bounce off hard rock. He squeezed the muzzle, and felt the descender unlatch from its harness. Drake familiarized himself with the process of turning it into an ascender, before moving off to where Dahl and half a dozen men stood waiting.

The floor crunched alarmingly under his boots, but he put it down to mummified debris.

"This cavern is oddly small compared to what we saw on the GPR," Dahl said. "It could have miscalculated. Spread out and look for a tunnel or something. And be careful where you stand. No one has set foot down here in many years."

The Swede shrugged. Drake inched around the cavern, studying the uneven walls and shivering despite the heavy coat he'd been given. Thousands of tons of rock and earth pressed down above him, and here he was, looking to go deeper. Sounded like a soldier's life to him.

Dahl was communicating with Parnevik through a two-way videophone. The professor was shouting out so many "suggestions" that Dahl muted the thing after two minutes. The soldiers shuffled and bumped their way around the cave until one of the Delta guys shouted, "I got a carving here. Tiny-ass thing, though."

Dahl un-muted the videophone. Parnevik's persistent voice came through loud and clear, and then stopped when Dahl held the cellphone to the wall.

"You see that?"

"Ja! *Det ar bra! Bra!*" Parnevik forgot his English in his excitement. "The *Valknut*. The slain warriors' knot. It is Odin's symbol, the triple triangle, or Borromean Triangle, connected with the idea of glorious death in battle."

Drake looked reflective. . "Reminds me of a few good days."

"This symbol is often found on 'picture stones' that depict the death of heroic warriors either travelling by boat or on horseback to Valhalla. This further cements the idea that we have found a worldly Valhalla."

"Sorry to piss on your parade, pal," a blunt SAS staff-sergeant said, "but this wall's about as thick as my mother-in-law. There's nothing behind it."

They all took a step back, sweeping their helmet-lights across the unbroken surface.

"It *has* to be a false wall." Parnevik almost screamed in his excitement. "Has to be!"

"Wait," Drake heard Ben's young voice say. "It says here that the Valknut is also called the Death Knot—a symbol that signified Odin's followers, most of whom had a tendency to die violently. I do believe it could be a *warning*."

"Bollocks." Drake's sigh was heartfelt.

"Here's a thought," Kennedy's voice cut across. "How about searching *all* the walls more closely. If you get more Valknuts, but then find a blank wall—I'd choose that one."

"Easy for you to say," Drake murmured. "Being up there and all."

They split up, combing the rocky walls inch by inch. They scraped at age-old dust and waved at cobwebs and kicked mold away. In the end, they found three more Valknuts.

"Great," Drake said. "That's four walls, four knots. What the hell do we do now?"

"Are they all identical?" the professor asked in surprise. "Don't touch any of them."

One of the soldiers tapped Parnevik's image on the videophone screen. "Well, I don't know about you guys, but I'm sure done listening to *him*." He squatted and pressed his hand against a Valknut.

"Wait," Ben's voice said. "The eyes are in Mimir's Well, not..." his voice was lost beneath a hiss of static and then the screen went blank. Dahl shook it and switched it on and off, but to no avail.

"Does anyone know what was he trying to say?"

The floor cracked and groaned beneath their feet. Drake thought the sound might be getting louder. He shouted at the soldier to take his hand away from the death knot.

Then the videophone burst into life again and Ben's face filled the screen. "Don't know what happened there. But listen—the eyes are in Mimir's Well, not the cavern beneath it. Understand?"

"Yes. So we passed them on the way down?"

"I think so."

"But why?" Dahl asked in disbelief. "Why create this cavern at all then? The GPR showed clearly that a massive space exists *beneath* this one. Surely the piece would be down there."

"Unless—" Drake felt a terrible chill as he remembered the pit of the World Tree and its many pitfalls. "Unless this place is the *trap*."

Dahl now looked unsure. "How so?"

"The Valknuts? That *space* beneath us? What if it's a bottomless pit?"

"That means you're standing on clay hardpan!" Parnevik shouted in terror. "It needs some kind of a catalyst to make it shatter, but I'd advise you to get out of there now!"

They stared at each other for one timeless moment of desperate mortality. They all wanted to live so badly. And then everything changed. The squatting soldier had started a chain reaction. What had at one moment been a fissure in the concrete-hard floor was now the hardpan cracking open. That odd tearing sound wasn't the rock shifting, but the floor fracturing slowly from end to end.

With the endless pit below them...

Six men leapt fiercely for two ascenders. When they gained the stable ground, still alive, Dahl shouted to regain order.

"You two, go first. Be snappy, for all our sakes."

"No, don't rush on your way up," Parnevik commented, "be

especially aware of your surroundings. We don't want to miss the artefact."

"Don't be a fool, Parnevik." Dahl was beside himself with apprehension. Drake hadn't seen him like this before. "The last two will check as they go," he said, staring at Drake. "That's you and me, pal."

Again the videophone squawked and went dead. Dahl shook it, as if he was trying to throttle it.

It took three minutes for the first pair to rise. Then another three for the second. Drake thought about everything that could happen in six minutes—a veritable lifetime of experience or nothing at all. For him it was the latter. Nothing but creaking clay, the groan of shifting rock, the rasp of chance deciding to reward him with life or death.

The hardpan floor near the first symbol crumbled away. There was no warning; it was as if the floor just gave up the ghost and tumbled into oblivion. Drake climbed as far up the well as he could, gripping the rocky sides, rather than trusting the fragile cavern floor. Dahl hugged the opposite side of the well, hanging onto a length of green twine with both hands, the ring on his wedding finger reflecting Drake's helmet light.

Drake kept his gaze upwards, searching for any sturdy lengths of twine they could attach to their harnesses. Then he heard Dahl shout "*Shit!*" and glanced down just in time to see the videophone cartwheel end over end in wicked slow-motion, before hitting the cavern floor with a crunch.

Weakened, the hardpan gave way, dropping into the black pit. A gale whooshed up to meet them, murky air set free, rustling with unspeakable darkness from a place where blind things slithered.

Looking down into that pit of endless shadow, Drake rediscovered his childhood belief in monsters.

There was a faint rustling noise, and a line fell from above. Drake grabbed it gratefully and attached it to his harness. Dahl did the same, looking equally white, and they both clicked their respective buttons.

Drake watched the altimeter click by. He studied his half of the well, whilst Dahl did the same on the other side. Several times they stopped and swayed forward to make a closer inspection, but each time they found nothing. One hundred feet passed, and then ninety. Drake stopped often, scraping his hands bloody, but found nothing. On they went, now passing fifty feet. Then, on one of Drake's closer inspections, he realized there was a wide plank of wood embedded in the wall, jagged around its edges, untouched by damp or mold, yet Drake could see carvings on its surface. It took him a while to angle his helmet properly, but when he did...

Eyes. The symbolic representation of Odin's eyes, carved into wood and left here...by whom?

By Odin himself? Millennia ago? By Heidi? Was that more, or less, believable? Either way, it was an incredibly important piece.

Dahl cast an anxious glance below. "That's a woodcut, Drake. Two of the nine pieces of Odin, so for all our sakes, grab it and don't drop it."

THIRTY-THREE

OSTERGOTLAND, SWEDEN

Drake emerged from Mimir's Well holding the woodcut aloft like a trophy. He knew that the find was a major step forward in their own quest. But before he could utter a word, he was plucked roughly out of his harness and thrown to the ground.

"Hey, steady on—" He looked up into the barrel of an HK Dream Machine, one of the new ones. He rolled slightly, and saw injured soldiers lying on the grass—Delta, SGG, SAS—and beyond them Kennedy, kneeling with a gun held to her head.

He saw Ben being forced to stand upright in a choke hold, Alicia Myles's merciless hands tight around his neck. Drake gritted his teeth when he saw Ben still clutching his cellphone in his hand. Clinging on till the last gasp...

"Alicia," he shouted. "What happened to you? There was a time when I considered you my closest friend."

"Let the Brit stand." Colby Taylor, the cultist leader, came into Drake's eyeline, an expression of disdain twisting his features. "You think we wouldn't notice you taking the professor back in Hawaii? You didn't think we might let that happen so we could track you? Let him watch his friends die—proof I can take all his pieces away before I take his pathetic life."

Drake let the fire of battle infuse his limbs. "You prove only that this place is as stated in the guide book—a land of monsters. And you, Alicia—" he turned baleful eyes on her. "I guess it had to be you who took out our sentries. What the hell is wrong with you?"

"Such a poetic guidebook," the billionaire chortled. "But true.

Give me the eyes." He held his hands out like a child asking for more. A mercenary took the woodcut of Odin's eyes and handed it to Taylor. "Good. Now where's your plane, Drake? I want your pieces, and then to quit this crap-hole."

"You won't get anywhere without the shield," Drake said, playing for time, saying the first thing that entered his head. "And then you'll need to figure out how it maps the way to Ragnarok."

"Fool," Taylor laughed nastily. "I know that. The only reason the *Forn Sidr* are here today and not twenty years ago is because the shield's only just been found. But I'm sure you already know that too. Are you trying to slow us down? Think we'll slip up and give you another chance? Well, Mr. Drake, let me tell you. *She—*" he pointed at Alicia, "doesn't slip up. She's hard-ass gold, that's what she is."

Drake watched as his ex-colleague slowly throttled Ben to death. "She'll sell you out to the highest bidder."

"I am the highest bidder, you washed-up piece of shit. I'm richer than the Blood King, and I don't even need the backing of the Shadow Elite."

Drake glowered. He'd heard that phrase before. Once as a soldier, and once more recently. But still he had no idea who the Shadow Elite were. If he survived this he might have to do more digging. —?

By a stroke of providence, someone used that moment to fire a bullet. The report echoed loudly, cracking through the woods. One of Taylor's mercenaries collapsed with a new third eye, dead in an instant.

Colby Taylor looked incredulous for a second. Then one of his own mercenaries crashed into him, knocking him to the ground, the mercenary bleeding, screaming and thrashing as he died. Drake was down beside them in a heartbeat as lead shredded the air above.

Everything happened at once. Kennedy slammed her body upwards. The top of her skull connected so solidly with the chin of her guard that he never knew what had happened. Instant lights out.

"*Who's firing?*" Taylor screamed into the damp earth.

A barrage of bullets flew back and forth; any mercenaries caught out in the open were decimated.

Torsten Dahl found freedom when the mercenary struggling to hold him was thrown off his feet, hit by a third echoing rifle shot. The SGG commander crab-walked to Professor Parnevik's side and started dragging the old man toward a bunch of scrub.

Drake's first thought was for Ben. As he prepared to make a desperate bid to save his friend, disbelief made him freeze. Alicia had thrown the boy aside and was advancing on Drake himself. A pistol appeared in her hand.

She raised her hand and centered on him.

Drake held his hands apart in a confused gesture. *Why?*

She squeezed the trigger. Drake flinched, expecting the heat, the numbness and then the pain, but his mind's eye caught up with his brain, and he saw she'd switched her aim at the last instant.

And pumped three bullets into the mercenary covering Colby Taylor's indignant form.

Two SAS soldiers and two Delta Marines had survived. The SAS had grabbed Ben and were dragging him away. What remained of the Delta team geared up to return fire into the nearby stand of trees.

More shots rang out. A Delta soldier twisted and fell. The other scrambled away on his belly toward Wells on the far side of Mimir's Well. Wells's prone body twitched as the American dragged him away, proof of life.

Alicia cried out in anger and leapt after the American soldier. When he turned and confronted her with his fists, she stopped for a second.

"Turn away, soldier," Drake heard her say. "Just go."

"I won't leave my man behind."

"You Americans, just give it a rest," she said, before unleashing hell, delivering punches and kicks to the man's most vulnerable areas. America's finest backed away, fighting hard but stumbling through the thick grass, first leading with one arm then staggering when it was broken, before losing the sight in one eye due to bruising and finally collapsing without even a twitch.

Drake was shouting, running at Alicia when she lifted Wells by the throat..

"Are you mad?" he shouted. "Have you gone absolutely *mad?*"

"He goes down the hole," Alicia's eyes were murderous. "You can join him or not. Your decision."

"What the hell, Alicia? *Why?*"

"One day, if you live through this, you'll find out why I hate him. And it will be the worst day of *your* life, Drake. Believe me."

Drake paused for breath. What did she know about his old commander? But to lose focus now was to invite death as surely as committing suicide. He struck at her with a straight-up boxer's jab, jab, cross. She parried, making sure she struck his wrist each time with bruising force, but he was in close now. Where he wanted to be.

He finger-jabbed at her neck. She sidestepped, right into his rising knee—aimed to crack a few ribs and slow her down.

But she rolled inside his knee so they were shockingly close, an inch apart, eye to eye.

Great eyes. Wonderful eyes.

That belonged to one of the world's greatest predators.

"You're weak as a wickle babe, Matt."

Her whisper chilled his bones as she stepped right in, extended an arm and threw him skyward. He landed on his back, winded. Before a second passed she was on top of him, knees ramming his solar plexus, forehead striking his own, making him see stars.

Again eye to eye, she whispered, "Stay down. There's a future for us somewhere."

But the choice wasn't his to make. It was all he could do to raise an arm, to roll sideways and watch as she half-dragged a semi-conscious Wells to the edge of the bottomless pit known as Mimir's Well.

Drake screamed with the effort of rising to his knees. Embarrassed by defeat, shocked by how much edge he'd lost since joining the human race, he struggled to breathe.

Alicia rolled Wells over the edge of the well. The SAS commander went over the edge without making a sound.

Drake swayed as he lurched to his feet, head and body aching. Alicia was approaching Colby Taylor now, still as fresh and agile as a spring lamb.

Alicia dragged the dead merc's body off Taylor. The billionaire scrambled up, eyes wide, staring from Myles to Drake to the trees.

Figures emerged from between the mist-wreathed trunks, like ghosts at home in this fabled land. The illusion shattered when the figures drifted close enough to see the deadly modern weaponry they carried.

Drake had circled around now. He could see the men approaching, knew it was the Germans, alerted by Alicia Myles, come to claim all the spoils.

Drake eyed the instrument of their victory with bewilderment. Alicia simply grabbed the Canadian billionaire, smiled at his bewilderment, and marched him over to Mimir's Well before angling his head over the edge.

Drake could have tried again, but realized he had higher priorities. He skirted the action, using Alicia and Taylor as a shield. He reached the scrub and kept going, edging slowly up a gentle grassy knoll.

Alicia pointed into the pit and shook Taylor until he screamed for mercy. "Maybe you'll find something to collect down *there*," she hissed and threw him bodily into the endless void. His screams echoed for a short while, then cut off. Drake wondered if a man who fell into a bottomless pit screamed forever, and if there was no one to hear him, did it really count?

By now Milo had reached his girlfriend. Drake heard him say, "Why'd the hell did you do that? The boss would've liked that asshole alive."

And Alicia's answer, "Shut up, Milo. Job's done. You ready to go?"

Milo grinned nastily up toward the top of the knoll. "We not gonna finish them off?"

"Don't be an arse. They're still armed and they hold the high ground. Do you have what we came for?"

"All on the plane. All Nine Pieces of Odin present and correct. Oh, and your plane is toast!" he cried in Drake's direction. "Have a ball out in this wasteland tonight!"

Drake watched the Germans beat a wary retreat. Their worlds had just teetered over the brink. They'd come all this way, made a ton of sacrifices, beaten themselves into the ground, only to lose everything to the Germans at the last hurdle.

"Yeah." Ben caught his eye with a humorless grin, as if reading his mind. "How life imitates football, eh?"

THIRTY-FOUR

OSTERGOTLAND, SWEDEN

The sun set slowly over a bleak horizon as the Europeans and their remaining American allies limped to higher ground. A thin, cold breeze whipped at their exposed flesh. A quick assessment found that one of the SAS soldiers was wounded, and Professor Parnevik was suffering from shock. No surprise there, given what he'd been through.

Dahl was radioing in their position by satphone. Help was about two hours away.

They stopped amidst a tiny stand of barren trees, open grassland all around them. Drake plonked himself down beside Ben.

Ben's first words: "I know people have died, Matt, but I just hope Karin and Hayden are okay. I'm sorry."

Drake nodded. "Don't worry. It's natural. Chances are extremely good for Karin, fair for Hayden," he admitted, having lost his sugarcoating abilities somewhere along the course of the mission. "How are *you* holding up, mate?"

Ben raised his cellphone. "I'm still alive."

"We've come a long way since the fashion show."

"I barely remember it," Ben said, seriously. "Matt, I *barely* remember what my life was like before this Odin thing began. And it's been...days?"

"I could remind you if you want. You were the Wall of Sleep frontman. You swooned over Taylor Momsen. There were cellphone overcharges. Rent arrears. Many rent arrears."

"We've lost everything. All the pieces. Hayden. Even the friggin' plane."

"We couldn't have gotten even this far without you."

"You know me, mate. I'd help anyone." It was a standard reply, but Drake could tell he was pleased with the praise. He hadn't forgotten that Ben was outthinking even the Nordic professor.

No doubt that was what Hayden had seen in him. She saw the man inside starting to shine through. Drake prayed for her safety, but there was nothing he could do for her right now.

Kennedy dropped beside them. "Hope I'm not interrupting you guys. You look kinda tight."

"No, not you," Drake said and Ben nodded. "You're one of us now."

"Thanks, I guess. That a compliment?"

Drake lightened the mood. "Anyone who can segue a few DinoRock titles with me is a brother for life."

"All night long, dude, all night long."

Ben groaned. "So," he glanced around, "it just got dark."

Drake considered the endless grasslands. A last sliver of deep red dripped down the farthest horizon. "I bet it gets awful cold here at night."

Dahl walked up to them. "Is this over then, men? Are we done? The world needs us."

A biting wind tore his words into shreds, scattering them across the plains.

Parnevik spoke from where he rested with his back against a tree. "There is good news, though, no? You told me you had the only known depiction of the pieces in their true arrangement."

"Yes, but the thing went on tour in the '60s," Dahl explained. "We can't be positive it hasn't been copied, especially by one of these Viking history freaks."

The professor was well enough to murmur, "Oh, thanks."

Full dark fell, and a million stars twinkled overhead. Branches swayed and leaves rustled. Ben instinctively inched closer to Drake on one side. Kennedy did the same on the other.

Where Kennedy's hip touched his own, Drake felt fire. It was all he could do to concentrate on what Dahl was saying.

"The shield," the Swede was saying, "is our last hope."

Drake found it hard to stay focused, despite everything. It was a long time since he'd felt this way. It took him back to when girls were girls and boys were nervous—wearing T-shirts in the snow, and walking their girlfriends around town on a Saturday afternoon before buying them their favorite single and sharing popcorn and a straw at the cinema.

Innocent days, long gone. Long remembered and sadly lost.

"Shield?" he blurted into the conversation. "Huh?"

Dahl frowned at him. "Keep up, you thick Yorkshire bastard. We were *saying* that the shield is the principal piece. Nothing can be achieved without it, since it gives the location of Ragnarok. It's also made of different *material* than the other pieces—something unknown."

"Like what?"

Dahl swore in his best Oxford accent. "How the hell do I know? Ask me one on sport."

"Okay. Why the hell did Leeds United ever sign Tomas Brolin?"

Dahl's face fell and then hardened. He was about to retort, when a peculiar noise shattered the stillness.

A wail. A moan from out of the darkness, a sound that triggered an irrational, primordial fear.

"Listen." Drake whispered. "What—?"

It came again. A yowl. Animal-like but throaty, as if from something large. It made the Drake's skin crawl.

"You remember?" Ben said in a whisper stilted by terror. "This is Grendel's country. The monster from *Beowulf*. There are still tales that monsters haunt this area."

"The only thing I really remember from *Beowulf* is Angelina Jolie," Drake said fondly. "But then I suppose the same could be said about most of her movies."

"Shhh!" Kennedy hissed. "What the hell is that *noise?*"

The howling came again, closer now. Drake tried desperately to distinguish anything through the darkness, imagining bare fangs that dripped saliva exploding toward him, strips of rotten flesh caught between jagged teeth.

He raised his gun, not wanting to frighten the others but just too uncertain to take any risks.

Torsten Dahl leveled his own rifle. The fit SAS trooper unsheathed a knife. Silence gripped the night.

A faint sound. A *clunk*. Something that resembled a light footfall...

But are they human feet? Drake wondered.

If he heard the clicking of claws he might well squeeze off his entire magazine in terror.

His heart leapt when Ben's cellphone suddenly exploded into life. Ben threw it in the air with shock, but then commendably caught it on the way down.

"*Bollocks,*" he whispered before realizing he'd answered it. "Hi, Mum."

Drake tried to quiet the thumping of blood through his brain. "Cut it off. *Cut it off!*"

Ben said, "In the loo. Call you later!"

Drake listened. The moaning came again, thin and anguished, followed by a distant thud, as if the noise-maker had thrown a rock. Another weeping cry, and then a howl...

This time definitely human. Drake rushed into action. "That's Wells," he said, and raced into the dark, instinct sending him to Mimir's Well and stopping his feet at the rim.

"Help me," Wells moaned, lifting cracked and bloodied fingers over the edge of the well. "Caught one of the ropes...on the way down. Nearly broke my arm. That bitch has...has to do more than that to kill me."

Drake took his weight, saving him from freefalling back into infinite night.

With Wells warmly wrapped and resting, Drake just held the man's eyes and shook his head in disgust.

Wells croaked, "I never meant to start a war between soldiers."

"That's okay then, 'cause Alicia and I are no longer soldiers. And what did she mean back there?"

Wells started coughing, ignoring the question.

Beside him, Ben was questioning Parnevik as if nothing had happened. "You think the shield is some sort of key?"

"The shield is everything."

"What are you two doing?" Drake asked, his attention caught by the bright glow of Ben's iPhone.

"Pulling up an image." Ben was googling "Odin's Shield" at the speed of a geek. The image that appeared was small, but Ben zoomed in faster than Drake could even think.

Ben held the iPhone at arm's length, letting everyone crowd around.

"It's easy," Kennedy said. "Ragnarok's in Vegas. Everything's in Vegas."

Parnevik rubbed his chin. "The layout of the shield shows four separate parts that surround a circular hub, the answer to our riddle. You see? Let's label them north, east, south and west, so we know what we're referring to."

"Neat," Ben said. "Well, west is obvious. I see a spear and two eyes."

"South is a horse and two wolves, I think." Drake squinted as best he could.

"Of course," Parnevik said. "You are right. Because east has to be two Valkyries. Yes? You see?"

Drake blinked hard, at last discerning two warrior women sat atop a pair of winged horses. The screen was worryingly small. "I blame Starbucks." He cursed. "A cafe with free Wi-Fi on every corner of the world except this one!"

"So..." Kennedy said haltingly, "no picture of the shield shown on the, umm, shield?"

The professor studied hard, getting in Ben's eyeline and receiving a friendly swat. "Can you zoom in a bit more?"

"Nah. That's its limit."

"I see no other markings in the eastern section," Dahl said from his standing position. "But north's pretty interesting."

Drake flicked his attention, and felt a jolt of shock. "That's the symbol of Odin. Three interlocking triangles. Same thing we saw down the well."

"But what's *that?*" Dahl pointed out a tiny symbol positioned at the bottom left of one of the triangles. When Ben scrolled up they all spoke in unison, "It's the shield."

A confused silence reigned. Drake wracked his brain. Why had the shield symbol been placed within the triangles? Obviously a clue, just not a very clear one.

"This would be a lot easier on a bigger *screen,*" the professor huffed.

"Stop whining," Ben said. "Don't let it beat you."

"Here's a thought," Kennedy spoke up. "Could the triangles

stand for something other than this 'Odin's Knot'"

"A secret purpose for a mystical symbol attached to a god previously thought mere legend?" Parnevik scoffed. "Surely not."

Drake rubbed his ribs where Alicia Myles had taught him that seven years out took a heavy toll on the level of your combat performance. She'd humiliated him, but he took comfort in the fact that he remained alive and they were still in the game.

Dahl tried to calm everyone. "The chopper will have onboard internet. It will be here in about…oh, thirty minutes."

"Okay, well, what about the central section?" Drake did his bit. "Two outlines that look like a child's drawing of three udders and a jellyfish."

"*And* the shield again," Ben zoomed in on the jellyfish's eye. "Same representation as the north section. So we have *two* depictions of the shield on the shield itself. A centerpiece composed of two random outlines, *and* the three Odinic triangles," he said, nodding at Kennedy. "That may not be triangles at all."

"Well, at least it proves my theory of the shield being the principal piece," Parnevik pointed out.

"Doesn't prove a thing," Ben said in an undertone.

"Those outlines remind me of something," Dahl mused. "I just can't say what."

Drake could think of several sardonic personal comebacks, but held himself in check. *Well, that's progress,* he thought. The proficient Swede had come a long way with them, and had earned more than a little respect.

"Look," Ben shouted out, making them all jump. "There's a thin, almost irrelevant, line connecting both shield images."

"Which actually tells us nothing," Parnevik grouched as he squinted.

"Or…" Drake mused, thinking back to his school days, "or…if you consider it a different way—we know the shield is a map to Ragnarok. The two images could be the same destination point but with two different *views*…only one is the elevation view and the other—"

"Is the *plan* view." Ben said.

At that moment there was the sound of a chopper approaching.

Dahl talked it in, showing his old-school dependencies by shutting off the GPRS. He squinted into the dark along with everyone else as the big, black shape approached.

"Well, we don't have much choice," he said with half a smile. "We're going to have to wing it."

Once aboard and settled, Dahl booted up a 17" Sony Vaio laptop that used its own portable modem, like an iPhone. Depending on the cell network coverage, they would have Internet access.

"It's a map." Drake continued his line of thought. "So let's treat it like one. Clearly the middle, the centerpiece, is the *plan* view. Copy the outline, use some kind of geographical recognition software, and see what comes up."

"Hmm," Parnevik studied the enlarged view dubiously. "Why include that other so-called udder-like image if the shield symbol lies inside your..." he paused reluctantly, then said, "jellyfish image."

"A point of reference?" Kennedy ventured.

The chopper swayed, buffeted by high winds. The pilot had been told to head for Oslo until he received further instructions. A second SGG team awaited them there.

"Try the software, Torsten."

"I already have, but I don't need it," Dahl replied in sudden wonder. "I *knew* that outline looked familiar. It's Scandinavia on a map. The *udders* are Norway, Sweden and Finland. The jellyfish is Iceland."

A split-second later, the laptop pinged with a total of three possible matches. The geographical recognition software had weighted the closest at 98 percent—it was Scandinavia.

Drake nodded at Dahl in respect.

"Ragnarok's in Iceland?" Parnevik questioned.

"Get those coordinates to the pilot," Drake jabbed at the coastline of Iceland and the position of the shield symbol. "Now. We're already hours behind."

"But we don't have the *pieces*," Ben said plaintively. "The Germans have them. And only *they* can use the pieces to find the Tomb of the Gods."

Torsten Dahl actually laughed for the first time since they'd met, making Drake do a double-take. "Oh, no," the Swede said "I have a *much* more intelligent idea. Why stoop to fiddling about with those friggin' pieces when we live in such an advanced technological age? Who needs a jigsaw puzzle when we have cutting-edge equipment right here? This was always Plan B, but in my eyes the *better* plan. We don't physically need the pieces. We just to be near them and let the Germans do all the hard work."

"Let me think here– wasn't Iceland where the shield was found?" Ben asked, impressing Drake again with his clear thinking under pressure.

"Yes, and if that's also the ancient site of Ragnarok," Parnevik said, "it makes perfect sense that Odin's Shield would have fallen where he died."

"Oh, it makes sense now, Professor," Kennedy teased him. "Now these guys have worked it all out for ya."

"Well, if it helps, we still have the greatest mystery to solve," Ben said with a slight smile. "The meaning of the ancient symbol of Odin—the three triangles."

THIRTY-FIVE

ICELAND

The Icelandic coastline is ice-laden, rugged, and awash with color, sheared in some parts by great glaciers, and beaten smooth in others by lashing waves and scouring winds. There are coasts of lava and black cliffs, majestic icebergs, and, overall, a kind of Zen-like calm. Danger and beauty stand hand-in-hand, ready to lull the unwary traveler to an untimely end.

Reykjavik passed beneath them in a matter of minutes, its bright red roofs, white buildings, and surrounding snow-covered mountains guaranteed to stir even the most jaded of hearts.

They stopped briefly at a sparse military base to refuel and upload snowsuits, ammunition and rations, and anything else Dahl could think of in the ten minutes they were at a standstill. The sheer amount of gear he brought astounded them; everything from tin cans to safety harnesses for climbing, rope and handheld GPS units.

But the people on board the black military chopper saw little of it. They were connected as a group—discussing the same objective—but their inner thoughts were of their own mortality —of how scared and apprehensive they were, and how worried for others.

Drake was as anxious as anyone. He couldn't envisage how to keep everyone safe. If this was Ragnarok they had found, then the legendary Tomb of the Gods was next, and their lives had just become a game of roulette.

And now in addition to Ben and Kennedy— two people he would protect with his life—Drake had to consider both Hayden and Karin, too. The real battle was coming, and he, a man who had escaped the ordeals of war once, now stood as a soldier in the vanguard.

War diminished you. It chipped chunks from your soul, took the man and molded him into a darker shadow of his real self. But Drake was ready to stand up and fight again.

Endgames were being played out in every corner. Abel Frey, equipped with all nine pieces, had already begun his and it would have been meticulously planned over countless years. Alicia and Milo might have one of their own, but Drake suspected his ex-SRT colleague had a killer surprise in store that even her boyfriend hadn't anticipated.

Torsten Dahl and Wells had rarely been off the phone since they crossed the coast of Iceland, receiving orders, hints and whispered advice from their respective governments. As they progressed, Kennedy answered a call that made her sit up straight for a few minutes and shake her head wearily in shock.

She turned only to Drake. "You know Hayden? The *secretary?* Yeah, she's just doing her job, right?"

"Is she okay?" Drake asked immediately.

"I don't know that, but I do know she's only a part of the American effort here. And she's right where they want her to be. In the middle of all this bullshit and as close to the enemy as it's possible to get."

"Bollocks." Drake sent a troubled glance at Ben, but still fancied she harbored a soft spot for his friend. Was it just Drake's heart feeding him romantic notions, telling him Hayden's feelings had been true, or was she leading them all on to get closer?

"That was an advisor to an advisor of the Secretary of Defense," Kennedy went on matter-of-factly. "Since I'm the only American on site, they want to be 'kept in the loop'."

"Indeed." Drake nodded toward Dahl and Wells. "And, over there, that's just history repeating." He looked tiredly through the window. "Can you believe, Kennedy, after the last week or so, that we're still in the game?"

"Can you believe," Kennedy said, "that everyone's buying into this tomb of the gods theory?"

"Gods don't have to be *Gods*," he said with weary aplomb "They only have to be men worshipped as Gods."

But then Kennedy gasped and leaned across to take a look out of the window. Drake felt her entire frame stiffen.

"Oh wow," she said. "That's the...'

"I know," Drake interrupted, staring. "Dahl, look at that."

The Swede stared over and quickly ended his call. A brief glance through the window made him frown in confusion. "It's just Eyjafjallajokul. And yes, yes, Drake, I know, it's easy for me to say, and yes it's the one that made all the news in earlier this year" he paused, riveted, expectant.

Parnevik's eyes were bugging. Swedish swear words shot from him like poisoned darts.

Now Ben scooted close to the window. "Wow. It's Iceland's most famous volcano and it's still erupting it seems, albeit gently."

"Yes." Drake said. "Fire will consume us. The friggin' *volcano*."

"And now, more importantly," Kennedy finally managed to continue, "look at the shield's image in elevation."

Parnevik nodded and found his flow. "Three *mountains—not* three triangles as has always been thought. The ancient scholars erred. It seems Odin's most famous symbol was decoded wrongly. Oh dear."

Drake looked beyond the erupting volcano, and saw two even taller mountains flanking it, that, when looked at in elevation, closely resembled Odin's symbol.

Parnevik swore again. "Our eyes do play a trick here, because although those three mountains appear to be beside Eyjafjallajokul, they are in fact hundreds of miles away. But they are part of the *chain* of Icelandic volcanoes, all connected."

"The Tomb of the Gods," Dahl breathed, "is *inside* the erupting volcano, judging by the map."

"Wait!" Dahl was watching the satellite image now that told them when they would reach the "jellyfish's" eye. "We still need a bit of help with the directions and, as I explained, this has always been my Plan B. That's one enormous mountain there, and Abel Frey's going to show us right through the secret door."

"How?" at least two voices asked.

Dahl winked and spoke to the pilot. "Take us higher."

*

They were now so high that Drake couldn't see even the mountains through the clouds. His new-found respect for the SGG commander was in dire need of a boost.

"Alright, Torville, put the peasants outta their misery, eh? Explain."

"Tor*sten*," Dahl corrected, before realizing he was being goaded. "Oh, I see. Okay then, try to keep up if you can. This is my army specialty, or *was*, before I joined the SGG. Aerial reconnaissance photography, in particular, orthophotos."

"That's brilliant," Drake said. "What the hell are those?"

"They are photographs taken from an infinite distance, looking straight down, that are then geometrically altered to the accepted standard of a map. Once the Germans align the pieces and the photo is uploaded, all we have to do is match it with real-world coordinates, then..." he shrugged.

"*Boom!*" Kennedy laughed. "You mean like Google Earth, right? Only without the 3D?"

"Indeed."

Drake made a face. "Hope this works, Dahl. Without the nine pieces, we're dead. It's our only chance to get ahead of the endgame."

"It will. And not only that, when the computer calculates the coordinates, we will know *exactly* where the entrance to the Tomb of the Gods is. Even the Germans, in full possession of all nine pieces, will have to estimate. You see, having the pieces has always been essential to finding the tomb, but not necessarily having them *in our hands*."

"Assuming the Germans arrange all the pieces correctly," Ben said with a humorless smile.

"Well, that's true. We can only hope that Abel Frey knows what he's doing. He's certainly had enough time to practice."

Drake slid out of his seat and looked for Wells; saw him tapping his cellphone against the window in frustration.

"Any news on Frey's chateau, mate?"

The SAS commander snorted. "Surrounded. But covertly—the chateau's security is unaware of its new-found attention. German cops are there. Interpol. *Representatives* from most of the world's governments. But still no Mai. She's gone. One of my intelligence guys thinks she's in the States. I'll not lie to you, Matt, that chateau is going to be one hard rock to crack without a shitload of losses."

Drake nodded, thinking of Karin. He knew the odds, having played them many times. "So we'll do the tomb first...then see where we're at."

Just then there was a grunt of excitement from the front of the cramped chopper. Dahl turned around with a happy smile on his face. "Frey's down there now. Arranging the pieces. If we set this baby on full res and a snap-happy one-frame-per-second, we'll be inside that tomb within the hour."

"Have some respect," Parnevik said reverently. "That's Ragnarok down there. One of the greatest fabled battlefields in known history, and possibly the site of at least one Armageddon. Gods died screaming in that ice. *Gods.*"

"And so will Abel Frey," Ben Blake said quietly. "If he's harmed my sister."

THIRTY-SIX

THE TOMB OF THE GODS

The game was up.

When Drake and his companions dropped altitude and overflew Ragnarok, heading for the smoking mountain, they knew the Germans would see and start hightailing it after them. The chopper descended rapidly into a soft basin, jarred violently by random gusts of wind and a rebounding downdraught. Everyone except the professor, who was feeling the trauma and fatigue of the last few days, shouldered as much gear as they were able. The pilot finessed the collective until the chopper hovered as close as it was going to get, six feet off the ground, then shouted at everyone to jump down.

"Fix the coordinates of the nine pieces," Dahl ordered the pilot. "I have a nasty feeling we're by no means done with them yet." He turned to the rest of the aircraft. "Clock's ticking!" He shouted, jumped and, as soon as his boots hit solid earth, started to run. "Let's move!"

Drake reached out to steady Ben, before surveying their surroundings. The tiny basin had seemed the best drop-off point, being only a mile from the small entrance they had surveyed and the only land within reasonable distance that wasn't too rocky or a potential magma tube. An extra bonus was it might help confuse Frey as to the tomb's exact location.

It was a bleak landscape. Drake thought it looked like the end of the world. Layers of gray ash, drab-colored mountainsides, and blackened deposits of lava did nothing to increase his confidence as he waited for Dahl to pinpoint the entrance on his

GPR device. He half expected a bedraggled hobbit to come crawling out of the dim mists, claiming he'd reached Mordor. The wind wasn't strong, but its sporadic gusts struck at his face like an angry viper.

"This way." Dahl took off across a drift of ash. High above them the volcano's mushroom cloud plumed into the sky. Dahl aimed for a thick black crevice in the mountain ahead.

"Why would anyone put such an important and sacred site inside a volcano?" Kennedy asked as she trudged beside Drake.

"Maybe it was never meant to last," he shrugged. "Just a final resting place. Iceland's been exploding for centuries. Who would've thought that *this* volcano would erupt so often without going full scale?"

The skies overhead were laden with snow and drifting ash, enforcing a premature dusk. The sun didn't shine here; it was as if hell had gained its first foothold in the earthly realm and was holding on tight.

Dahl negotiated the uneven ground, stumbling sometimes through unexpectedly deep drifts of gray powder. When he reached the stark cliff, the rag-tag group had ceased to talk—their mettle leached away by the depressing wilderness.

"Up here." The Swede gestured with his gun. "About twenty feet." He squinted. "Can't see anything obvious."

"Now, if Cook had said that off the coast of Hawaii, we'd never have had Dole pineapple," Drake chided gently, hoping for a laugh.

"Or Kona coffee." Kennedy licked her lips at him, then blushed when he winked back.

"After you," he said, indicating the thirty-degree incline with a flourish.

"Not a chance, perv." Now she did manage a smile.

"Well, so long as you promise not to stare at *my* arse." Drake attacked the rocky slope with gusto, testing every hold before distributing his weight, and keeping a close eye on Dahl and the lone SAS soldier above him. Kennedy came next, then Ben, and finally the professor and Wells.

No one had wanted to be left out of this particular mission.

Dahl clattered on ahead for a time. Drake cast a glance behind them, but saw no signs of pursuit. A moment later, Dahl's voice penetrated the cloak of silence.

"Whoa, got something here, lads. There's a rock outcropping, then a left turn behind it..." His voice faded. "A vertical shaft with...yes, with steps carved into the rock. A bit tight. *Helvite!* Those old gods must've been skinny!"

Drake reached the outcropping and shimmied behind it. "Did you just swear, Dahl, and crack a joke? Or try to, at least. So you may be human after all. Hope we're not in a hurry to leave."

With that alarming thought, he helped Dahl fix a safety line before squeezing the Swede down the black hole. Several ripostes came to mind but this wasn't the time or the place. Without room to aim a flashlight below, poor Torsten Dahl was climbing down blind, a step at a time.

"If you smell brimstone," Drake couldn't resist, "stop."

Dahl took his time, planting every foot with care. After a few minutes he disappeared, and all Drake could see was the dim glow from his firefighter's helmet growing fainter and fainter.

"You okay?"

"I hit rock bottom!" Dahl's voice echoed up.

Kennedy glanced around. "Is that another joke?"

"Well, let's get out of this cold." Drake gripped the black-rock rim and gingerly lowered himself over the edge. Using his feet to scrabble for purchase, he gently lowered himself inch by perilous inch. The hole was so tight he scraped his nose and cheeks at every move. "Ow! Just take it slow," he called up to the others. "Try to move your upper body as little as possible."

After a few minutes he heard Dahl say, "Six feet," and sensed the rock at his back become empty space.

"Be careful," Dahl warned. "We're on a ledge now. About two foot wide. Sheer rock wall to our right, the customary bottomless pit to our left. Only one way to go."

Drake used his own light to verify the Swede's findings as the others made their lengthy descents. As they approached, Drake said, "I'd estimate that shaft to be barely the size of the shield. I wonder if the measurements are intentional."

Dahl shrugged. "Everything about this quest seems intentional." He urged the rest of the team down.

Once everyone was warned and prepared, Dahl began to inch along the ledge. Utter darkness enveloped them, speared only by their helmet flashlights which danced about like fireflies in the bayou.

"This reminds me of one of those old dinosaur films," Professor Parnevik said. "You remember? *The Land That Time Forgot*, I think?"

"The one with Raquel Welch?" Wells asked. "No? Ah well, people from my era, they think dinosaur—they think Raquel Welch. Never mind."

Drake pressed his back to the rock and sidestepped forward, arms spread out, ensuring both Ben and Kennedy followed his example before moving off. The murky void faced them, and now a faint rumbling came to their ears, deep and far away.

"That would be Eyjafjallajokul, the mountain, erupting gently," Professor Parnevik whispered along the line. "My best guess is that we are in a side chamber, well insulated from the magma chamber and from the conduit pipe that feeds the eruptions. There might be dozens upon dozens of ash and lava layers between us and the rising magma, shielding us and the tomb. We may even be inside a bedrock anomaly, where it rises at a steeper angle than the sides of the mountain."

Dahl shouted into the gloom. "*Helvite!* We have a low wall coming up, crossing our path at a ninety-degree angle. It's not high, so don't worry, just be careful."

"Some kind of trap?" Parnevik ventured.

Drake saw the obstacle and thought the same. With great care, he followed the SGG commander over the knee-high barrier. They both saw the first tomb at the same time.

"*Whoa*," but then Dahl's grasp on words failed him.

Drake just whistled, awestruck by the sight.

A great niche had been carved into the mountainside, travelling possibly a hundred feet into the core of the volcano—toward the magma chamber. The entrance had been formed into an arch, perhaps a hundred feet high. As everyone gathered around and took out their heavy-duty flashlights, the stunning spectacle of the first tomb unfolded.

"Amazing," Kennedy breathed. Her light illuminated shelf

upon shelf cut into the rocky walls, each adorned by and filled with treasures: necklaces and spears, breast-plates and helmets. Swords...

"Who *was* this guy?"

Parnevik was predictably studying the far facing wall, effectively the god's arched tombstone. A fantastic carving stood in sharp relief there, easily the equal in skill of any of the latter-day Renaissance men, even Michelangelo.

"It is the tomb of Mars," the professor stated. "The Roman God of War."

Drake saw a depiction of a muscle-bound figure wearing a chest plate and skirt, holding a great spear over one massive shoulder whilst staring over the other. In the background stood a majestic horse and a round building that closely resembled the Colosseum in Rome.

"Beats me how they decided who gets to be buried here," Kennedy murmured. "Roman gods. Norse gods..."

"Me too," Parnevik said. "Perhaps it was just by the whim of Zeus."

"Or Odin?" Drake raised an eyebrow.

All eyes flicked inevitably to an enormous sarcophagus that stood beneath the carved mural. Drake's imagination took hold. If they looked inside would they find the bones of a god, or a human venerated as one?

"We don't have time!" Dahl sounded frustrated, worn and harassed. "Let's go. We have no idea how many gods may be buried down here."

Parnevik picked up one of the items, a gleaming necklace. "We—and I mean the archaeological and scientific world—have known about these crazy anomalous items for hundreds of years. You see, the more science advances, the easier we spot our past mistakes. And some of them, we don't like to admit. In particular the ones that would force us to redefine our entire thinking, the ones that might challenge all we know about evolution. They are 'ooparts'—out of place artefacts that have been found in strata long before humans were believed to have existed. They simply can't be there. It is impossible. Any yet they are. This..." he spread his arms wide. "This tomb may shed more light on their existence. It proves some kind of life existed before we thought it did."

Kennedy frowned at Drake, and looked along the ledge as it disappeared into the blackness. "That's a rather narrow, fragile track of rock we're following. And I bet my 401K the god count isn't just *one or two.*"

"We can't trust anything now," he said. "Only each other. C'mon. The Germans are coming."

They filed out of Mars's burial chamber, each person stealing a longing, backward glance at its relative safety and incalculable significance as they left. More rumblings shook a far-flung cave and echoed around their own. Drake looked up, and fancied he could see a similar ledge far above him. *Bollocks.* This thing could wind up and around all night.

On the plus side, there were still no signs of pursuit. Maybe Frey and Alicia and their gang were having trouble fitting the shield down the entry tube. Drake guessed they had gained a good lead on the Germans, but knew some kind of confrontation was inevitable. He just hoped they could find the bones of Odin before it happened.

A second ledge appeared ahead, and beyond it another magnificent niche set back into the mountain. This one was adorned by rank upon rank of gold objects, the side walls fairly glowing with golden light.

"*Incredible!*" Kennedy breathed. "I've never seen anything like this. Who *is* that? The god of treasure?"

Parnevik squinted at the rock carving that dominated a massive sarcophagus. He shook his head for a moment, frowning. "Wait, are those feathers? Is that god clothed in feathers?"

"Could be, Prof," Ben was already looking past the niche and into the stretch of black night that awaited them. "Does it matter? It's not Odin."

Parnevik ignored him. "Of course it matters. That's *Quetzalcoatl! The Aztec God!* Which makes all this..." he gestured at the shining walls.

"*Aztec gold,*" Wells breathed, awestruck despite himself. "Fantastic."

"This place..." Kennedy was practically hyperventilating, "is the greatest archaeological find of *all time*. You get that? There's not just one civilization's deity here, but *many*. And all the traditions and treasures that accompany them. This is...staggering."

Drake glanced away from the depiction of Quetzalcoatl, adorned in feathers and brandishing an axe. Parnevik was saying that the Aztec god had been known—by accepted clerical sources—as the *God Ruler*; an expression intimating that he had indeed been real in some form or other.

"Quetzalcoatl means 'flying reptile' or 'feathered serpent'. Which is—" Parnevik paused for effect, then seemed to realize that everyone else had filed back to the ledge, "a dragon," he said to himself, sounding pleased.

"Does he have anything in common with Mars?" the lone SAS staff-sergeant—a man called Jim Marsters—asked.

Drake watched Parnevik step out onto the ledge, his lips pursed. "Only one," his breathy speculation carried past everyone on the ledge. "That they can, and have at some time, both signified death."

At a third niche, equally as breathtaking as the last, Drake found himself staring at a carving of a stunning naked lady.

A fortune in statuettes lined the walls. Dolphins, mirrors, swans. A necklace of sculpted doves large enough to span the Statue of Liberty's neck.

"Well," Drake said. "Even I know who that is."

Kennedy made a face. "Yeah, you would."

"The original slut," Parnevik said harshly. "Aphrodite."

"Hey, hey," Wells said. "You're calling the Goddess Aphrodite a slut? Down here? This close to her tomb?"

Parnevik rushed on with careless bullishness. "Known to have slept with gods and men, including Adonis. *Offered* Helen of Troy to Paris, then sealed the deal by inflaming Paris's ardor the moment he laid eyes on her. Born near Paphos from Uranus's newly castrated testicles. I have to say she's a—"

"We get the message," Drake said drily, still staring at the carving. He smiled when he noticed Kennedy shaking her head at him.

"Jealous, love?"

"Sexually frustrated much?" She pushed past him to be second in line after Dahl.

He stared after her. "Well, now you mention it..."

"C'mon, Matt." Ben slipped by him too. "Wow!"

His exclamation made them all jump. They turned to see him scrambling back on all fours, terror etched into his face. Drake wondered if he'd just seen the Devil himself borne on wings of demons, rising up from the cookhouse of hell.

"This tomb—" he gasped. "It's on a platform...floating in air...*there's nothing on the other side!*"

Drake's heart froze. He remembered Mimir's Well and its false floor.

Dahl jumped several times. "The rock feels sturdy enough. This can't be the end of the line."

"*Don't do that!*" Ben squeaked. "What if it breaks away?"

Stillness reigned. Everyone stared at each other with wide eyes. Some ventured a glance back along the way they had come, the safe way, Wells and Ben amongst them.

At that moment, at the furthest range of hearing, a faint clattering sound could be heard. The sound of a stone dropped down a well.

"That's the Germans," Dahl said with conviction. "Testing the depth of the shaft. Now, we either find a way off this platform, or we die."

Drake nudged Kennedy. "See up there?" He shone his flashlight above them at a higher ledge. "There must be another set of niches or caves above us. But see...see how the rock edge seems to *curve*."

"Right." Kennedy hurried to the edge of Aphrodite's niche. Then, hugging the jagged rock, she leaned around the corner. "Some kind of structure here. Oh, man."

Drake held her shoulders and peered into the dark. "Oh no."

There, stretching away beyond the reach of their lights, was a thin ledge that turned into an even thinner spiral staircase. The staircase stretched up above them, heading for the next level.

"Talk about vertigo," Drake said. "This just took the biscuit *and* the jar."

THIRTY-SEVEN

THE TOMB OF THE GODS

The spiral staircase felt solid enough, even though it wound through seemingly empty air above an endless pit and its architects had inconsiderately failed to fit any kind of railing. Drake's well-trained nerves juddered faster than a flea on a jackhammer.

One complete circle led them about a quarter of the way up Aphrodite's niche, so Drake figured they had another three circuits to do. He moved up a step at a time, following Ben, trying to keep everyone's fear at bay with constant reassurance, taking deep breaths and always looking ahead to their goal.

Sixty feet to go. Fifty. Forty.

When he neared thirty feet, he saw Ben stop and sit for a moment. The boy's eyes were petrified with fear. Drake sat gingerly on the step below him.

"This isn't the time to start composing a new track, mate."

Then the SAS soldier's voice echoed up from below them. "What's going on? We're hanging in the wind down here. Get movin'."

SAS soldiers, Drake thought. Didn't make 'em like they used to.

"Take a break," he shouted back. "Just be a minute."

"*A break! A fu—*" Drake heard Wells's low tones, then silence. He felt Kennedy sit near his feet, saw her tight smile, and felt her shaking body through his toes.

"How's the kid?"

"Missing college," Drake made himself laugh. "And fellow band members. Also the pubs of York. Free cinema night. Pizza. *Call of Duty.* You know, student boy things."

Kennedy peered more closely. "That's not what student boys and girls do in *my* experience."

Now Ben opened his eyes and tried a strained smile. He inched himself around on hands and knees. Once he was facing upwards again, still on hands and knees, he started to climb one grueling step after another.

Inch by inch, step by perilous step, they ascended. Dahl stayed close to the Professor, lending a hand when needed. Drake felt the stress making his own head and heart ache. If Ben fell he would willingly block the boy's fall with his own body, if only to save him.

Without question or hesitation.

Another full circle and they were about twenty feet from their goal—a ledge that mirrored the one they had just traversed. Drake studied it in the flickering light. It led back toward the entrance shaft but obviously one level up.

Level up? he thought, and groaned in silence. He'd been "retro-ing" it too much with Sonic the bloody Hedgehog.

Above him he saw Dahl waver; he was half-carrying the professor. The Swede had stood up too fast, overbalanced, and now had too much weight on his back foot. There were no sounds, just the struggle as he fought to regain his balance. He could only imagine the tortures flooding through Dahl's mind: the space at his back, the safety in front, the thought of the long, torturous drop.

Then the Swede flung himself forward, hit the steps, and clung on for dear life, still clutching hold of Parnevik. Drake heard both men's heavy breathing from ten feet down.

A few minutes later and the arduous climb continued. At last, Dahl stepped off the stairs and onto the ledge, then crawled forward on hands and knees to make space. Drake followed not long after, pulling a still sprightly Kennedy with him, feeling stunned relief at returning to a narrow ledge that still left them only a slip from screaming death.

When they were all accounted for, Dahl sighed. "Let's get to the next niche and call a rest," he said. "I, for one, need a breather."

After five more minutes of shuffling their sore bodies and

fighting off increasing muscle strains they stumbled into the fourth niche, the one that stood directly above Aphrodite's tomb.

No one saw the resident god at first. They were all on their knees resting and panting. Drake thought wryly that this was what civilian life had led him to, and only looked up when Parnevik uttered an expletive that would have seemed odd coming from anyone else.

"Woof!"

"What?"

The eccentric professor laughed. "Dog head. It's Anubis."

"The jackal?" Wells sat back and gripped his knees to his chest. "Well. I'll be..."

"An *Egyptian* deity," Parnevik said. "And this one is undoubtedly linked to death. I believe I also shouldn't have to remind you of Euhemerus at this point?"

"Please don't," Drake said, but Parnevik forged ahead.

"Here we have cast-iron proof that Euhemeristic theory was right all along. That gods were actually revered men. Yes, this takes it to a whole new level, agreed, but Gods and myths and legends *must* derive from something real. Not only is myth proven to be a distorted account of historical events, it's true protagonists are *real*."

"Don't forget, we haven't looked inside any of the coffins yet," Ben said. "We don't know what's inside."

Drake took in row upon row of mummies and coal-colored jackal statuettes. Gold-inlaid coffins and emerald-studded ankhs. Unimpressed, he turned his back on the god's burial chamber and broke into a KitKat. A moment later, Kennedy was seated by his side.

"So," she said, unwrapping her own food and drink.

"Woah, you're good with the chat-up lines." Drake grinned. "I'm feeling encouraged already."

"Listen, buddy, if I wanted you *encouraged* then you'd be putty in my hands." Kennedy shot him a grin, both cheeky and exasperated. "You guys can't quit it for a minute, can you?"

"Okay, okay, I'm sorry. Just messing about. What's up?"

He watched Kennedy peer off into the void, saw her eyes widen when she caught the faint sound of Frey's soldiers catching them up. "This...thing...we've been skirting around for a while. Do you think we've actually got something, Drake?"

"I certainly think Odin's here."

Kennedy rose, about to walk away, but Drake put a hand on her knee to stop her. The touch almost produced sparks.

"There," he said. "What do you think?"

"I don't think I'll have much of a job when we get back," she whispered. "What with the Thomas Kaleb situation. That bastard killed again, you know, the day before we got to Manhattan."

"*What?*"

"Yes. I went to walk the murder scene. To pay my respects."

"I'm so sorry." Drake refrained from hugging her, recognizing it was the last thing she needed right now

"Thank you. You're one of the most honest men I've ever known, Drake. Maybe that's why I like you so much."

"Despite my annoying comments?"

"Very much *despite* those."

Drake finished the last of his chocolate, and decided against tossing his KitKat wrapper into the void. Knowing his luck, he'd trigger an ancient litter-trap.

"But no job means no ties," Kennedy went on. "I have no true friends in New York, can you believe that? Not anymore. No family. I guess I might need to disappear from the public eye, anyway."

"Well," Drake mused, "you're an enticing prospect, I can see." He gave her goofy eyes. "Maybe you could say bollocks to gay ole Paris and come visit merry old York."

"But where would I stay?"

Drake heard Dahl mustering the troops. "There's at least one place I can think of." He waited until she had climbed to her feet then caught hold of her shoulders and gazed into her sparkling eyes.

"Seriously, Kennedy, the answer to all your questions is 'Yes'. But I can't deal with that now. I have my own baggage that we should discuss, and we need to stay focused." He nodded at the void. "Down there is Alicia Myles. You might think our journey so far has been dangerous, that this tomb is dangerous, but, believe me, they're *nothing* compared to what that she can do."

"He's right." Wells came up and caught the last comment. "And I'm seeing no other way out of here, Drake. No way to avoid her."

"We can't block the route behind us because we need a way out," Drake nodded. "Yes, I've trawled through every scenario too."

"Knew you would have." Wells smiled, as if he'd known all along that Drake was still one of his boys. "C'mon, the Swede's bellowing."

Drake followed his old boss to the ledge, then took his place behind a refreshed Ben and Dahl. The professor was running on sheer excitement and probably had more energy than any of them. A final appraising glance saw everyone looking jittery about the way ahead.

"Four down," Dahl said, and shuffled away across the ledge, the mountain at his back.

The next niche was a surprise and gave them all a fortifying boost. It was the Tomb of Thor, son of Odin.

Parnevik was beside himself, suddenly filled with pure adrenalin. The professor of Nordic mythology had located the Tomb of Thor, arguably the best known Nordic figure of all time, thanks in part to Marvel comics.

Wild elation barely covered it.

And for Drake, the presence of Thor suddenly made it all real. These were the coffins of men and women who had passed into history as Gods. All powerful, all conquering, or not – these people, or their legends handed down through centuries, had elevated them beyond mortal man and turned them into worshipped, deified beings

There was a respectful silence. Everyone knew of Thor, or at least some incarnation of the Viking god of thunder and lightning. Parnevik lectured about how Vikings referred to Thorsday, or as we now know it—Thursday. This interlaced with Wednesday—what used to be Wodensday, or Odinsday. Thor was the greatest warrior-god known to man, a hammer-wielding, enemy-felling *tour de force*. The pure epitome of red-blooded Viking manhood.

It was all they could do to drag Parnevik away and stop him examining Thor's tomb there and then. The next niche, the sixth, contained Loki, the brother of Thor and another of Odin's sons.

"Trail's hotting up," Dahl said, with barely a glance inside the niche before continuing along the ledge that ended against the mountainside—a solid black mass.

Drake joined the Swede, Ben and Kennedy as they ran flashlights over the rock face.

"Footholds," Ben said. "And handholds. Looks like we're going up."

Drake craned his neck. The rock-hewn ladder ran up into infinite dark, and they would have nothing but the empty, musty air at their back.

First a test of nerve, now what? Strength? Vitality?

Again Dahl went first, Parnevik partly tethered to his back. The Swede climbed fast for twenty feet or so before seeming to slow as the blackness engulfed him. Ben chose to go next, then Kennedy.

"Guess you can watch my back now," she said with half a smile. "Make sure it doesn't go flying past you."

Drake winked. "Promise I won't take my eyes off it."

He reached for three perfect holds before moving his fourth limb. In this way he rose slowly up the sheer rock face into the volcanic air.

The rumblings continued all about them; distant complaints of the mountain. Drake imagined the magma chamber sitting not too far away, bubbling, spitting hellfire and discharging it across the walls, spewing up toward the distant blue Icelandic skies.

A foot scraped above him, slipping off its little ledge. He held himself stock still, knowing there was little he could do if someone came barreling past him, but prepared, just in case.

Kennedy's foot swayed in space about a meter above his head.

He reached out, balanced precariously, but managed to grab the sole of her boot and guide it back to its ledge. A short whisper of thanks drifted down.

On he went, fingers starting to ache in every joint. The tips of his toes bore the weight of his body for every small ascension. Sweat slicked every pore. He began to worry about Ben. The lad wouldn't be able to take much more of this.

He estimated about fifty feet of safe but terrifying hand and footholds passed before they reached the comparative safety of another ledge.

"What now?" Wells was flat out on his back, groaning. "Another bloody ledge-walk?"

"No," Dahl didn't even have the strength to make a joke. "A tunnel."

"Balls."

On their knees, they crawled forward. The tunnel led into an inky darkness that made Drake start to believe he was dreaming awake before he abruptly ran into Kennedy's stationary behind— face first.

"Ow! Could've warned me."

"Difficult when I was suffering the same fate," came back a dry voice. "Dahl was the only one who came out of that pile-up sans bruised nose, I think."

"It's my heart I worry about," Dahl called back wearily. "The tunnel finishes at the first step of another staircase that runs at a forty-five-degree angle. Nothing to left and right, at least nothing I can *see*. Prepare yourself."

"These things must be attached somewhere," Drake muttered as he crawled on bruised knees. "They can't just be suspended in mid-air."

"Maybe they can," Parnevik said. "For a *god's sake*. Ha ha. Not a bad joke, but seriously, my best guess is a series of flying buttresses."

"Hidden beneath us," Drake said. "Sure. Must've taken a hell of a workforce. Or a couple of really strong gods."

"Maybe they asked Hercules and Atlas for a hand."

Drake edged out onto the first step, the creepy feeling of vertigo invading his brain, and started to ascend the rough stone risers. It was not a grueling climb, this stage, but it did invoke a sense of lightheadedness. The group rose slowly, finally finding another niche upon a suspended platform.

Dahl met his hopeful gaze with a jaded shake of his head. "Nope, not Odin. This one's Poseidon."

"Impressive."

Drake sank again to his knees. He hoped the Germans were having it just as hard. At the end, instead of a battle maybe they could just duke it out with rock, paper, scissors.

The Greek God of the Sea carried his usual trident and a roomful of fabulous wealth. This was the seventh god they had passed. The figure nine began to gnaw at Drake's mind.

Wasn't the number nine the most sacred figure in Viking mythology?

He mentioned it to Parnevik whilst they rested.

"Yes, but this place clearly isn't just Nordic," the professor jabbed a finger at the trident-bearer behind them. "Could be a hundred of them."

"Well, we clearly aren't going to survive *a hundred* of them," Kennedy snapped. "Unless someone built a Ho-Jo's up ahead."

"Or better still, a bacon butty shop." Drake smacked his lips. "I could tackle one of those bad boys about now."

"Crusty," Ben laughed and slapped his leg. "You're about ten years out of date. But don't worry—you still have entertainment value."

It was five more minutes before they felt rested enough to continue. Wells and Marsters listened out for their pursuers, but no sounds drifted through the perennial night.

"Maybe they all fell off." Kennedy shrugged. "It could happen. If this were a Michael Bay movie, someone would have fallen by now."

"Indeed." Dahl led the way up another suspended staircase, a short one this time. As fate dictated, this was the one where Wells lost his grip and slipped two steps down, cracking his chin against stone each time.

He tasted blood at the back of his mouth.

Drake grabbed him by the shoulders of his big coat. The man below him—Marsters—gripped his thighs with superhuman strength.

"Not going anywhere, old man. Not yet."

The fifty-five-year-old was manhandled back up the staircase with Kennedy supporting Drake's back and Marsters ensuring he didn't slip any lower. By the time they reached the eighth niche, Wells was back in good humor.

"Yeah, did it on purpose, boys. Just fancied the rest."

But he clasped Marsters' arm and whispered a heartfelt thanks to Drake when no one was looking.

"No worries, old mate. Just hang in there. You haven't had your Mai-time yet."

The eighth niche was a bit of a showstopper.

"Oh, Lord." Parnevik's wonder infected them all. "It's Zeus: the Father of Man. Even gods address him as a deity—a paternal figure. This is...beyond Odin...way beyond, and that's coming from a Scandinavian."

"Wasn't Odin identified as Zeus among the early Germanic tribes?" Ben asked, clearly remembering his research.

"He was, lad." Parnevik looked thoughtful.

The King of the Gods stood high and supreme, a thunderbolt grasped in one massive hand. Inside his niche, apart from the now familiar coffin, was arrayed an abundance of glittering treasure, full to overflowing with tribute beyond anything one single man could amass today.

And then Drake heard a curse, loud, and in German. It echoed up from below.

"They've just breached the tunnel," Dahl closed his eyes in exasperation. "That puts them only fifteen minutes behind us. We have no bloody luck! Follow me!"

Another staircase beckoned, this one swinging way out and above Zeus's tomb before becoming vertical for the last ten steps. They tackled it as best they could, courage turned to ash by the creeping dark. It was as if the absence of light quashed the stuttering spirit.

Talk about vertigo, Drake thought. *Talk about your balls shrinking to the size of peanuts.* Those last ten steps, suspended above the pitch black, climbing through the crawling night, almost overwhelmed him. He had no idea how the others managed it—all he could do was review the mistakes of his past and sift through them—Alyson and the baby she'd been carrying. The baby neither of them ever saw. The SRT campaign in Iraq that screwed it all up—the one in Vienna he'd never finished. He planted every fault and blunder at the forefront of his mind to exclude the intense fear of falling. To overcome.

He put one hand above the other. One foot above the next. He pushed the others to forge ahead, verbally and physically, using every ounce of his strength. Vertically upwards he went, infinity at his back, gusts of some nameless wind tugging at his clothes. Distant thunderous roars could have been the volcano's song, but they could have been other things, too. Indescribable horrors, so ghastly they would never see the light of day. Dreadful beasts, slithering through rock, mud and muck, piping out ghastly tunes that invoked blood-red visions of madness.

Drake crawled over the last rocky step and onto a level surface. Rough stone scraped his scrabbling hands. With a last wrenching effort, he raised his head and saw everyone else sprawled out around him, but beyond them he saw Torsten Dahl—the mad Swede—literally creeping forward on his belly toward a niche larger than anything they had seen so far.

The mad Swede. But the guy was beyond good. He was a bloody hero. He had practically carried Parnevik the whole way.

The niche was suspended on one side but attached to the heart of the mountain on the other.

"*Thank you,*" Dahl said weakly. "It's Odin. We've found the Tomb of Odin."

He could only smile as Parnevik found yet another new lease of life.

THIRTY-EIGHT

THE TOMB OF THE GODS

A masculine cry shot through his torpor.

No, a scream. A bloodcurdling wail that spoke of pure horror. Drake opened his eyes—they'd only been closed a second—but the rock surface was too close to focus on. He groaned, continuing to lie there and get his breath back.

And found himself thinking: *How far would a man fall down a bottomless cavern before he died?*

The Germans were here. One of their brethren must have just fallen off the staircase.

Drake struggled upright, every muscle sore, but feeling the adrenalin firing his blood and clearing his thoughts. He inched toward Ben, who was lying prone near one of the platform's edges. Drake dragged him into Odin's niche. A brief glance back told him the Germans hadn't arrived yet, but his ears told him they were mere minutes away.

He heard Abel Frey's cursing. The clunk of safety gear. Milo shouting bloody murder at one of the soldiers.

A chance to show your mettle, he thought. It was something Wells used to say on the toughest days in boot camp.

He dragged Ben around, propping him with his back against Odin's sizeable sarcophagus. The boy's eyelids were fluttering. Kennedy stumbled over. "You get ready for the fight. I'll sort him." She slapped his cheek lightly.

Drake lingered, meeting her eyes for one brief second. "Later."

The first of the Germans came over the top. A soldier that promptly collapsed in exhaustion, followed immediately by a second. Drake hesitated to do what he knew should be done, but Torsten Dahl shot past him, exhibiting no such qualms. Wells and Marsters were shuffling forward too.

A third enemy combatant crawled over the top, this one a great shambling hulk of a man. Milo. Blood, sweat and real tears made a grotesque mask of his already alarming face. But he was tough and quick enough to heave himself over the top, roll, and raise a tiny handgun.

One shot exploded out of the barrel. Drake and his colleagues instinctively ducked, but the bullet flew wide.

The shrieking voice of Abel Frey shattered the stillness that followed the discharge. "*No guns, Dumbkopf. Narr! Narr! Listen to me!*"

Milo screwed his face up and sent a nasty smile at Drake. "What an asshole, hey, buddy?"

The gun was swallowed by an oversized fist and replaced by a serrated blade. Drake recognized it as a Special Forces knife. He sidestepped around the big man, giving Dahl the opportunity to kick one of the fallen soldiers off into space.

The second German fell to his knees. Marsters sliced him a new smile then threw the limp body to the side. By now three more had gained the platform, dragging themselves over the top, and then Alicia sprang up from below to land in a poised crouch, a knife in each hand. She was the most drained Drake had ever seen her, and she still looked like she could take on the Ninja elite.

"No guns you say?" Dahl managed between forced breaths. "You finally believe the Armageddon theory, Frey?"

The big German designer had hauled himself over the edge. "Don't be a fool, soldier boy," he panted. "There is no ancient Armageddon. But a prize like Odin's tomb should be unspoiled. My collection has room for excellence only."

"Which you see as a reflection of yourself, I assume," said Dahl, stalling whilst his team got their breath back.

Frey snorted. "I once heard perfection was in the eye of the beholder. What a load of claptrap. Perfection is created by *power.*"

Dahl made a face. "You have an odd view of the world."

"But a true one. I *own* my view. I created it. I enhance it."

Drake backed away from Milo. "Really? With all those crappy dress designs? Don't think so, man."

Frey looked grim. "You are a fool if you believe that I sully my hands with the fashion industry, save for appearances. I own people to do that. But it is time to stop stalling. And time—" he grinned without humor. "To die."

There was a pause as the men assessed each other. Drake backed away a little more from Milo, moving unwittingly toward Odin's tomb where Ben and the professor still sat side by side, guarded only by Kennedy. He was waiting for one more...

...hoping ...

And then a shattered groan came from the staircase, a faint plea for help. Frey glanced down. "*You left her?*" he spat at Alicia. "Down there with the shield? Are you dumb as well as crazy, Myles?"

Alicia's eyes flashed with deadly intent. "What did you say?" But then her greater need got the better of her and she turned back to the edge of the platform. "Jeez, girl, I help you with that thing all the way here and you can't even carry it the last few yards? What kinda pack-donkey are ya?"

Frey looked like he was going into shock. "Help her. *Help her. Watch* her. She can't be trusted without you at her back and she can't do it alone. The shield is the principal piece!"

The warrior woman grunted haughtily, then extended a hand over the side. With one tug she hauled Hayden over the top. The American CIA agent was spent from the long climb, but even more so from carrying the heavy weight the Germans had strapped to her back.

The Shield of Odin, wrapped in canvas.

Parnevik's voice rang out. "He brought the shield here! But why?"

"*Because* it's the principal piece of the Nine, you idiot." Frey fired at him. "And forged with some unknown element. It is both map and weapon. Why on earth would I *not* bring it?" The maniac shook his head in disdain and turned to Alicia. "Finish these pathetic cretins. I have Odin to appease, and a party to get back to."

Alicia laughed maniacally. *"My turn!"* she cried, and threw her safety gear into the middle of the rocky dais. Amidst the distraction she leapt for Wells, showing no surprise at his presence. Drake focused on his own fight, lunging at Milo and sidestepping a deft swipe of the blade, then jabbing in with a hard elbow to Milo's jaw.

Bone cracked. Drake danced away, swaying and staying light on his feet. This would be his strategy then, hit and run, striking with the hardest points of his body, aiming to break bone and cartilage. He was faster than Milo, but not as strong, so if the giant caught up with him...

Thunder echoed through the mountain, the growl and crash of rising magma and shifting stone.

Milo winced in agony. Drake led with a double side-kick, two taps—the sort of thing you might see Van Damme deftly execute on the TV—absolutely useless for real life street-fighting. Milo knew that, and batted the attack aside with a snarl. But Drake knew it too, and when Milo launched his bulk forward, Drake threw another solid elbow strike into his opponent's face, devastating his nose and eye socket, knocking him solidly to the floor.

Milo hit the ground like a felled rhino. Once down against an opponent of Drake's caliber there was no way back. Drake stamped on his wrist and knee, breaking both major bones, and then scooped up the discarded army knife.

He surveyed the scene as best he could, squinting by the glow of the flashlights.

Marsters, the SAS soldier, had made short work of two Germans and was now struggling with the third. To neutralize three men in a few minutes was a tall order for anyone, even an SAS soldier, and Marsters was carrying a minor injury. Wells was dancing with Alicia along the rim of the platform, more *running* than dancing actually, but keeping her busy. His strategy was sound. At close quarters she'd gut him in a second.

Kennedy was dragging Hayden's tired body away from the center of battle. Ben had run to her aid. Parnevik was studying Odin's tomb, showing a shocking lack of interest in his or anyone else's welfare.

Abel Frey had confronted Torsten Dahl. *Not the best move,* Drake thought, but then the German certainly appeared to have an inflated view of his own prowess. The Swede was besting the German in every way, his movements becoming smarter by the second as strength returned to his aching limbs.

Good, Drake thought. They were easily on top.

Not relishing a confrontation with Alicia, he nevertheless moved toward Wells. Despite his train, the fifty-five-year-old needed the most help. When his old teammate clapped eyes on Drake, she stood back from the fight.

"Destroyed you once already this week, Drake. You that much of a sadist you want it again?"

"You got lucky, Alicia. By the way, you train your boyfriend?" he nodded back at Milo, who was barely moving where Drake had left him.

"Only in obedience." She flipped both knives up and caught them in a single motion. "Come on! I just love me a threesome!"

Her nature might have been wild, but her actions were, as always, controlled and calculating. She jabbed at Drake whilst slyly trying to push Wells back again toward an endless void. Wells saw her intentions at the last possible second and hurled himself away.

Drake fended off both her knives, turning each blade to the side and trying not to get his wrists broken or slashed in the process. It wasn't just that she was good...it was that she was *consistently* good.

Abel Frey suddenly shot past them. It seemed that, unable to best Dahl, he had resorted to sprinting past the Swede in his headlong quest for Odin's tomb.

And in that split second, Drake saw Marsters and the last German soldier locked in a deadly struggle on the very edge of the platform. Then, with shocking abruptness, both men stumbled and fell off.

Dying screams echoed into the void.

Drake compartmentalized it, said a prayer for the man, and then swept his body around and took off after Frey. He couldn't leave Ben exposed back there. Kennedy was blocking the designer's path, steeling herself, but as he sprinted forward

Drake noticed a small black object clasped in Frey's hand.

Radio or cellphone. Some kind of transmitter. He screamed: "Do you have my signal? Then, yes, do it now. *Do it now!*"

What the—?

It was beyond comprehension what happened next. In an event of mind-boggling recklessness the side of the mountain suddenly *imploded*. There was a heavy *whump* and then giant boulders and chunks of rocky shale blasted in all directions. Stones of every shape and size cracked and shot across the void like bullets.

A great hole appeared in the side of the volcano, as if a hammer had smashed through thin plasterboard. Drab daylight shone through the gap. Another *whump* and the hole widened even further. A hail of rubble cascaded down into the bottomless pit in an eerie, profound silence.

Drake hit the floor, holding his head in his hands. Some of that detonated rock smashed into Odin's tomb and was bound to have damaged the other priceless tombs. *What's Frey doing?*

THIRTY-NINE

THE TOMB OF THE GODS

A chopper appeared in the newly made hole, hovering cautiously for a second before flying through.

Four heavy rappel lines already dangled from the base of the helicopter.

It beggared belief. Abel Frey had ordered the cracking of a mountainside. A mountainside that was part of an active volcano.

To enhance his *collection*.

Drake didn't have to wonder how he'd chosen the right point to break through. Devices were available not only to the military but also through the Internet—devices like the SASW-G, a spectral analyzer of surface waves, designed to measure the wave velocity of rock without the need for a borehole. Choose the best point of entry by following a transmitter attached to Frey, make the calculation and employ explosives.

The man was deranged. He was laughing maniacally even now. When Drake raised his eyes, he saw Frey had not moved an inch, but stood solidly upright as debris from the exploding mountain fizzed around him.

Safe in his tyrannical cocoon, believing in his madness that somehow, he was protected.

Alicia left Wells and stumbled to Frey's side, even her crazy composure having slipped a little. Beyond them Professor Parnevik, Ben and Kennedy had been shielded by the walls of Odin's niche. Hayden was flat out, motionless. Had she come all this way to die in fiery madness? Wells knelt to one side, clutching his stomach.

The helicopter drifted closer, its motor screaming. Frey raised a machine pistol and gestured everyone back from Odin's massive sarcophagus. Drake didn't have to wonder why he hadn't used it before now. The man's obsession had unhinged him. He delighted in the madness, the power of being able to change the rules on a whim. Before Drake could even think about calling Frey's bluff and making his people stay in the niche—knowing Frey's fear that bullets might damage Odin's tomb—they had moved clear. A brief flurry reinforced Frey's request, bullets firing wide of priceless gold Viking relics in the form of shields, swords, breastplates and horned helmets. Gold coins, no doubt shifted by Parnevik and the mountain's rumblings, began to rain down from the shelves like Times Square confetti.

Frey waved the chopper in.

Drake got to his knees. "You move that coffin, you risk destroying the tomb!" he screamed, his voice barely audible above the heavy thud of rotor blades.

"Don't be a wimp! The coffin holds the bones of *Odin*. It is everything," Frey shouted back, his face twisted out of shape by a reckless glee. "Admit it, Drake. I beat you!"

"It's not about winning!" Drake cried back, but now the chopper was directly overhead and he could barely hear himself speak. He watched as Frey guided it in, accidentally spraying bullets as he waved his hands. Drake prayed that his friends didn't catch a stray round.

The German had lost it. Being this close to his lifelong obsession, finally, had unhinged him.

Dahl was now beside Drake. They watched Frey and Alicia guide the heavy chains lower until they could loop them around both ends of the sarcophagus. Alicia made sure they were secure.

The helicopter took the weight. Nothing happened.

Frey shrieked into his handset. The helicopter tried to lift the coffin again, this time its engines roaring like an infuriated dinosaur. The chains tightened and there was a distinct cracking sound, the noise of rock being sundered and shattered.

Odin's coffin shifted.

"This is our last chance!" Dahl screamed into Drake's ear. *"Slim as it is, we grab Milo's gun and go for the chopper."*

The Swede leapt for Milo's weapon. Drake leapfrogged forward just as Dahl began rummaging through Milo's clothing. In the next second, the Swede stumbled back in surprise as Milo launched his body upright, the American hunched over in agony but mobile, and starting to limp toward the edge of the platform and one of the rappel lines.

Drake paused in shock. The helicopter's engines shrieked once more and the dreadful crack of fracturing rock filled the cavern. In another moment, Odin's outsize sarcophagus shifted and pulled free of its moorings, swinging untold tons of crushing death alarmingly in Drake's direction.

"*Noooo,*" Dahl's cry echoed Parnevik's.

There was a shriek, a crazy shriek like a vent hole being superheated, a sound like all the demons in hell being burned alive. From the newly uncovered hole beneath Odin's sarcophagus a narrow blast of sulfuric air shot up. An astonishing heat filled the cavern.

"Shit!" Drake cried and rolled away. "Take cover."

Frey and Alicia lunged aside, narrowly missing being burned alive as they clambered atop the swinging coffin. Frey shouted, "Do not come after us, Drake! I have insurance!" Then the German seemed to get an idea, a vouchsafe of security. He shouted at Drake's companions, "Now! *Follow the coffin or you die!*" Frey encouraged them by waving his machine pistol. They had no choice but to edge around the column of steam.

Dahl turned his haunted eyes on Drake. "We have to stop him," he said. "For...for our friends."

Drake nodded. Of course. He followed the SGG commander, carefully skirting the swinging sarcophagus that now passed above them, their grinning enemies safely on top and his companions following its trajectory from the other side.

They were covered by the weapon and the whim of a maniac. The only reason Frey hadn't shot them yet was because he'd seen the fury unleashed by the uncovering of the vent hole.

Drake reached the rent in the rock floor. The steam was a scalding, writhing tower. Untouchable. Drake closed in as far as he could before turning around to watch their enemies' progress.

Hayden had stayed flat out on the ground, obviously feigning unconsciousness for she now sat up and shrugged out of the straps that secured Odin's Shield to her back. "What can I do?"

Drake gave her a momentary glance. "Have the FBI got any contingency plans to shut down a volcano?"

The FBI liaison looked momentarily abashed before shaking her head. "Only the obvious. Stick a crazy German down the vent pipe." She flung off the shield with a cry of relief. All three of them watched it roll on its rim like a noisy coin. "You surely don't think this could start an eruption?"

"Of course not, but it could end up bloody melting us."

The pressure escaping from the pipe increased. Hayden, looking none the worse for wear after her rough stint in enemy hands, stared at the steam vent as if it might eat her alive.

Then, with a sound like a herd of animals trapped in a burning forest, another steam vent spewed forth from below, the piercing shriek of its eruption almost deafening. The sulfuric stench thickened the air around them, turning it into a toxic miasma. Drake and his two companions doubled over, coughing. For a long moment they could only gasp for air. The mountain's faint rumblings, for so long their constant companion, were becoming more like thunder. To Drake, struggling to stand, it seemed like the very walls were shaking.

"Newsflash," he said. "Plan B is now in effect. For future reference that means I don't know what the hell else to do."

Drake finally turned his attention back to Frey. As he did so, horror filled his heart beyond anything he could imagine, even now.

The chopper was rising, straining to lift Odin's weighty coffin which swung gently beneath it. Both Frey and Alicia sat atop the coffin, hands wrapped firmly around the harness that secured it to the helicopter.

Ben, Kennedy, and Professor Parnevik were strapped tightly to three of the other rappel lines that dangled beneath the chopper, no doubt coerced there at gun point whilst Drake, and Hayden had been felled by the steam vents.

They were hanging over the void, swaying as the helicopter rose, being kidnapped right from under Drake's nose.

"*Nooooo!*"

He ran—a lone man, sprinting with an energy born of rage and loss and love—a man who launched himself out over the bottomless pit and into black space, shouting for what was being taken away from him and grasping desperately for one of the swinging lines as he fell.

FORTY

THE TOMB OF THE GODS

Drake's world stopped as he leapt into the dark—a three-inch-thick piece of swinging rope his only goal.

His fingers brushed the rope and *failed to close.*

His body, at last affected by gravity, began to plummet. At the last second, his flailing left hand closed over a rope that dangled below the others and gripped with reflexive venom.

His fall arrested, his shoulder muscles on fire, he grasped the rope with both hands and closed his eyes to still his rapidly beating heart. From somewhere above came raucous applause. Alicia venting her sarcasm.

"Is that what Wells used to mean by *show your mettle?* Always wondered what that crazy fossil meant."

Drake looked up, acutely aware of the pit beckoning hungrily below, feeling a wash of vertigo like never before. But his muscles were powered by new-found purpose and adrenalin, and most of the old fire was back in him now, desperate to be unleashed.

He climbed the rope, hand above hand, gripping it with his knees, moving fast. Frey waved his machine pistol, laughing as he took careful aim, but then Hayden gave a despairing shout. Drake saw her standing near Odin's tomb, aiming Wells's gun at Frey—the old commander slumped next to her, but still breathing.

Hayden gestured with the gun. "Let him climb!"

The chopper was still hovering, its pilot unsure of his orders. Frey hesitated, caught in a stand-off, snarling—a child parted from its favorite toy. "Okay. *Hündin!* I should have dropped you out of the plane!"

Drake smirked when he heard Hayden's reply. "Yeah, I get that a lot."

Kennedy, Ben, and Parnevik were staring wide-eyed at the proceedings, hardly daring to draw breath.

"Go get him!" Frey then screamed at Alicia. "Hand to hand. Get him and let's go. The woman won't shoot you. She's *government issue.*"

Drake carefully watched Alicia leap off the sarcophagus and catch hold of a parallel rope to Drake's. Alicia scooted down the rope like a monkey, soon level with Drake. She faced him, perfect face full of malice.

"I *can* swing both ways." She leapt into the air, feet first, drawing a graceful arch in the gloom, totally airborne for a moment. Then her feet connected solidly with Drake's breastbone and she whiplashed her body forward, briefly grabbing his rope before swinging to the next.

"Fuckin' *baboon,*" Drake muttered, his chest on fire, his grip weakened.

Alicia used her momentum to swing around the rope, legs out, and crashed into his belly. Drake managed to swing to the right to lessen the blow, but still felt the harsh stab of pain in his ribs.

He snarled at her, compartmentalized the hurt, and climbed higher. A glint entered her eyes, along with a new respect.

"At last," she breathed. "You're back. Now we'll see who's best."

She shuffled up the rope, confidence radiating from her every move. With a single leap she bypassed Drake's own rope, grabbed another, and again used her momentum to come back on the return swing, legs aiming this time for his head.

But Drake was ready. With supreme skill he let go of his rope, ignoring the intense vertigo, and caught it two feet further down. Alicia sailed by harmlessly above him, stunned by his move, still flailing.

Drake leapt up the rope a foot at a time. By the time his adversary realized what he had done he was above her. He stomped hard on her head.

He saw her fingers let go of the rope. She fell, but only a few inches. The hard nut within her kicked in and she regained her grip.

Frey bellowed from above. "No good! Die, you stupid English unbeliever!" In less than a heartbeat, the German whipped out a knife and sliced through Drake's rope.

Drake saw it all in slow motion. The glint of the blade, the wicked shine of the cutting edge. The sudden unravelling of his lifeline—the way it started to bulge and wriggle above him.

The immediate weightlessness of his body. The frozen instant of terror and disbelief. The knowledge that everything he had ever felt and everything his future held had just been eradicated.

And then the fall...seeing Alicia, climbing hand over fist to get back on top of the sarcophagus...seeing Ben's mouth twist into a scream...Kennedy's face turning into a death mask...and through his peripheral vision...Dahl...what the...?

Torsten Dahl, the mad Swede, sprinted across the platform, one of the safety harnesses strapped to his body, then literally *launched* himself out into the black pit just as Drake himself had done a few minutes before.

The safety harness unraveled behind the Swede, anchored and wrapped several times around a pillar in Odin's niche and also held tightly by Hayden. Dahl's crazy dive...down and down...brought him close enough to grab Drake's arms and grasp them tightly.

Drake's rush of hope was quashed as both he and Dahl now fell together, safety line playing out...time stopped and anticipation became an agony of suspense...then came the sudden, painful jerk as the pillar took most of the strain and Hayden tried to hang on. Drake was almost torn from Dahl's hands but the strong Swede managed to hold on.

Then the hoping. The slow, painful heaves of rescue. Drake watched Dahl's eyes, not speaking, not emitting an ounce of emotion as he climbed up the man's body and then grasped the taut rope above, helped the Swede get his own hands up and then climbed inch by inch to safety.

The chopper pilot must have received panicked orders, for he began to rise quickly until he was ready to fire a third missile, this one out of the mountain, designed to widen the gap enough to fit the sarcophagus through without risking it being damaged. Drake imagined it was also the reason Frey wasn't hanging around and trying to finish them off. Retrieving Odin's sarcophagus trumped everything in the fanatic's mind.

Within three minutes Odin's coffin was gone. The chopper's thudding rotor blades a distant memory. As were Ben, Kennedy, and Parnevik.

At last, Dahl and Drake dragged themselves over the rocky edges of the precipice. Drake wanted to rush off in pursuit, but his body wouldn't respond. It was all he could do to lie there, absorbing the trauma, rerouting the pain to a cordoned off part of his brain.

And as he lay there, he heard the sound of rotary blades approaching. Was the chopper returning? No, this was the same chopper that had brought them here. And it was both their means of rescue and pursuit.

Drake could only stare into Torsten Dahl's exhausted eyes. "You are a *god,* mate." The significance of the place they were in was not lost on him. "A true god."

FORTY-ONE

GERMANY

Every time Kennedy Moore so much as shifted in her hard seat, Alicia Myles gave her a fierce glare. The Englishwoman was an uber-warrior blessed with a cop's sixth sense of suspicion.

They had stopped only once during the three-hour flight from Iceland to Germany. Early on, only a few minutes after they'd exited the volcano, they had winched up and steadied the coffin, and brought everyone on board.

Abel Frey had immediately retired to a rear compartment. She had not seen him since. The madman was probably greasing the wheels of theft and industry. Alicia had practically thrown Kennedy, Ben and Parnevik into their seats, then perched next to her boyfriend, the injured Milo. The chunky American seemed to be clutching every part of his body, but chiefly his balls, a fact Alicia seemed to find alternately amusing and worrying.

Three other guards also sat inside the chopper, flicking their watchful eyes between the captives and the odd companionship that existed between Alicia and Milo— which, in turns, was sad and then brimming with fury.

Kennedy had no clear idea where they were when the chopper began to descend. Her thoughts had drifted during the last hour—from Drake and their adventures in Paris and Sweden, to her old life at the NYPD which she had loved, but which got in the way of every relationship she'd ever tried to start. There was a time when she'd accepted her future was going to be a twelve-hour day followed by a microwave meal and a bottle of red wine, and that hadn't worried her too much. She could have lived with that. The everyday good deeds she did more than made up for a vacuous life. But she always returned to Thomas Kaleb—the serial killer she had set free. Memories of his victims assailed her. The crime scene she had walked a few days ago—*his* crime scene—remained as fresh in her memory as newly spilled blood. She realized she hadn't seen a news report since.

Maybe they had caught him.

Don't even dare to dream...

No. In her dreams they never caught him, never even got close. He killed again and again, taunted her. And guilt rode her like an avenging demon until she gave it all up. From a woman content, she had become a woman possessed simply because she'd tried to do the right thing. The good and bad of it all ate at her soul, tearing it apart strip by strip. The only salvation was this adventure she'd become a part of, and that only because it stopped her from dwelling on what she couldn't help but think were her sins, not Kaleb's.

But that wasn't quite true, she thought. Now there was Drake...could his open desire to help everyone he met save her soul?

The chopper dropped fast, yanking her out of a vision she couldn't bear to face. The private compartment at the rear opened and Abel Frey strode out, issuing orders.

"Alicia, Milo, with me. Bring the prisoners. Guards, you will accompany the sarcophagus to my viewing room. The custodian there has instructions to contact me as soon as it's prepared. Odin may have awaited Frey for thousands of years, but Frey doesn't wait for Odin."

"What do you expect to find in there?" Kennedy asked. "A man? A god?"

"In truth, the bones of a man long revered. The bones of a man who, at one time, performed deeds so great that his people worshipped him. But it doesn't matter. The sarcophagus is mine now, just mine. Forever more."

"The whole world knows what you've done," Kennedy said. "Fashion designer, my ass. Even if you were, you never will be again. How long do you think you'll stay out of jail?"

"American self-importance," Frey snapped, "and stupidity

makes you believe you can speak out loud, hmm? The superior mind always triumphs. Do you really think your friends made it out? We set traps in there, idiot. They won't make it back past Poseidon." He motioned violently toward Alicia. "Please hurt her for me."

Alicia leaned in immediately, face so close their noses were practically touching. A surprising whisper crossed her lips as they almost brushed Kennedy's.

"Scream now."

Kennedy complied, unhurt, wondering what on earth had gotten into the zany Englishwoman. Remorse? A change of heart? Only Drake would be able to figure that one out.

Kennedy opened her mouth to protest again, but noticed Ben's brief headshake. *Survive first, fight later.* She silently quoted Vanna Bonta—*I would rather have an inferiority complex and be pleasantly surprised, than have a superiority complex and be rudely awakened.*

Frey couldn't possibly know their own chopper had remained hidden at a higher altitude whilst they'd searched the tomb. And pride reassured him that his intellect trumped theirs.

Let him think that way. The surprise would be all the sweeter.

The chopper landed with a jolt. Frey marched forward and jumped off first, shouting orders at men on the ground. Alicia rose and made a motion with her forefinger. "You three first. Heads down. Keep moving till I say otherwise."

Kennedy exited the chopper behind Ben, feeling the ache of exhaustion deep in every muscle. What she saw outside made her forget her tiredness for a minute, in fact it took her breath away.

This was clearly Frey's German chateau; the designer's den of iniquity, where the entertainment never stopped. Their landing pad faced the main entrance—double oak doors inlaid with gold studs were framed by Italian marble pillars that led into a grand entrance hall. As Kennedy watched, two expensive cars rolled up, a white Lamborghini and a red Maserati, from which four ecstatic twenty-somethings rolled out and tottered up the steps into the chateau. The heavy beats of dance music drifted through the door.

Above them, a wide stone-clad facade was topped by a row of triangular crenulations, and two taller towers to either end, giving the vast structure the whole Gothic Revival appearance. *Imposing,* Kennedy thought, and a little stunning. She fancied being invited to a party at this place would be an upcoming model's dream.

And Abel Frey preyed on dreams.

Someone shoved her towards the doors. Alicia watched the guests carefully as they bypassed the burbling supercars and walked up the marble steps, through the doors and into an echoing entry hall. To the left, a leather-bound gate led into a nightclub complete with upbeat music, multi-colored lights, and cubicles that swayed above the crowd where one could prove how well one could dance. Kennedy stopped immediately and screamed.

"Help!" she cried, staring straight at the patrons of the club. "Help us!"

Several people took a moment to lower their half-full glasses and stare. After a second they began to laugh. A classic Swedish blonde raised her bottle in the universal *cheers* sign; a dark-skinned Italian male gave her the eye. The rest went back to their disco inferno.

Kennedy groaned as Alicia grabbed her hair and dragged her across the marble floor. Ben cried out in protest, but a slap to the face almost felled him. More laughter rang out from the party guests amidst several bawdy comments. Alicia flung Kennedy against the great staircase so that she banged her ribs, hard.

"Stupid," she hissed. "Can you not see they are enamored of their host? And that they're high? They will never think badly of him. Now...walk."

She gestured upwards with the small gun that had appeared in her hand. Kennedy considered resisting but, after what had just happened, decided to roll with it. Up the stairs they marched, toward another wing of the chateau. Once they left the staircase and stepped into a long, unfurnished corridor—a bridge between wings—the dance music died down and they could have been the only people in residence.

Beyond the corridor, they were marched into what might once

have been a spacious ballroom. But now the area had been divided up into half a dozen separate rooms—rooms with bars on the outside instead of walls and doors.

Cells.

Kennedy, Ben and Parnevik were hustled into the nearest. A loud clang signified the closing of the door. Alicia pointed to the ceiling. "You *are* being watched. Enjoy."

In the resounding silence that followed, Kennedy ran her fingers through her long black hair, smoothed out her pantsuit as best she could and took a deep breath. None of this was easing her conscience.

"Well—" she started to say.

"Hey, *kids!*" Abel Frey appeared at the front of their cell, grinning like the god of hellfire. "Welcome to my party chateau. I somehow doubt you'll enjoy the experience quite as much as my more affluent guests. Especially you." He smirked at Kennedy.

He waved his own remark away before they could respond. "Don't bother speaking. Your words hold little interest for me. So," he made a pretend pondering gesture, "who do we have? Well, yes, of course, there's Ben Blake. The pleasure's all yours, I'm sure."

Ben ran to the bars and wrenched at them as hard as he could. "Where's my sister, you bastard?"

"You mean the feisty blonde with the—" he kicked out a leg wildly. "*Enter the Dragon* fighting style? You want details? Let me explain—she met her match."

Frey took a moment to fish a remote control out of a pocket of the silk dressing gown he had quickly changed into. He flicked it toward a portable TV Kennedy hadn't even noticed. The picture came on—a music channel.

Ben emitted a guttural sound deep from his belly. "Is she okay? *Is she okay?*"

Frey flicked the remote again. The screen switched to another, grainier image. Kennedy realized she was looking at a tiny room. There was a girl with short-cropped blond hair lying despondently on the bed.

"What do you think?" Frey goaded. "She's alive. For now."

"Karin!" Ben ran toward the TV, but then stopped, suddenly

overcome. Sobs wracked his entire body.

Frey laughed. "What more do you want?" He made another show of thinking, and then switched the channel again, this time to CNN. Immediately, a news report of the New York City serial killer—Thomas Kaleb—appeared on the screen.

"Recorded this for you earlier," the madman said to Kennedy with glee. "Thought you'd like to watch."

She felt her body go rigid, but listened despite herself, heard the dreaded news that Kaleb continued to stalk the New York streets, emancipated, a ghost.

"I believe you liberated him," Frey said pointedly at Kennedy's back. "Nice going. The predator is back where he belongs, in the wild, no longer a caged animal in a city zoo."

The report flicked back over archive footage of the case— standard stuff—her face, the dirty cop's face, the victims' faces. Always the victims' faces.

The same ones that haunted her nightmares every day.

"Bet you know all their names don't you?" Frey taunted. "Their families' addresses. The way they died."

"*Shut up!*" Kennedy held her head in her hands. *Shut it out! Please!*

"And you," she heard Frey whisper, "Professor Parnevik." He spat out the words as if they were bad meat caught between his teeth. "You should have stayed with me."

A gunshot rang out. Kennedy screamed in shock. The next second she heard a body collapse and turned to see the old man hit the ground, a hole blown through his chest. Blood seeped across the floor.

Her mouth dropped open, disbelief shutting down her brain. She could only stare as Frey turned to her one more time.

"Kennedy Moore, your time is coming. We will soon explore the depths to which *you* are capable of sinking."

With a turn of heel and a grin, he was gone.

FORTY-TWO

LA VEREIN, GERMANY

Abel Frey chuckled to himself as he headed for his private quarters. An inventive few moments and he'd trodden those idiots into the ground. Broken both of them and finally killed that old fool Parnevik stone dead.

Wonderful. Now to even more pleasurable pursuits.

He opened the door to his private quarters and found both Milo and Alicia sprawled out on his sofa, just the way he'd left them. The big American was still carrying an injury, wincing with every movement, courtesy of Matt Drake.

"Any news from next door?" Frey asked immediately. "Has Hudson called?"

Next door was the CCTV control center, currently being overseen by one of Frey's more radical cohorts—Tim Hudson. Known about the chateau as "Mainframe Man" for his extensive computer expertise, Hudson had been one of Frey's earliest disciples, willing to go to any extremes for his fanatical boss. They were monitoring progress of the installation of Odin's sarcophagus, with Hudson at the helm. Frey was eager to see the sarcophagus set in its rightful place for his initial visit. Part of the CCTV was also being used to survey Karin's quarters, and the cells of his new inmates.

And the party of course. Hudson had designed a system that put every inch of the club under some kind of scrutiny, be it infra-red or standard feed, and every action of Frey's elite guests was being recorded and examined for its weight in leverage.

*

He had come to realize that knowledge was not power after all. Power was actually hard proof. The discreet photograph. The HD video. Entrapment might be illegal, but if the victim was sufficiently terrified then the legality of anything was but an irrelevant obstacle.

Abel Frey could engineer a "date night" with a starlet or a rock-chick any time he chose. He could acquire a "lost" painting or a sculpture from its unscrupulous owner, obtain front row seats to the hottest show in the glitziest town at a moment's notice, attain the unattainable, whenever the whim took him.

"Nothing yet from Hudson," Alicia said, lounging with her head propped on her hands and her legs draped over the edge of his sofa.

Frey watched Milo groan and hold his ribs. He felt a jolt of electricity raise his heart rate as he saw Alicia raise an eyebrow and the delicious idea of lust and danger mingled in his mind.

Alicia swung her legs down. "On second thoughts, Milo, why don't you go check again? And get a full report from Hudson, hmm? Boss" –she nodded at a silver platter of nibbles– "fancy something?"

Frey studied the plate as Milo sent a pretend glare at his girlfriend then groaned and limped out of the room.

Frey said, "Biscotti looks good."

No sooner had the door clicked into place than Alicia handed the plate of biscuits to Frey and climbed up on his desk.

"Want some fine English ass with that?"

Frey flicked the secret button under his desk. Immediately, a fake painting slid aside to reveal a bank of video screens. He said "Six" and one of the screens flashed into life.

"My battle arena," he breathed. "It's already prepared for what's to come. Yes?"

Alicia wriggled seductively. "Yes."

Frey felt a different kind of excitement. "Then I have about ten minutes. It will have to be quick."

"Story of my life."

Frey turned his attention to her, always aware of Milo only twenty feet away behind an unlocked door, but even with that, and the sensual presence of Alicia Myles, he still found it hard to tear his eyes away from the lavish cell that housed one of his newly acquired captives.

The serial killer—Thomas Kaleb, located through the New York criminal network system and apparently happy to help.

The ultimate face-off between the serial killer and the New York cop who had arrested him was imminent.

FORTY-THREE

LA VEREIN, GERMANY

Kennedy rattled the bars when Abel Frey and his guards appeared outside. She screamed at them to remove the professor's body and let them go free, then felt a rush of trepidation when they did just that.

She stopped outside the cell. One of the guards gestured with his gun, making it clear where she was to go. They walked deeper into the prison complex, past several more unoccupied cells. Though it was empty, the scope of it all chilled her to the bone. She wondered what terrible crimes Frey was capable of perpetrating.

It was then she understood he might be worse than Kaleb. Worse than all of them. She hoped Drake, Dahl and a backup army were closing in, but she had to face the fact that they may be on their own. How could she hope to protect Ben as Drake had? The young lad trailed along at her side. He'd barely spoken a word since Parnevik had died. In fact, he'd spoken only a few words since they'd fled the tomb.

Had he lost all hope of saving Karin? Kennedy had always been good at gauging people. She could identify the man who would try to flee the scene from the man who wouldn't hesitate to fire first. She knew how to read the man who held dreadful secrets, the woman who protected him. But Ben Blake—he was a tough one. Probably because he was still changing, developing. Would his plight make him or break him? One thing she knew for certain, his cellphone still sat safely in his pocket, switched to vibrate.

"We're actually in the right place now," Kennedy whispered out of the side of her mouth. "Believe it or not. Keep your wits about you and think of Karin."

"Shut up!" Frey spat. "You should worry about your own fate, Miss Moore."

Kennedy sent him a fleeting look. "What's that supposed to mean? You gonna make me wear one of your designer gowns?"

The German raised an eyebrow. "We'll see how long you stay feisty."

Beyond the cell complex they entered another, far dingier section of the house. They were angling sharply downward now, the rooms and corridors in disrepair. Knowing Frey as she did, though, the shabbiness was likely purposeful misdirection to help ward snoopers off.

They traveled along a final corridor and stopped outside an arched door with shiny metal straps across its hinges. One of the guards keyed in an eight-figure number on a wireless keypad and the heavy doors creaked open.

Kennedy saw a chest-high metal rail encircling the room within. About thirty to forty people stood around the rail, drinks in hand, laughing. Playboys and drug barons, high-class male and female prostitutes, royalty and Fortune 500 chairmen. Widows with vast inheritance money, oil-rich sheiks and millionaires' daughters, visiting or holidaying at the party chateau. In a way, their presence was good. The authorities outside would be more than interested in their illicit pastimes.

These people didn't simply stand against the barrier, they *adorned* it, sipping their Bollinger and *Romanee Conti*, nibbling their delicacies and exuding their culture and class.

When Kennedy walked in, they all turned to stare. Were they evaluating her? Whispers ran around the dusty walls and prickled across her ears.

That's her? The cop?

He's going to annihilate her in, oh, four minutes, tops.

I'll take that and raise you ten thousand, Zak. What do you say?

Seven minutes. I wager she's stronger than she looks. And, well, she'll be a mite pissed don't you think?

A refined laugh. *Mr. Block, you have a good point.*

What the hell were they talking about?

Kennedy felt a rude kick to her back and stumbled into the room. The assemblage laughed. Frey glided after her.

"*People!*" He laughed. "*My friends!* This is one fine offering, don't you think? And she's going to give us one fine night!"

Kennedy stared around, intimidated despite herself. What the hell were they talking about? *Stay prickly,* she remembered Captain Lipkind's favorite saying. Stay on your game. She tried to focus, but the shock and the surreal surroundings threatened to undo her.

"I won't *perform* for you," she muttered at Frey's back. "In any way."

Frey turned to her and his knowing smile was startling. "Won't you? For something *precious?* I think you overestimate yourself, and your kind. But I *really* think you will, dear Kennedy." He gestured her forward.

Kennedy stepped to the circular rail. About twelve feet below her was a rough, circular pit, dug unevenly out of the earth, its floor dotted with rocks, its walls clad in dirt and stone.

An old-fashioned gladiator arena. A fighting pit.

Metal ladders were hauled beside her and lifted over the rail into the pit. Frey indicated that she should climb down.

"Not a chance," Kennedy whispered. Three guns were leveled at Ben.

Frey shrugged. "I need you, but I don't need the boy. We could start with a bullet to the knee, then an elbow. Work around and see how long it takes for you to do my bidding." His hellfire smile persuaded her that he'd be glad to prove the truth in his words.

She gritted her teeth and spent a second smoothing her trousers down. The affluent mob inspected her with interest, as they might a caged animal. Glasses were emptied and nibbles nibbled. Waiters and waitresses flitted amongst them, unseen by them, refilling and refreshing.

"What's with the pit?" she said in an attempt to barter for time, now seeing no way out of this debacle and trying to give Drake every precious extra second.

"This is my Battle Arena," Frey said obligingly. "Where you live in glorious memory or die in shame. The choice, my dear Kennedy, *is in your hands.*"

Stay prickly.

One of the guards nudged her with the barrel of his pistol. Somehow she managed to find an encouraging look for Ben, and reached out for the ladder.

Kennedy swung onto it, feeling unreal and detached. Whatever was happening didn't sound good. It sounded like she was going to be fighting for her life.

As she descended the ladder, cries of bloodlust and obscenities curdled the air. Bets were staked: some that she would die in less than a minute, others that she would lose her nerve in under thirty seconds. One or two offered some encouragement, but most gambled that *he* would desecrate her dead body after he had pulverized it.

The richest of the rich, the most powerful scum on earth, a shadowy elite; if this was what wealth and power got you then the world was indeed broken.

All too quickly, her feet touched the hard earth. She dismounted, feeling cold and exposed, and looked around. There was a hole in the wall opposite. Currently it was blocked by a set of thick bars.

A figure trapped on the other side of them rushed forward, smashing against them with a bloodcurdling shriek of fury. He shook them so hard they bounced, his face little more than a twisted snarl.

But despite that, and despite her bizarre surroundings, Kennedy recognized him in less time than it took to think his name.

Thomas Kaleb, serial killer. Here, in Germany. With her. Two mortal enemies placed in the battle arena.

Abel Frey's plan, hatched back in New York, had come to fruition. The madman must have tracked Kaleb down using his extensive criminal contacts, perhaps even offering her as a sweetener, and flown him out of the country.

A sheer rush of hatred arrowed from Kennedy's toes up to her brain and back down again.

"You *bastard!*" she cried, seething. "*You absolute bastard!*"

Then the bars clicked open, and Kaleb leapt toward her.

*

Drake exited the helicopter before it touched down, still a step behind Torsten Dahl, and ran toward a lively hotel that had been commandeered by a joint coalition of international forces. A mixed army to be sure, but a determined and capable one.

They were 1.2 miles north of La Verein.

Army and civilian vehicles were convoyed up outside, engines ticking over, at the ready.

The foyer was a mass of activity: commandos and Special Forces, intelligence agents and soldiers all grubbing up, cleaning up, and gearing up.

Dahl made his presence known by jumping onto the hotel's front desk and hollering so loudly everyone turned to stare. A respectful silence fell.

They already knew him, as well as Drake and the others. They were well aware of what had been achieved in Iceland. Every man here had been briefed by video link established between the Swede's chopper and the hotel's first-rate conferencing facilities.

"We ready?" Dahl shouted. "To take this criminal down?"

"Vehicles prepped," a commander shouted. "Snipers in place. We're so hot we could restart that volcano, sir!"

Dahl nodded. "Then what are we waiting for?"

The noise level climbed a hundred notches. Troops filed out of the doors, slapping each other's backs and agreeing to meet for post-battle beers to bolster bravado. Engines started to roar as the assembled vehicles pulled away.

Drake joined Dahl in the third one, a military Hummer. Through the last few hours of briefings he knew they had about two hundred men, enough to deluge Frey's small army of roughly a hundred, but the German held the higher ground and was expected to have some tricks up his sleeve.

But the one thing he didn't have was the element of surprise. His narcissism wouldn't allow him to believe in failure.

Drake bounced along in the front seat, gripping his rifle, his thoughts focused on Ben and Kennedy. Hayden sat behind them, bruised and bedraggled but tooled up and kitted out for war. Wells, with his stomach wound, had been left at the hotel.

Drake turned to Hayden. "You okay?"

"I'll feel better in about an hour, I hope."

"Right. Well, don't worry. Trust me. Trust Dahl. We have your back on this one."

The FBI agent tried to hide a look of sudden but fond amusement. "Thanks for that."

The convoy rounded a sharp bend and there was La Verein, lit up like a Christmas tree against the darkness that surrounded it and before the black face of the mountain that towered above. Its gates were wide open, demonstrating the insolent audacity of the man they had come to dethrone.

Dahl keyed his mic. "Last call. We're going in hot. Speed will save lives here, men. You know the targets and you know our best guesstimate of where Odin's coffin will be. Let's stick it to that PIG, soldiers."

The reference stood for Polite Intelligent Gentleman. Heavy on the irony. Drake held on with white knuckles as the Hummer shot through Frey's gatehouse with barely an inch to spare on either side. The guards in the watchtowers raised the alarm.

The first shots were fired, bouncing off the lead cars. When the convoy came to a slewing, grinding halt, Drake opened his door and rolled. They hadn't used air support because Frey might have RPGs. They needed to abandon their vehicles quickly for that very same reason.

Get in, and turn the land of the PIG into a bacon factory.

Drake headed for some thick shrubbery that grew under a ground floor window. The lead SAS team were already securing the nightclub area and its civilians. Bullets flew from the chateau's windows, peppering the gatehouse's walls as vehicles flooded through the gate. The coalition force returned fire with a vengeance, smashing glass, striking flesh and bone, and chipping the stone facade into mush. Shouts and screams and calls for reinforcements rang out.

Chaos reigned inside the chateau. An RPG screamed from a top floor window, crashing into Frey's own gatehouse, destroying part of the wall. Rubble cascaded down onto the invading soldiers. Machine gunfire was returned, and one German mercenary toppled from up high, screaming and tumbling until he struck the ground with a horrendous crack.

THE BONES OF ODIN

Dahl and another soldier fired through the front doors. Their bullets took out two men. Dahl ran forward. Hayden was somewhere in the melee behind him.

"We need to get inside this hellhole! *Now!*"

More explosions shook the night. A second RPG blasted a massive crater a few feet east of Drake's Hummer. A shower of dirt and rock plumed into the sky.

Drake ran, crouch style, staying below the crisscrossing tracery of bullets that riddled the air above his head.

The war had truly begun.

The crowd betrayed its thirst for blood before Kennedy and Kaleb even came close. Kennedy circled carefully, her feet testing for rock and earth, moving erratically so as not to be predictable. Her brain struggled to make sense of it all, but already she'd spotted a weakness in her opponent—the way his eyes drank in the figure that her formless pantsuit conservatively covered.

So that was one way to distract the killer. She concentrated on finding another.

Kaleb made the first move. Spittle flew from his lips as he lunged at her, arms flailing. Kennedy batted him away and sidestepped. The crowd bayed for blood. Someone threw red wine on the earth, a symbolic gesture of the blood they wanted spilled. She heard Frey, the sick bastard, egging on Kaleb, the heartless psychopath.

Kaleb lunged again. Kennedy found her back against the wall. She'd lost concentration, distracted by the crowd.

Then Kaleb was on her, his bare arms around her neck, sweaty, disgusting. The arms of a killer...smearing their putrid filth all over her skin. Warning bells tolled in her mind. *You have to stop thinking like this! Focus and fight! Take on the fight and the fighter standing before you, not the horrible legend you've created in your head.*

The crowd howled again. They banged their bottles and glasses against the fence, braying like beasts, yearning for a kill.

And here was Kaleb, so close after everything that had happened. The monster rammed a fist into her side whilst pulling her head against his chest. His dirty, sweaty chest. Then he hit her again. Pain exploded in her ribcage. She staggered. Red wine showered over her, spilled from above.

"That's it," Kaleb taunted her. "No bitch cop will ever get the best of me."

The crowd roared. Kaleb wiped his disgusting hands on her face and laughed with a quiet, fatal malice.

Kennedy flinched and fell backwards. She tried to shuffle away from him, but he got a tight hold on her pants. He pulled her back toward him, grinning like a death's head savage. She had no choice. She unbuttoned her pants and let them slide down her legs. She used his instant surprise to squirm away. The crowd bayed. Kaleb, with the twisted vision of a psychopath, held her pants up in triumph, not having the slightest idea it was Kennedy's way of splintering his single-minded fury. He stood there for a while, attention divided, then lunged forward but she kicked him savagely in the face, gratified to see his nose twang sideways, bloody and broken. She sat there a moment, staring up at her nemesis and found that she couldn't look away from his blood-flecked eyes.

Drake rolled into a wide entry hall. The SAS had indeed secured the nightclub area and were covering the grand staircase. The rest of the chateau wouldn't be so easy.

Dahl tapped his breast pocket. "Blueprints show the vault room to our right and then into the far east wing. Let's not second-guess anything though. We agreed that's the most logical place for Frey, our friends and the sarcophagus."

"Wouldn't dream of it," Hayden deadpanned.

With a force of men scrambling behind him, Drake followed Dahl into the eastern wing. Once the door was opened, more bullets strafed the air. Drake rolled and came up firing.

Suddenly, Frey's men were amongst them. Knives flashed. Handguns fired. Soldiers went down to the left and right. Drake rammed the barrel of his gun against the temple of one of Frey's guards, then let the weapon swing into firing position just in time to put a bullet into an attacker. A guard thrust at him from the left. Drake evaded the lunge and jabbed an elbow in the guy's face. He bent down over the unconscious man, picked up his knife and threw it end over end into another who was about to execute a Delta commando.

A gun fired next to his ear; the weapon of choice of the SGG. Hayden used a Glock and an army-issue knife. A multinational force for a multinational incident.

Drake rolled flat under a guard's sideswipe. He flung his body around, legs first, sweeping the man off his feet. When he landed heavily on his spine, Drake ended his life.

He spied Dahl a dozen steps ahead. Their enemy was thinning now—probably just a few dozen martyrs sent out to wear down the invaders. The real army would be elsewhere.

"Good for a warm up." The Swede grinned, blood coating his mouth. "Now *come on!*"

They went through another door, swept a room clear of booby traps, then another room, where snipers took three good men before they were eliminated. They found themselves facing a high rock wall complete with loopholes through which machine guns rattled. At the center of the wall was an even more formidable steel door, reminiscent of a bank vault.

"That's it," Dahl said as he ducked back. "Frey's viewing room."

"Looks like a tough bastard," said Drake, sheltering behind him, holding up a hand as dozens of troops ran to his side. He looked for Hayden, but failed to see her slim frame amongst the men. *Where the hell had she gone? Oh, please, please, don't let her be lying back there...*

"Fort Knox tough," a Delta commando said after taking a look.

Drake and Dahl shared a look. "*Grapplers!*" they both said at the same time, sticking to their speed-and-no-messing-around policy.

Two big guns were passed carefully up the line, soldiers grinning as they watched. The powerful guns, like rocket launchers, had solid steel grappling hooks attached to their barrels.

Two soldiers sprinted back the way they had come with the optional steel cables cradled in their arms. The cables were attached to a hollow chamber in the launchers' rear.

Dahl double-clicked his comms. "Say when it's a go."

Seconds passed, then the answer came. "*Go!*"

Delta and SGG soldiers laid down covering fire. Drake and
Dahl stepped out, launchers poised on their shoulders, took aim,
and squeezed the triggers.

Two steel grappling hooks shot out at rocket-like speed,
embedding themselves deep into the stone wall of Frey's vault
before bursting through the other side. Once they encountered
empty space, a sensor triggered a device that deployed the hooks
themselves, making them clamp hard to the far side of the wall.

Dahl tapped his ear. "Do it."

Even from down here Drake heard the sound of two Hummers
slammed into reverse, cables attached to their reinforced
bumpers.

Frey's allegedly impenetrable wall exploded.

Kennedy kicked out as Kaleb shambled toward her, catching his
knee and making him stagger. She scrambled to her feet. Kaleb
lunged again and she slapped his ear with the back of her hand.

The crowd above bleated their pleasure. Thousands of dollars'
worth of rare wine and fine whisky splattered as it hit the dirt of
the arena. A pair of women's lacy panties floated down. A man's
tie. A pair of Gucci cufflinks, one bouncing off Kaleb's hairy back.

"Kill her!" Frey screamed.

Kaleb attacked like a freight train; arms spread, guttural
sounds coming from deep in his belly. Kennedy tried to skip
away, but he caught her and lifted her bodily into the air.

Airborne, Kennedy could only cringe in anticipation of the
landing. And it came hard, rock and earth slamming into her
spine, driving the air from her lungs. Her legs kicked, but Kaleb
landed inside them and planted himself on top of her, elbows
first.

"More like it," the killer grunted. "Now you'll squeal.
Eeeeeee!" His voice was manic, a pig's slaughter screeching in
her ear. "*Eeeeeeeeeee!*"

Searing agony made Kennedy's body convulse. The bastard
was an inch away now, lips dripping saliva onto her cheeks, eyes
shining with crazy, abhorrent inhumanity.

For a moment she was helpless, still trying to catch a breath.
His fist slammed into her belly. His left hand was about to do the

same when it paused. A heartbeat of thought, and then it snaked up to her throat and began to squeeze.

Kennedy choked, gasping for air. Kaleb giggled like a madman. He squeezed harder. He studied her eyes, staring as if transfixed. He bore down on her body, pinning her with his weight.

She kicked out with all her might, knocking him to the side. She was well aware she'd just received a pass. The bastard's twisted needs had saved her life.

She snaked away again. The crowd jeered at her—at her performance, at her dirty clothes, at her bleeding legs. Kaleb rose like a boxer from the edge of defeat and spread his arms wide, laughing.

And then she heard a voice, weak but spearing through the raucous cacophony.

Ben's voice. "Drake's coming, Kennedy. The guards are talking about it. He's coming!"

But he wouldn't find them here. She couldn't imagine that of all the places in the chateau, he'd search this area first. His most likely target would be the vault room or the cells. It could be hours...

Ben still needed her. Kaleb's victims still needed her.

To stand up and shout when they couldn't.

Kaleb ran at her, reckless in his bloodthirstiness. Kennedy feigned terror, then planted her back foot and sent an elbow slamming straight into his onrushing face.

Blood spouted over her arm. Kaleb stopped, as if he'd run into a brick wall. Kennedy pushed her advantage, hammering his chest with her fists, punching his already broken nose, kicking at his knees. She used any method she could to disable the executioner.

The crowd's roar increased, but she barely heard it. One swift kick to the groin sent the asshole to his knees, another to the chin flipped him onto his back. Kennedy fell into the dirt beside him, panting through exhaustion, and stared into his disbelieving eyes.

There was a thud close to her right knee. Kennedy looked over to see a broken wine bottle embedded neck up in the dirt. A merlot, still dripping its liquid red promise.

Kaleb swung at her. She took the blow on her face without flinching. "You need to die," she hissed. "For Olivia Dunn." She wrenched the broken bottle out of the ground. "For Selena Tyler." She raised it above his head. "For Miranda Drury," she added. Her first blow shattered teeth. "And for Emma Sulke." Her second broke bone. "For Emily Jane Winters." Her final blow stopped his heart.

She knelt there in the bloodied earth, victorious, the adrenalin firing her veins and pounding through her brain, trying to claw back the humanity that had momentarily deserted her.

FORTY-FOUR

LA VEREIN, GERMANY

Kennedy was ordered back up the ladder at gunpoint. The body of Thomas Kaleb was left where it lay.

Frey looked unhappy as he spoke into a cellphone. "The vault," he rasped. "Save the vault at all costs, Hudson. I don't *care* about anything else. Just do what I pay you for!"

He ended the connection and stared at Kennedy. "It appears your army friends broke into my house."

Kennedy turned on the gathered elite. "Seems like you rich idiots are gonna get a little of what you deserve."

There was quiet laughter, the tinkle of glasses. Frey joined in for a moment before saying, "Finish your drinks, my friends. Then leave in the usual way."

Kennedy summoned some bravado and gave Ben a wink. Her body ached. Her head pounded and her legs throbbed; her skin was ripped and her hands were covered in sticky blood.

She held them out to Frey. "Can I clean this off?"

"Use your shirt," he sneered. "It's no more than a rag anyway. No doubt it mirrors the rest of your closet."

He waved a hand in the royal manner. "Bring her. And the boy."

Kennedy smiled despite the situation. "This is how it ends for you, Frey. Prison or a bullet. Now *you* get to choose."

Frey chortled. "One such as I, a man of great wealth, has more than one level of protection in place, my dear. Indeed, more than a dozen."

"We've already breached your chateau."

Now Frey laughed hard. "I didn't say security. I said protection. The difference is vast, believe me. Instead of a camera it's a prominent name. Instead of an order given to a guard it's a whisper in the ear of an influential man. Instead of a group of mercenaries it's a group of lawyers."

They exited the arena, Kennedy feeling the exhaustion and trying to still her spinning head. The ramifications of what she'd done would live with her for decades, but now wasn't the time to dwell. Ben was at her side and, from the look on his face, clearly attempting a form of telepathic encouragement.

"Thanks, man," she said, heedless of the guards. "Was nothing but a cakewalk."

They followed a left-hand fork that ran away from their cell block. Kennedy summoned her wits.

Just survive, she thought. *Just stay alive.*

Frey received another call. *"What? They're at the vault? Moron! You...you..."* he sputtered, enraged. *"Hudson you...send in the whole army!"*

An electronic shriek severed the connection as abruptly as a guillotine.

"Take them to the housing block!" Frey turned on his guards. "It seems there are more of your *friends* than we first thought, dear Kennedy. I'll be back to tend your wounds later."

With that, the deranged German marched away at pace. Kennedy became acutely aware she and Ben were now alone with four guards. "Keep going." One of them prodded her toward a door at the end of the hallway.

When they passed through it, Kennedy blinked in surprise.

This part of the chateau had been completely gutted, a new arched roof built overhead, and small brick "houses" lined two sides of the space. Little more than large sheds, there were about eight of them. Kennedy knew instantly that more than a handful of captives had passed through this place in its time.

A man worse than Thomas Kaleb?

Meet Abel Frey.

Her situation was worsening by the second. The guards maneuvered both Ben and her toward one of the houses. Once inside, it was game over. *You lose.*

She could take one out, maybe even two. But four? She had no chance.

Unless...

She peered behind at the nearest guard, caught him staring at her. "Hey, is this it? You gonna put us in there?"

"Those are my orders."

"Look. This kid here—he's come a long way to save his sister. You think maybe he could see her? Just once."

"Orders from Frey. We're not allowed."

Kennedy let her gaze travel between all four guards. "So? Who's to know? Recklessness is the spice of life, right?"

The guard snapped at her, "You blind? Haven't you *seen* the cameras in this place?"

"Frey's busy fighting an army he can't beat." Kennedy smiled. "Why'd you think he took off so quick? You know who's out there—the Swedes, the British and the friggin' Americans. You're done, all of you. You guys let Ben see his sister, then maybe I'll cut you some slack when the new bosses get here."

The guards stole glances at each other, and soon two of them were unlocking Karin's door whilst the others made a show of protesting.

Two minutes later, they brought her out. She staggered between them, looking drawn, her blond hair bedraggled and her face defeated.

But then she saw Ben, and her eyes lit up like lightning in a storm. Strength seemed to pour back into her frame.

Kennedy caught her eyes as the two groups met, trying hard to convey the urgency, the danger, the last chance scenario of her crazy idea all in one look.

Karin shrugged off the guards and snarled, "*Come get some, motherfuckers.*"

Torsten Dahl led the charge, gun held out like a raised sword, shouting for all he was worth. Drake was at his side, sprinting at full pace even before the vault wall had collapsed. Smoke and debris plumed through the small space. As Drake ran, he sensed other coalition troops fanning out to either side. They were a rushing phalanx of death, bearing down on their enemies with deadly intent.

Drake's instincts kicked in as the smoke swirled and thinned. To the left, a huddle of guards stood, frozen in fear, slow to react. He fired a burst into their midst, taking down at least three bodies. From ahead, he heard some return fire. Soldiers fell to his left and right, some simply flailing hard into the collapsed wall with their momentum.

Blood sprayed right before his eyes as a man pirouetted in sudden death, not fast enough to dodge a bullet.

Drake dived for cover. Sharp rock and concrete shredded the flesh of his arms as he hit the floor. Rolling, he fired a few bursts into the corners. Men screamed. An exhibit exploded under intense gunfire. Old bones spun through the air in slow motion.

More gunfire from ahead and Drake saw a mass of moving men. *Jesus!* Frey's army was right here, arrayed in its own deadly formation, and coming forward faster and faster as it sensed it had the edge.

Karin used her martial arts training and surprise to incapacitate her opponents within seconds. Kennedy delivered a sharp backhand to her guard's chin, then stepped in and headbutted him so hard *she* saw stars. After a second she saw that her second opponent, the fourth guard, had leapt away to create some space between them.

Her heart sank. So the fourth guard *had* been a bridge too far, even for two of them.

The guard looked petrified as he raised his rifle. Finger trembling, he swept the area, seeking help. Kennedy held her hands palms outwards.

"Calm down, dude. Just stay calm."

His trigger finger flexed in fear. A shot rang out, bouncing off the ceiling.

Kennedy cringed. Tension thickened the air into nervous soup.

Ben almost screamed as his cellphone cut a raucous tune through the unease. Seether's *Effigy* cranked up to max.

The guard jumped too, squeezing off another involuntary shot. Kennedy felt the wind of the bullet pass by her skull. Pure fright riveted her to the spot.

Please, she thought. *Don't be an idiot. Remember your training.*

Ben threw his phone at the guard. Kennedy saw him flinch and swiftly dropped to the floor to create more distraction. She scrabbled for a discarded rifle. By the time the guard had batted the phone away and refocused, Kennedy had shouldered the third guard's weapon.

Karin, though, had guested here for a while. She had experienced the worst of La Verein. She fired instantly. The guard staggered back as a red puff exploded from his jacket. Then a dark stain spread across his shoulder and he looked bewildered, then angry.

He fired, point-blank, at Ben. Kennedy screamed.

But the shot went wild, the miss caused by the guard's head exploding a millisecond before he'd pulled the trigger.

Behind him, framed by his spray of blood, stood Hayden, Glock in hand.

Kennedy looked at Ben and Karin, saw them staring at each other with elation, love and sorrow. It seemed prudent to give them a minute. Then Hayden was at her side, nodding with relief at Ben.

"How's he doin'?"

Kennedy winked. "He'll be happier now you've arrived."

Then she sobered. "We got other captives to rescue in here, Hayden. Let's get 'em and quit this hellhole."

The two armies met with a clash, the coalition force shooting their opponents where they stood, the Germans wielding knives and trying to get up close.

For a moment Drake found this knife-play futile, utter madness, but then remembered who their boss was. Abel Frey. The madman wouldn't want his own side using bullets just in case they marred his priceless exhibits.

In amongst it, Drake felled foe after foe. Soldiers grunted and struck at each other all around him, using force that broke bones. Men screamed. Battle combat was a total melee. Survival was down to pure luck and instinct rather than skill.

As he fired and punched and scrapped his way through, he caught sight of a figure up ahead. A whirling dervish of death.

Alicia Myles, cutting a swathe through the international super-troops.

Drake faced her. The battle noise fell away. They were near the back of the vault, Odin's sarcophagus beside them, open now, a rack of spotlights arrayed above it.

"Well, well," she laughed. "The Drakester. How's it hanging, pal?"

"Same as ever."

"Mmm, I remember. Though can't say it *hung* for too long, eh? Nice catfight up on the ropes by the way. Not bad for a one-time soldier-cum-civilian."

"You too. Where's your BBF?"

"BBF?"

Two struggling soldiers crashed into Drake. He shoved them away with Alicia's help, both of them savoring what was to come.

"Best Boyfriend Forever? Remember him? Milo?"

"Oh, yeah. Had to kill him. Bastard caught Frey and me in an awkward position." She sniggered. "Got mad. Got dead." She made a face. "Just another dearly departed fool."

"Who thought he could tame you." Drake nodded. "I remember."

"Why'd you have to be here now, Drake? I really don't want to have to kill you."

Drake shook his head in bemusement. "There's a term—*beautiful liar*. Those two words sum you up, Myles."

"So?" Alicia rolled up her sleeves with a grin and kicked off her shoes. "You ready to get your balls handed to you?"

Out of the corner of his eye Drake saw Abel Frey creeping away and shouting at someone called Hudson. It seemed Myles had been guarding them as they directed their force, but now she had other priorities. Torsten Dahl, ever reliable, stepped in front of the crazy German and launched an attack.

Drake clenched his fists. "Not gonna happen, Myles."

FORTY-FIVE

LA VEREIN

Alicia shocked Drake by ripping off her jacket, swirling it around itself until it became as tight as a rope, then swinging it two-handed around his neck. He struggled, but her improvised harness dragged him in.

Straight into her rising knees—Thai-boxing style. One. Two. Three.

He twisted around the first. Turned again. The second crunched by his ribs. The third caught him fully in the balls. Pain thudded through his belly, sickening, and he fell onto his backside.

Alicia stood above him, grinning. "What did I say? Tell me, Drakey, what *exactly* did I say." She made a motion of handing him something. "Your balls."

She dropped a hip and twisted, shooting out a side-kick aimed at his nose. Drake brought up both hands and blocked it. She turned so she was facing him dead-on, swinging one leg high and over in an arc, then bringing the heel sharply down toward his forehead.

Axe kick.

Drake rolled back, but the kick struck his chest painfully.

She stamped on his ankle.

Drake screamed. His body was being systematically beaten, bruised and lamed. She was breaking him, piece by piece, taking advantage of the easy civilian years. But then—could he even blame the lay-off? She had always been good. But had she always been *this* good?

Civilian break or not, he was still ex-SAS, and she was painting the floor with his blood.

He shuffled backward. A trio of fighters fell over him, crashing all around. Drake enjoyed the respite of elbowing a German in the throat. He heard cartilage crack, felt a little better.

He stood up, aware that Myles had allowed him. She danced from foot to foot, eyes lit from within by devilry and brimstone. Beyond her, Dahl, Frey and Hudson were locked together, wrestling across the side of Odin's coffin, faces constricted with pain.

Alicia again flicked out her jacket at him. It connected like a whip, burning the left side of his face. She struck again and he caught it, and pulled with intense strength. She came stumbling into his arms.

"Hi."

He jammed both thumbs just below her ears, pressing hard. Instantly she began to writhe, all semblance of cockiness gone. He was pressing the nerve cluster hard enough to cause any normal man to black out.

Myles bucked and kicked like a rodeo bull.

He pressed harder. Finally, she leaned back in his harsh embrace, letting him take her weight, limp, no doubt trying to compartmentalize the pain. Then she shot upright and thrust both thumbs under his armpits.

Straight into his own nerve cluster. Agony blasted through his body.

And so they were locked: two fearsome enemies, battling through waves of pain, barely moving, staring into each other's eyes like long-lost lovers, till death do they part.

Drake grunted, unable to hide his suffering. "This. . .is. . .crazy.... Why work for this...this man?"

"Means...to an...end."

Neither Drake nor Alicia would back down. Around them the fight began to draw to a close. More coalition troops remained standing than Germans. But they battled on. And out of the corner of his eye Drake was aware that Dahl and Frey were now locked in a similar, deadly embrace.

Drake fell to his knees, taking Alicia with him. Black spots danced before his eyes. He realized that if she found a way to break his hold, he was well and truly done for. Energy drained from him by the second.

He wilted. She pressed harder, that ultimate killer instinct digging in. His thumbs slipped away. Alicia fell forward, striking with an elbow to his chin. Drake saw it coming but didn't have the energy to stop it.

Sparks exploded behind his eyes. He fell flat on his back, staring up at Frey's gothic ceiling. Alicia crawled over and blocked his line of sight with her pain-riddled face.

None of the soldiers around them tried to stop her. This would not end until one of the combatants either called a truce or died.

"Not bad," she coughed. "You still got it in you, Drake, but you need a lot of retraining. I'm still better than you."

He sighed. "I know. For now."

"What?"

"You have...that edge. That killer instinct. Battle fury. It makes the difference. That's why I quit."

"The Devil lives in me," she smirked. "My dad always told me that, the bastard. Now I know. But why would losing the edge make you want to quit the army?"

"Once you care about something *outside* the job," he said, "that changes everything. And you don't have to be *bad*, Alicia. You just have to try to change."

Her fist was raised, ready to crush his throat. A moment passed. Then she said, "A life for a life?"

Drake was starting to feel the energy trickling slowly back into his limbs. "After everything I've done today I think they owe me that much."

Alicia stepped back and held an arm out to help him to his feet. "I actually bloody rolled Wells *toward* the ropes at Mimir's Well. I *didn't* kill him at Odin's tomb. I also diverted Frey's attention *away* from Ben Blake. I helped Kennedy. I'm not in this to destroy the world, Drake, I'm just here to have me some fun. We'll see each other again."

"Acknowledged." Drake steadied himself, just as Torsten Dahl heaved Abel Frey's limp body off the wide rim of Odin's coffin. It hit the floor with a wet crack, flopping lifelessly against the priceless Italian pavers.

A cheer went up, echoing through the coalition troops.

Dahl pumped a fist as he stared inside the coffin.

"The bastard never got to see this prize," he laughed. "His life's work. The genuine bones of Odin, straight from the Tomb of the Gods. Hey guys, you've gotta see this."

Jubilantly, he urged everyone across to see what he had found.

FORTY-SIX

STOCKHOLM

A day later, Drake managed to escape the endless round of debriefings to catch up on a few hours' sleep at a nearby hotel, one of Stockholm's oldest and finest.

In the lobby, he waited for the elevator and wondered why all his thought processes were shot. They'd been rendered inoperable by lack of sleep, constant beatings and intense pressure. He needed several days of recuperation.

The elevator dinged. A figure appeared behind him, and then moved to his side.

Kennedy—dressed in Saturday's pantsuit, hair tightly swept back, surveying him with those deep, tortured eyes.

"Hey."

Words weren't enough. To ask her if she was okay was beyond lame, it was downright foolish.

"Hey, yourself."

"Same floor?"

"Sure. They're keeping us all boxed off together."

They got in, stared at their shattered reflections in the mirror, avoided contact with the requisite video camera. Drake pressed the button for nineteen.

"You getting through this as well as I am, Kennedy?"

She laughed, genuinely. "A crazy week, or *weeks*. Not sure. It blows my mind that I ended up fighting my nemesis and clearing my name at the end of all this. At least on paper. Doesn't change what Kaleb did."

Drake shrugged. "As did I. Ironic, eh?"

"Where did Alicia go?"

"Into the night where all the darkest secrets go; her and that computer geek, Hudson," Drake shrugged. "Gone before anyone who really mattered noticed."

"You did the right thing. They weren't the masterminds here. Alicia's dangerous but she's no psychopath. She actually gave me a break on the chopper for some reason, saved me some pain. And Hayden," she went on as the elevator doors closed and the old car began to rise. "You think she'll stick with Ben?"

"I really hope so. But they're whole levels apart. If not, well at least he's had sex now, I think."

Kennedy punched his shoulder. "Don't count them chickens, buddy. Maybe he'll write her a song instead."

"Call it—*three and a half minutes with you.*"

They were clicking slowly past the seventh floor. "Reminds me: back at Odin's tomb, what was it you said? Something about me staying in York."

Drake stared at her. She gave him a seductive smile.

"Well...I..." then he sighed and relented. "Am hopelessly out of practice at this."

"At what?" Kennedy's eyes glinted with mischief.

"An old DinoRock group called it the *Immaculate Seduction.* In Yorkshire we just say we're 'chatting up a bird'. We're simple folk, tha knows."

As the elevator clicked past the fourteenth floor, Kennedy unbuttoned her shirt. Underneath, she wore a red bra.

"What are you doing?" Drake felt his heart jump as if it had been electro-shocked.

"What the hell do you think?"

Kennedy unbuttoned her pants and let them pool to the floor. She wore a matching pair of red panties. The elevator dinged as it arrived at their floor. Drake felt his spirits and everything else start to rise. The door slid open.

A young couple were waiting. The woman giggled. The guy grinned at Drake. Kennedy pulled Drake out of the elevator and into the corridor, leaving her pantsuit behind.

Drake glanced back. "Don't want it?"

"Don't need it anymore."

Drake swept her up into his arms. "My room's not far."
Kennedy let her hair down.

THE END

Other Books by David Leadbeater:

The Matt Drake Series

The Matt Drake series is a constantly evolving, action-packed romp based in the action-adventure genre. Parts 1-18 are available now with part 19 slated for an October 2018 release.

The Bones of Odin (Matt Drake #1)
The Blood King Conspiracy (Matt Drake #2)
The Gates of Hell (Matt Drake 3)
The Tomb of the Gods (Matt Drake #4)
Brothers in Arms (Matt Drake #5)
The Swords of Babylon (Matt Drake #6)
Blood Vengeance (Matt Drake #7)
Last Man Standing (Matt Drake #8)
The Plagues of Pandora (Matt Drake #9)
The Lost Kingdom (Matt Drake #10)
The Ghost Ships of Arizona (Matt Drake #11)
The Last Bazaar (Matt Drake #12)
The Edge of Armageddon (Matt Drake #13)
The Treasures of Saint Germain (Matt Drake #14)
Inca Kings (Matt Drake #15)
The Four Corners of the Earth (Matt Drake #16)
The Seven Seals of Egypt (Matt Drake #17)
Weapons of the Gods (Matt Drake #18)

The Alicia Myles Series
Aztec Gold (Alicia Myles #1)
Crusader's Gold (Alicia Myles #2)
Caribbean Gold (Alicia Myles #3)
Chasing Gold (Alicia Myles #4)

The Torsten Dahl Thriller Series
Stand Your Ground (Dahl Thriller #1)

The Relic Hunters Series
The Relic Hunters (Relic Hunters #1)
The Atlantis Cipher (Relic Hunters #2)

The Disavowed Series:
The Razor's Edge (Disavowed #1)
In Harm's Way (Disavowed #2)
Threat Level: Red (Disavowed #3)

The Chosen Few Series
Chosen (The Chosen Trilogy #1)
Guardians (The Chosen Tribology #2)

Short Stories
Walking with Ghosts (A short story)
A Whispering of Ghosts (A short story)

All genuine comments are very welcome at:

davidleadbeater2011@hotmail.co.uk

Twitter: @dleadbeater2011

Visit David's website for the latest news and information:
davidleadbeater.com

CPSIA information can be obtained
at www.ICGtesting.com
Printed in the USA
LVHW020528090322
712938LV00010B/1518

9 781482 504354